A RELUCTANT BRIDE

The king has decreed that his loyal servant, Lord Alex de Monteneau, will rule the Lady Talia's lands and determine whom the fiery maiden will wed. The groom he chooses, however, will certainly *not* be himself, for the noble knight desires a far richer castle and a docile wife—not this infuriating, iron-willed beauty who resists his authority at every turn. Yet the woman's charm, strength, and smoldering sensuality are rapidly becoming a serious distraction . . . .

In the past, Lady Talia has managed to save her humble ancestral castle—and her virtue—from numerous self-proclaimed "husbands." But the unnervingly attractive warrior who has "rescued" her from yet another unwanted wedding seems the most dangerous of the lot. No man will *ever* decide her future! But how can Talia hope to retain her cherished independence when she secretly, passionately longs for Alex to share her bed?

D1040597

Other Avon Romantic Treasures by
Linda Needham

MY WICKED EARL
THE MAIDEN BRIDE
THE WEDDING NIGHT

LINDA NEEDHAM

THE BRIDE BED

An Avon Romantic Treasure

AVON BOOKS

An Imprint of HarperCollinsPublishers

This is a work of fiction. Names, characters, places, and incidents are products of the author's imagination or are used fictitiously and are not to be construed as real. Any resemblance to actual events, locales, organizations, or persons, living or dead, is entirely coincidental.

AVON BOOKS
An Imprint of HarperCollins*Publishers*
10 East 53rd Street
New York, New York 10022-5299

Copyright © 2002 by Linda Needham
ISBN: 0-380-81524-9
www.avonromance.com

First Avon Books paperback printing: October 2002

Avon Trademark Reg. U.S. Pat. Off. and in Other Countries, Marca Registrada, Hecho en U.S.A.
HarperCollins® is a registered trademark of HarperCollins Publishers Inc.

Printed in the U.S.A.

10 9 8 7 6 5 4 3 2 1

Chapter 1

Carrisford Castle
Devonshire, 1145

"By the rood, Lady Talia, that bloody Lord Rufus be the meanest, ugliest bugger there ever was!"

Mustn't forget cruel, malicious, and stone-stupid, Talia thought, but didn't dare say to Leod, else the dear old warrior and his compatriots might take the matter of Lord Rufus into their own hands.

"Mean and ugly or no," Talia whispered, swallowing the cold panic that had settled against her heart, "in just a few minutes Lord Rufus will be my husband."

Husband. Dear Lord, the word tasted bitter.

"Hell's hoary hound, girl, y'can't marry that pig-snouted bastard!"

"It's not a matter of choice, Quigley," Talia said, a darkly distant thunder shifting her off-balance as she stepped into the firelit shadows of her castle courtyard. "I'm Rufus's ward."

And this time there would be no escaping the inevitable.

No escaping the horrid ogre waiting for her to join him on the chapel steps.

To marry him.

This time there'd be no army to come crashing through the castle gates, like the last time.

No act of God, like the time before, no broken siege.

No royal warrant in trade for her wardship, like the first.

No escape at all from this marriage to Rufus.

"When you reach the chapel steps, my lady, stand clear of the blighter, and I'll put an arrow through 'is empty black heart."

"You'll do nothing of the sort, Jasper." That's just what she needed; Rufus's men tearing her father's old archers to pieces. She took hold of the man's bony arm. "You'll each behave yourselves tonight, else you'll have worse than Rufus to answer to."

Talia heard the three men grumbling as they all set off again toward the chapel. She suffered another soul-hollowing chill as the sky rumbled and thundered again, as the night wind slipped over the timber-picketed battlements, whirling together clouds of glistening leaves and sparks from the fire baskets.

"Gor, Rufus!" someone shouted over the milling mass of brutish soldiers. "There your lady be!"

The crowd laughed and parted only wide enough for Talia and her old champions.

"Mmmmmm . . . Tasty, she looks to me."

" 'E's waiting for ya, yer bridegroom is. Stiff as a pike, I'll wager."

On she went, through the serpentine corridor of jeering, ogling men, stinking with drink and neglect.

So like their master.

Rufus.

There he was, strutting around at the bottom of the chapel steps.

Her gluttonous, barely human guardian turned husband-to-be, downing a flagon of ale and grabbing another from a cowering page.

Rufus de Graffe.

Pillager. Waster.

Mother Mary, where was a true warrior when she needed one? Her very own Green Knight to slay these dragon whelps and their unspeakable master?

A man who would keep this unrelenting war at bay, who'd keep her people warm and fed and secure in their homes.

Who'd be a husband to cherish?

Just one more miracle. And I'll never ask again.

"There she is, Father John," Rufus bellowed, his ale-slitted eyes gleaming at her, "my little bride. All pink and clean and ready for me."

Aye, ready to lose her stomach as the ghastly man staggered and stumbled toward her through the drunken crowd.

Please God, let the great ass drink himself into a stupor long before our wedding chamber is blessed.

"Come here, girl." Rufus clenched her upper arm between his bruising fingers and yanked her up against his barrel chest, his foul breath flipping her stomach on end.

"Keep your bloody—" But Quigley's outraged shout ended behind Jasper's hand.

"Please, let's get on with it, Father John," Talia said, easily yanking out of Rufus's reeking embrace. She took the few steps toward the chapel, terrified that the old warriors would draw Rufus's wrath, relieved when Rufus trailed her, revolted by his nearness.

"Ah, now that's what a man needs in a wife, eh, priest: eagerness to be bedded."

Talia swallowed the bile in her throat and cursed the lot of brides, of women, of royal wards who must obey their unworthy guardians.

The thunder came again, more deeply, rumbling across the cobbles, seeping its oddly intimate warmth through the soles of her slippers, riding up her calves to soften her knees.

Father John cast Talia a look of helpless distress as he motioned toward the steps. "If you'll, uh-mmm, take your place beside Lord Rufus."

Her place. No. Rufus was far, far from the right man to stand with her here on the chapel steps, the lord of her beloved father's castle, her husband.

Her protector.

"No more lagging, priest," Rufus said, growling as he slid his hand over Talia's backside. "The lady has her needs."

Rufus squeezed hard and she slapped his hand away without thinking, hoping Leod wouldn't jump the man. "I'm not your wife yet, Rufus."

"Be damned, woman! You'll speak when you're asked to—" Rufus's beefy face reddened. He drew back his fist and Talia was about to dodge out of the way, when the force of his swing was caught by a wide-eyed soldier.

"Trouble, Your Lordship."

Another crash of thunder, closer, grazing her heart.

"Bloody impudent sot, can't you see I'm busy!" Rufus sent the guard sprawling into the muddy cobbles. "Now, on with it, priest!"

Father John had wound the twine of his wooden crucifix around his fist. "But, Lord Rufus, shouldn't you—"

"The wedding, dammit!" Rufus grabbed Father John by the front of his cowl and thrust him back against the door. "Begin now!"

But the thunder came again, rocking the very steps now, and her balance. Another shudder seemed to make the timbered wall of pickets dance along the stone parapet.

Father John's eyes bulged as he squawked out, "Bless, O Lord, this ri—"

"Sir! At the gate!" The guard had struggled to his knees, and now tugged at the hem of Rufus's hauberk. "They're coming through—"

They? Hope washed over her. *Please God, deliver us this one last time.*

Everything stopped in the next breath.

Stopped with a crash, then a splintering sound as a single stone catapulted into the courtyard and landed hard against the kitchen shed.

Another siege?

Oh, please, God, yes!

Then a great banging of wood and metal echoing through the courtyard as a sea of soldiers began spilling through the barbican gate and into the courtyard.

Wonderful, miraculous, glittering-helmed soldiers, easily overwhelming the few men who had tried to close the huge double doors against the surging assault.

The chaos slowed suddenly, and out of the

midst of it came a deep-voiced cheer that rose up from the tumult of hooves and clashing swords, that echoed from the gates and bounded through the barbican and into the courtyard.

At the center of the cheering crush rode a huge mounted warrior, his arm raised in savage triumph, his blade filling the night sky with a flash of lightning and moonlit steel.

Their leader, no doubt.

Her miracle.

And he seemed to be staring right at her.

Through her, probing and intimate.

"Buggering hell!" Rufus staggered sideways, slack-jawed, as wave after wave of mounted warriors coursed around their overwhelming leader and his massive destrier.

"Call the men to battle, sir. Please!"

This was a miracle, all right, a vast and sweeping one, pouring over the ramparts, swords flashing. Filling her heart with gratitude and her ears with the horribly familiar sounds of war.

A miracle that might kill them all.

"The men, sir! Pleeease!"

"Call 'em y'rself, Garlock!" And then Rufus skittered from the church steps, slinking off into the shadows, leaving his men armed with little more than empty mugs of ale and their bare fists.

"Ha! That'll show the bastard!" Jasper said, brushing his palms together, scowling after Rufus.

"One enemy replaced by another," Talia said, keeping the monstrous warrior in her sights, painfully aware that the trouble was far from finished. That the fires would doubtless start in a few moments, the sacking and the pillaging. "We've faced this all before, gentlemen."

"Seven times, by my count," the priest said, his fists buried deeply inside his sleeves, his face chalky as he fixed his gaze on the chaos in the courtyard.

"Aye, so Leod, you and Jasper go to my sisters in the keep. Guard them with your lives."

Leod snorted, working his frizzly brows into a single solid arch. "And where do you think you're goin', my lady, when you're all dressed up?"

"Go, Leod! Now!"

"Aye, my lady." The two old men grumbled at each other as they hobbled off into the clash of metal and smoke and men.

Damn this bloody civil war and all its demon players. Threatening and threatening and threatening again. Always clamoring at her door.

Like this new one, wielding his sword against the sky, bellowing orders that sent men in every direction.

Just another warlord. The next claimant to her wardship. To her marriage bed.

Inciting his troops to his own brand of savagery against her and the people she loved.

"Go, Father; hide the gold candlestick and the rood."

"Aye, and the altar cloth." He smiled ruefully and slipped through the chapel door.

"To the village, Quig. I'll ring the alarm from the tower. See that the villagers go into hiding until they hear the tithe bell, then come find me with the damage report. Or if there's trouble—"

"I can't leave you to—"

"Hurry please, Quigley. You know what has to be done."

"Aye, my lady. For your father and for you." The old warrior frowned through his deep moustache and vanished into the chaos.

Talia sped away from the chapel steps, losing sight of the huge warrior in the snarl of men and horses. Though for the first time she realized that it didn't matter this time. That it could never happen again.

Whoever you are, Sir Warlord, this time things will be different. As Rufus would have discovered had he stayed long enough to wed and bed her.

Your victory will be as short-lived as his. Because her plans were already in place to take back control of her life—as unstopped as the tide, as necessary as the sweet sea air.

Her heart uplifted with resolve, Talia kept to the perimeter of the courtyard and its gruesomely dancing shadows, dodged and ducked her way through the fighting, and finally managed to ring the alarm bell against the baketower wall, praying that the villagers had escaped in time.

Mother Mary, she really ought to be used to the terror by now, armies of men battering down her castle gates. Raiding her crippled village, slaughtering the men, violating the women, terrifying the children. Making orphans of the innocent.

Aye, but she *had* gotten used to it. And that had been the trouble: accepting defeat instead of turning to fight.

It wouldn't happen again.

Woe be to this new one, this massive invader with his shiny blade and arrogant victory.

He'd just made the biggest mistake of his iniquitous life.

She'd taken but three steps in the direction of the shop rows when she smelled smoke.

Straw, a dreaded smell, for it always meant the stables, the horses! One fire setting another until the courtyard was ablaze.

Talia skirted the riot, tracking the smoke to a grain storage bin in the front of the castle granary, expecting to find licking flames.

But instead of setting the fire, two soldiers were quickly dousing it, dumping the grain onto the ground, as another held one of Rufus's struggling pages by the scruff of the neck.

"Our lord de Monteneau keeps no hostages, boy," the soldier bellowed at the terrified young man. "You do know what that means, don't you?"

De Monteneau. The new one.

"Please, sir," the baleful young page said, squirming without success. "Don't kill me!"

Horrified that this de Monteneau devil would blithely order the death of a defenseless boy, Talia grabbed the soldier's sleeve. "You'll not kill this boy!"

The huge soldier paused, clearly annoyed but listening. "And you are . . . who?"

"My lady Talia, please don't let them kill me," the boy whimpered, taking a handful of her hem.

She grabbed his hand, fixed him with a stare. "Did you start the fire, Figgis? The truth, now."

He let out a mournful whine. "Rufus ordered me to as he escaped, my lady. I thought—"

"Great heavens, Figgis, if Rufus had told you to jump off the kitchen tower into the bay, would you have?"

He nodded. "Yes."

Talia sighed, then glared up at the bull-shouldered soldier and his companions. "The boy was minding orders, sir, ill conceived, though they be. You'll not kill him, do you hear me? You will hold him in the guardhouse."

"Our lord does not hold hostages."

Murdering monster.

"Where is this lord of yours?"

The man laughed, arrogant, amused, certain of

himself. "My lady, our lord is busy somewhere seizing this castle."

She was just forming a hard-edged curse on her tongue when she caught sight of another flame, far across the courtyard. A flare of light inside the chapel, a flame where it shouldn't be.

Please not the chapel!

"Keep the boy safe, soldier! Or you'll have me to answer to." Fearing the very worst, Talia ran back to the chapel, up the steps, and burst through the door.

There wasn't fire at all, nothing but a wildly flaring torch fixed into a sconce above the altar, its flame tossing dense shadows everywhere, masking everything not directly in its pale orange path.

"Father John!" Her voice echoed back at her, bumped against the vaulting and the sounds of the battle raging outside.

He wasn't there. Only a dark, empty silence . . . and a large, formless, encompassing shape against the altar.

A shape that breathed and shifted, then broke into two pieces.

One part remained a groveling lump on the ground, and the other grew even larger, darker, taller, stealing most of the light and nearly all of the air.

A man. No, not a man, a monster! As tall as the altar arch, and his shoulders as wide.

The lump on the floor rose up on his knees,

spoke in a broken voice. "Sir, 'tis our only holy relic—"

Father John!

The beast raised his arm above his head, clearly about to run the priest through with his dagger.

"Noooo!" Without another thought, Talia leaped onto the broad back of the immense soldier. "Unholy heathen! How dare you attack a priest!"

She scrambled to keep hold as his dagger clattered to the floor, wrapping her arm around his thick neck, clinging indelicately to his leather and mail-clad waist with her thighs.

Furious, she smacked him on the helm, bruising her hand as the faceplate shut with a clang. "And in a house of God!"

The fiend growled deeply, a sound that rattled her heart as he reached around her with his huge, gauntleted hand, and took hold of her knee. Then in a single, smooth motion, he grabbed her shoulder with his other hand and dragged her all the way around to the front of him, her legs still encircling his waist, the thick hilt of his sword trapped indecently between her legs.

"How dare you, sir!" She looked up into the dark, slitted void in his helm where his eyes ought to be, fathoms deep and threatening everything she held dear.

"Well, now," he said, his voice a forceful, intimate rumble that radiated through her chest and lit dark delving fires in her belly, "what have I caught here?"

More trouble than you know, she wanted to say. But she couldn't speak a single word. How could she when she was clinging to the muscular hips of a compelling, steamy soldier, staring up into his murderously dark eyes while his huge hands cupped her bottom.

Perfectly.

Privately.

"Release me, this second, before I—" Well, she didn't know what she could possibly threaten to do to him while he had her trapped in this insufferable position. "Before . . . I scream!"

"Scream as you will, madam," he breathed from behind the slits in his faceplate. "I doubt anyone would hear."

And she was quite sure that even fewer would care.

Chapter 2

❝I said put me down!" Mustering her courage and the shreds of her dignity, Talia shoved her palms against the middle of his chest, trying to push away from the man, to unbalance him and get away. But that only seemed to amuse the beast.

"Dammit, settle yourself, woman." He finally raised his faceplate with one hand, leaving her breathless again, her will abruptly trapped by a gaze darker than coal and a heat more fiery than the sun.

"Release me, you foul-smelling lout!" Not that he smelled foul in the least, or that she ought to be noticing his scent of leather and smoke. "Unhand me this instant!"

This time his laughter was darker, entered low

in her belly, vibrating the flat handle of his sword where it pressed the linen of her gown against her most intimate parts.

"Stop your squirming, madam, else you'll find yourself pierced through by more than my blade."

The barbarian's meaning couldn't have been more clear. He was taking liberties with her hem, sliding her already rucked kirtle up and up her thighs, his fingers traveling too quickly, too close, making her jump, and cling harder, higher against his neck till she was face-to-face with him.

"What are you doing, sir? Stop! I don't think you realize just whom you're molesting."

"Madam, were I molesting you," he said, his dark words echoing inside his helm before they found her, "I can guarantee that you'd be quite sure of it."

But the man only kept to his boorish quest, mauling her thighs, tugging at her kirtle until it was hiked nearly to her waist, leaving only the thin linen of her undershift between her most delicate flesh and his sword handle, raising a thrilling flush all over her body.

Not thrilling, entangling. Abashing. Sizzling.

"I said stop!" She slapped the side of his helm again and drew another growling curse.

"Quiet yourself, woman."

"I'll do nothing of the sort. I am Lady Talia, and this is my castle, and if you don't put me down this instant, I'll see that you spend the rest of your wicked days rotting in my dungeon."

The warrior stilled for a long moment, then drew her closer and murmured against her ear, "Your pardon, Lady Talia, but that is a prospect I fear I find far too tempting at the moment."

Steamy heat poured off him, seeped right through the front of her gown, flaming her cheeks and ruffling her thoughts. "Your meaning, sir?"

"We are *joined* together, madam, if you haven't yet noticed." He gave another yank at the front of her gown. "Now, for both our sakes, hold still."

"Joined?" Unimaginable. "We are not."

And yet, there was something very deliberate about his movements, efficient almost, as he glared fiercely into her eyes, his straight white teeth set together in a grimace of concentration, while he shifted his hand at her bottom and lifted her slightly off his hips.

Then the blackguard reached down between his belly and hers, heading directly, unerringly, to that private, nearly exposed place between her legs—

"Sir!" Another well-deserved slap against his helm. But it was Talia who gasped, whose heart gave that immodest leap.

"Still yourself!" he growled, still delving.

And just when she thought he was going to take the boldest liberty of all, the churl yanked at her kirtle just below her thigh and lifted her fully off his waist with those huge hands of his, leaving her free of him at last and feeling absurdly bereft as she felt herself dropping until her feet hit the floor.

Breathless, her pulse racing madly, Talia backed up into the altar, then leveled a threatening finger at the enormous man who was righting his hauberk and breathing in deep gusts, as though he'd just run a mile in all that mail and leather.

"You will leave this chapel immediately, soldier, else I'll have you in chains for stealing from the church and for arrogance and for . . . for . . ." For liberties! For *fondling* me! "Well, you know very well the full extent of your crimes!"

Father John appeared at her elbow, tugged on her sleeve. "But that wasn't the way of it, Lady Talia. He—"

He very well *had* fondled her! But perhaps the good priest hadn't seen that.

"Don't worry, Father." She pushed the stammering priest safely out of the way and grabbed a wooden chalice off the altar. "I'll have him brought to justice before whoever has just scaled my walls and plundered my castle."

"But my lady, he wasn't . . ."

"A pity that your lady is so thickheaded, Father John." The towering man advanced on her, his eyes glittering beneath his helm, his shoulders filling the chapel vaulting. "Has she always been this way?"

Talia stuck her arm out in front of her to stop him, but he simply came on like a landslide. "If you won't take your heathen self out of this place immediately, then I shall—"

"Lock me in your dungeon, madam?" Oh, the man possessed a haughty laugh, dark and profusely compelling.

Despite her outstretched arm and her dire warnings and her title, he'd backed her against the altar, his shoulders blotting out the torchlight, stealing her breath, making her wonder if she'd be found by her new guardian before his swordsman could assault her.

"Run, Father John! Take the candlestick with you while you have the chance!"

"But, my lady, 'tis what I've been trying to tell you! He's the one who *saved* the candlestick and the relic coffer from one of Rufus's louts."

Oh, innocent priest. "You didn't see him, Father, as I did. But when I came in, he was about to run you through!"

"Nay, my lady, he was helping me up from where I'd been thrown." Father John turned to his attacker. "I don't know who you are, kind sir, but I'm most grateful."

"Please, Father—" Talia ran to Father John's side, ready to haul him away from the danger, when a knot of soldiers came through the chapel door.

They stood at attention as one addressed the towering soldier. "My lord!"

My lord? So her tormentor was one of de Monteneau's officers.

The brute turned to the soldiers. "Have you secured the gatehouse, Sergeant?"

The sergeant bowed crisply. "And all of the towers, my lord."

Oh, how she hated this—listening to the state of her castle in the hands of another.

"What of de Graffe?" The man removed his gloves and tucked them into his sword belt, bringing a blaze of heat to Talia's cheeks as she recalled her recent position there.

"Stripped of his tunic and boots and on the run, my lord, as you commanded."

Talia nearly smiled. Oh, to have seen that.

"And now it seems we've gained a half dozen of his men-at-arms."

"Men to be trusted?"

"Every one of them eager and greatly honored to give their service to you, my lord Alexander."

To *him*? To the *beast*?

Mother Mary! This man, this scandalizing brute, was their leader? If so, please God, let him not also be her new guardian! Let him be a trusted officer, sent ahead by de Monteneau to lead the assault.

"See to their assignments then, Dougal."

"Yes, my lord." The man gave His Lordship a sharp salute, made the sign of the cross toward the rood screen, then sped out the door, only to have an even more eager soldier and two squires take his place.

"The quay and the village are secure, my lord."

"Excellent, Gordon."

Talia's stomach fell and rose again. Quigley! Did he make it to the village in time?

"Oddest thing though, my lord . . . about the village."

"Odd in what way?" The man pulled off his helm, and the leather cap with it, revealing a square, clean-shaven jaw, and thick, gleaming black hair that tumbled out onto his broad shoulders.

"Empty, my lord. Not a soul anywhere."

They got away!

"Indeed?" The warrior cast Talia a long, narrow look of suspicion, boring right through her, as though he sought a secret from her. "Thank you, Gordon. Post sentries along the roads, and see to the horses."

"Yes, my lord. But one more thing, if I might." The sergeant wore a half smile.

"Yes?" His lordship swabbed his sleeve across his face.

"Your banner now flies above the barbican."

A strangely deep emotion swept across the

man's hard-planed features, a startled pride, that seemed to lodge in his shoulders, broadening them. "Good. Thank you, Gordon."

"Pleased to serve you, my lord."

And Talia could no longer deny the horrible truth. *His* banner! That could only mean—

"De Monteneau!"

He turned slowly in all that leather and mail to stare at her for a long moment.

"Alexander de Monteneau, my lady." He nodded a careless, almost indiscernible bow in her direction. "The new lord of Carrisford. Which . . . I believe . . . makes you my ward."

His ward. His chattel.

His wife!

"I've been commissioned by his majesty, King Stephen, to unseat a rebel baron and fortify Carrisford." He handed his helm and cap to one of the squires, strode to the chapel door in a jangle of spurs, and threw it open with a sweep of his arm. "Which, it seems, I've done."

Another greedy, warring man to toss her around and threaten everything she loved.

Not for long, my lord. I've already seen to that.

"Well, isn't that thoughtful of the king to care." *You arrogant, rapacious bastard.* "As for you, de Monteneau, you need to understand from the outset that you may be my new guardian, that you may hold my lands at your pleasure, and steal my rents for your coffers, but there's one thing that I bloody well will not allow."

He frowned deeply, narrowing his eyes to thick-lashed slits. "And that is, madam?"

Her heart seething with resolution, Talia leveled a finger up at him. "I will not, no matter how you threaten or cajole, agree to marry you."

Chapter 3

*M*arry her?

Bloody hell, all Alex wanted to do was taste her glistening, upturned mouth and its pouting frown, to fully explore the ripe, round contours of her bottom.

His hands still burned, though they'd been shielded from that silky softness by the thick leather of his gloves.

This was far more dangerous than the kind of combat he was used to, utterly unexpected. This wild-limbed woman who had fearlessly leaped upon him from behind and battered his shoulders and head, who'd clung to him with surprising strength, who'd scowled and railed at him, nose to helm, even as he held her fast against him.

And bloody hell, he'd hardly been in a position

to object at the time, with his head full of her meadowy scent, and his focus transfixed on the intimate encircling strength of her legs around his waist, her heels digging into his buttocks.

His imagination had run completely amuck. 'Twas a great fortune that his thick sword had shielded her from the rutting shape and the fullness of him.

An even greater fortune that the woman was now scowling fiercely at him. Lips full and sulky, glinting in the torchlight, another volley of rebellion poised there on her mouth.

And her head full of some preposterous notion about denying him a marriage to her. Foolish woman. He'd come too far, made too much progress toward his objective to turn his plans back now. Lady Talia would soon understand just who was in charge.

"Lest you have forgotten in the chaos, madam," Alex said, filling the scented space between them, lifting her stubborn chin with the end of his finger, tempted to follow the clear column of her throat into the shadows beyond her chemise, to the hint of roundness there, "you are my ward."

Yet rather than lowering her gaze or cowering from him as a mild and proper ward ought to do, the blasted woman narrowed her glittering eyes at him. "Believe me, de Monteneau, I haven't forgotten. I know exactly the consequences of a wardship, my lord guardian, every degradation—"

Degradation?

"Every act of abasement and corruption."

Bloody hell, she was a madwoman. " 'Tis a legal arrangement, madam. Between King Steven and me."

"And *me*. Not that I count for anything more than that sconce over there. But I'm repeating my warning to you, my lord, that a marriage between us is impossible. I am sick to death of you and your sort breaking down my gates and destroying everything in sight. Taking your pleasure where you will." She straightened, tossed that cloud of red-gold hair over her shoulders and started away. "Now if you'll excuse me, I have a castle to rescue from your accursed invasion."

The woman had been damnably fascinating to watch, but his amusement fled as she tried to bolt from him, replaced by a singular flash of fury as he caught her by the upper arm and drew her against the length of him.

"Do not mistake *my* intentions, Lady Talia: I am lord here. *Your* lord. I have the right and the purpose to do whatever I please with your wardship. And you will obey me without question."

"You're a fool if you think that just climbing over my walls and erecting your standard on my ramparts makes you any kind of a guardian. You can't possibly know the extent of destruction a raid like this has on a castle and a village, the fields and the barns and the—"

"I'm a soldier, madam." He pulled her sharply closer, near enough to feel her breath on his cheek, to savor it breaking against the bridge of his nose. "I am intimately aware of the ill effects of war."

She frowned and blinked, then pulled away from him, outrage sparking from her lashes. "Then how could you possibly allow this to happen?"

"This?"

She tromped past him, startling him when she caught up his wrist in her warm fingers and led him like a lamb, out the door and onto the chapel landing. "*This*, de Monteneau! The pillaging and the plundering—"

"There damned well better not be any plundering—" His orders had been clear.

"And the fires..." Her voice rose as she pointed randomly to the courtyard and then the towers, to the dripping sky, her disappointment obvious in her sigh.

His own satisfaction at his swift success was difficult to hide. "Fires, madam? Where? I see nothing burning beyond a few basket braziers. Shall I have them put out for you?"

Her mouth became a firm line as she stared out at the scene, searching for what wasn't there. "There are always fires, de Monteneau."

Always. The word had shaken her voice, rattled that brash confidence.

She was decorated with bits of flowers, her hair

caught at her forehead in a leather band that attempted to rein it in. An odd desire to apologize for all the incivilities of war banged around inside his chest.

"Not this time, madam."

She shot him a scowl, a queen who had snatched back her crown. "I can only imagine what sort of terror the rest of your men are visiting upon my village. And if anything happens to my family, to the people I love . . ."

Family? Stephen had said nothing about the woman having family here. "Madam, I absolutely guarantee that nothing untoward will happen to you or your family, or to your villagers."

She snorted and glared up at him. "You cannot possibly guarantee anything of the sort, de Monteneau. Excuse me, I have work to do." She started off down the stairs without a backward glance at him, let alone begging his leave. An unfortunate habit that he meant to break.

He followed to stop her, but an elderly man caught her as she reached the bottom step. "My lady!"

"What is it, Quigley? What have we lost now?"

"Well, uhm . . . nothing that I could see, my lady," the old man said, casting a wary glance at Alex as he stepped in behind his ward. "It's just that . . ."

The old man's shaggy eyebrows became one as he frowned at the woman then back again at Alex.

"What's happened, Quigley?" She brushed the front of the man's tunic with her hand, a fond gesture that seemed to soothe him.

"Who be he?"

The woman gave a dismissive tsk. "De Monteneau. The new one. Never mind him. Go on."

The new one—as though he was merely a sack of onions brought up to the kitchen.

"I just thought you'd like to know, my lady, that I did that . . . *thing* you asked me to do." Those grey flicking brows confirmed what Alex had expected: deception already.

Alex stepped between his sputtering ward and her ancient minion, pleased to see the man quaking. "What *thing* would that be, Quigley?"

"Well, I . . . uh, my lord, I . . ."

Lady Talia stuck herself between them again. "I sent him off to inspect the grist mill and the quay and bring me a report."

"Both fine, my lady," Quigley shot back. "Not like the last time."

Which earned Alex another accusing frown as his ward took the man's hand. "Good then, Quig, if you'll see to the cellars and after that to the kitchen."

Bloody hell, this was *his* battlefield, not hers. "Hold one moment, both of you."

"Go," she said. And blast it all, if the old man didn't shoot away from them into the crowd.

Alex reached for her, but she managed only a

step away before a mob surrounded her, shouting questions.

Bloody hell, he didn't need this kind of distraction. He'd never given a thought to the woman that he would play warder to—she hadn't mattered to him in the least. Stephen had merely mentioned that she was in her early twenties and an heiress.

The king had left out beautiful, brazen, and capable of landing a stinging blow to his head, right through the thickness of his helmet.

Taking that bastard Rufus's castle had been simple—an easy walk through the gate, past the inebriated guards, and the rest had fallen into place, as it always did, with his highly skilled army of knights and archers.

And now he was the lord of a threadbare castle that was proving more trouble than gain.

His fiercely protective ward was shoulder deep in questions, flinging her orders far and wide.

"You can tell His Lordship's sergeant that the doves belong to me and that the dovecotes need to be secured, Flynn."

"Aye, my lady."

"Cap off all of the wellheads, Joscelyn. Hobbs, you and Rowley round up all these animals and see to their proper penning."

"The boats at the quay, my lady? Rufus's men took some of 'em."

"Then get a count. See which are still usable."

And on she went.

The last thing he needed was a beautiful, stubborn ward who refused to understand her place in his life. Though, indeed, a beautiful ward did have a certain value of her own. And a strategically placed castle, for all of its ruination, was ever a tempting conquest for any man.

As tempting as the woman who was gesturing to a tall, thin-boned man.

"Collin, take your surgeon's tools to the great hall; it'll have to serve as an infirmary as it did the last time. I'll pass the word."

Alex pushed through the crowd, caught his ward's shoulders and turned her. "Enough, madam. The great hall will serve as my headquarters tonight."

"Of all the arrogance, de Monteneau! The wounded need attention far above your comforts."

"There are no wounded."

She laughed as though he'd just suggested they stop to play a game of chess. "If you'll pardon me, my lord, my people need my help just now."

Her people.

Bloody hell! It was time to show the woman who was master here, to claim her wardship unequivocally in front of her people as well as his own.

"You'll come with me, madam." He left the woman occupied with meting out her orders, mounted his horse waiting nearby, heeled him through the crowd, and moments later had the sputtering woman sitting across his lap, clasping her tightly against his chest.

"How dare you, de Monteneau!" She whipped around inside his embrace and glared up at him, then twisted to get away. "Let me down this instant."

Alex only wheeled his horse and headed toward the barbican, trying not to think about the woman's scent, the incongruously sagging band of flowers woven into her hair.

"You'll hold yourself still, madam."

"Not until you put me down, else I'll—"

"Else what? You'll smack me in the head again? You're again in no position to issue threats, madam. I am your guardian; this castle is mine to administer as I see fit. And now I'm about to ensure that everyone, including you, understands."

Ensure *how*, Talia wondered, barely able to see beyond the beast's hulking arm banded across her shoulder, holding her fast against his chest, stunning her with the searing heat that poured off him.

Seven assaults on her castle and none had ever gone like this one: the courtyard returned to normal a half hour after the attack, no sign of fire, or bloodshed, or the usual thieving by the victorious soldiers, not a single head on a pike to warn of the perils of crossing the new warlord.

Most unbalancing of all, never once had she

been captured by their leader, let alone mounted on his lap like his bawdy wench and paraded through the bailey.

"No fires, no blood, no pillaging, madam," De Monteneau said against her ear. "Are you satisfied?"

"Not until you are gone from here." And that shouldn't be long at all, if everything went as she'd planned. A month or less and it would all be over and they'd be safe at last from men such as de Monteneau, and his king.

"You've no choice in my coming or my going, Lady Talia," the man whispered, his breath steamy hot and brushing against her temple. "And now you and I will set straight the way that things will be between us."

As though she wasn't already painfully aware of every detail.

He trotted his great destrier around the bailey, then into the barbican, the arrogant victor. Catching praises from his men-at-arms and tossing them back, saluting the watchmen, *his* watchmen, now pacing across the ramparts.

Everything just so. As though he'd been lord of Carrisford for years, not minutes.

Then de Monteneau rode with her right to the steps of the great hall and came off his horse with Talia tucked under his arm like a sack of dried peas.

"You have no right to manhandle me, de Monteneau!"

He set her gruffly on her feet and held her shoulders between his hands, any hint of amusement gone from his eyes. "You'll behave yourself inside the hall, madam, else you'll find yourself in *my* dungeon."

"Ah, so then you take *me* as your hostage, de Monteneau, instead of Rufus?"

The huge man went still as a mountain, his eyes flinty cold. "You are my ward, Lady Talia. I am your guardian. Nothing more. Now come."

He caught her elbow and led her up the stairs. Her great hall was now seething with de Monteneau's men. Knights, by the look of them, broad-shouldered, strutting giants; far from battle-weary, or slathering with bloodlust, or carousing on stolen ale. They certainly smelled better than Rufus's lot.

"My lord de Monteneau!"

A rolling, thunderous bellow of approval rose from them, then they surrounded de Monteneau and Talia.

A sea of smiling warriors' faces, hearty grunts of congratulations to their leader, whose heated hands freely rode her hips and the small of her back as he walked so palpably close behind her, who withstood a round of shoulder-slapping that would have felled an ordinary man.

But that was the trouble: De Monteneau was far from ordinary. Extraordinarily tall, with the shoulders of a bear, and hair as black as midnight.

And as arrogant as a bull in rut.

"Where are you taking me, de Monteneau? And where have you taken the wounded?"

"The wounded, madam?" he asked, as though he truly believed his own puffery.

"You heard me tell Collin to house the wounded here in my great hall, yet I see that your men have taken over with their celebrating. I demand to be shown to wherever you're keeping the wounded."

De Monteneau stopped Talia and turned her to face a man who'd been following at his elbow. "The wounded, Patrick—how many?"

Patrick shook his head. "None, my lord, I'm glad to say. At least none beyond a few of Rufus's men-at-arms. Nothing more serious than a scrape."

"That's impossible!" Talia said, her heart still aching from the loss of two of her most well-loved and loyal men, their lives stolen in the battle between Rufus and Aymon, the guardian who'd held her wardship before him. After three weeks of siege followed by Rufus storming the walls, the blood had run freely in the bailey of Carrisford Castle.

"Collin!" Talia pressed through the throng of

warriors and found Collin standing on a bench. "Where are they, Collin—all the wounded?"

Collin shrugged, looking confused. "I waited here for them, my lady, but there aren't any. 'Cept for Tunny's skinned-up elbows. He tripped over one of those loose piglets and slipped on the rainy cobbles. Cook's workin' up a poultice for him."

"Only Tunny? But that's not possible. They're probably hiding," she whispered, hoping the man wouldn't reveal where they were. "Gone to ground until the smoke settles."

But Collin only shrugged again. "'Pears to be no smoke either, my lady."

She'd seen that for herself: no smoke. No blood. No lasting terror.

No more new-made orphans to comfort and care for.

An unwelcome glimmer of hope flickered through her, tapped at her heart, a sensation she hadn't felt in years.

A feeling not to be trusted.

Just as she couldn't possibly trust de Monteneau.

Not with her careful plans to protect her people already in the works. The last thing she needed was a nosy, well-organized guardian to slow her progress.

"This way, madam." The huge man ignored her protest, merely turned her and increased the pressure of his fingers around her arm and against her back.

He was courtly and proud as he strode with her through the crowd, as though he was about to partner with her in a dance and waited only for the music to begin.

"Have you no sense of timeliness, de Monteneau? You've obviously never taken a castle before. There are many things to—"

"That's enough, madam." He laid his sultry warning against the ridge of her ear, just long enough to raise a deliciously, utterly uninvited shiver along her nape, lasting long enough to make her stumble and grab a breath.

And follow him as he stalked toward the raised dais at the screen end of the hall, where green boughs and ribbons incongruously draped the arches and the sconces. Remnants of the wedding that the bullheaded beast had so miraculously interrupted.

Some miracle! Just let him stand here on the dais and try to claim her in marriage as Rufus had done.

She was about to remind him of just that, but he encircled her waist with his powerful hands and raised her up to stand on the bench, eye to eye with him.

"Behave yourself, madam," he said on the end of a snarl. He then turned to his men, and they quieted as though on cue, waiting for him to speak.

"Well done, men." He'd barely finished this easy praise before another cheer filled the barreled ceiling, rattling the wattle between the timbered posts.

"To Lord Alex!" Hoots and hoorays and fists punched into the candle-smoked air.

De Monteneau raised his hand, and the cheering faded. "You've exceeded my hopes, as always."

Their new cheers exceeded the previous thunder. *Oh, what a load of self-righteous pig wallow.*

"I am here, gentlemen, at the behest of His Royal Majesty, King Stephen, the true and just ruler of Britain."

Yes, yes, more cheering, more table pounding approval from his rabble. More time wasting.

"In the king's name, and with his express permission, I do hereby claim Carrisford Castle, and with it, the royal wardship of Lady Talia."

Lord, curse them all, kings and guardians and men who encourage their crimes.

De Monteneau gave a flick of his brow, a humorless smile that she yearned to smack off his face. "There you see, Lady Talia, Carrisford is my castle now. Officially."

Then you and I are officially at war, my lord.

He turned toward her as though he'd read her

thoughts. "Now you'll announce your acceptance, madam, so that my men and your own people may hear and know that you will comply with my authority."

"And if I choose not to accept?"

"Choose, madam?" The man arched a menacing eyebrow, as though he'd never before been thwarted, and now found a feral delight in the possibility. "Don't ever think that you have a choice in the matter."

Or that all your official blustering will give you power over my life.

He settled his broad, possessive hand low across the width of her back. "Now you'll speak, madam, without condition, loudly and clearly."

Tired of playing shuttlecock to every warrior who happened to pass by her castle, Talia turned her most innocent smile on the man.

"Very well, my lord . . . de Monteneau."

The man's strong, white teeth gleamed as he said, "*Now*, madam."

Talia raised her chin to the nearly silent mob, marveling again at their easy discipline, wondering what their behavior meant about their leader.

Her guardian.

She stilled the trembling anger in her chest and cleared her voice. "I, Lady Talia, heiress of Carrisford Castle, do acknowledge the rights and privileges of Lord Alexander de Monteneau as official guardian over my wardship." As the crowd cheered, she turned to the impossibly tall man standing, fists against his hips, at her side. "Will that do, my lord?"

Instead of the red-jowled, flared-nostril anger that she'd come to expect from her guardians, de Monteneau merely said, "It'll do well enough for now, madam."

For now?

A marriage threat, to be sure. One that stirred a silky-hot memory of their first meeting, the breathless heat of him.

"Now this is finished, *my lord guardian*," she said, her jaw aching with anger at the raw effect he had on her thoughts, "you'll excuse me if I take your leave to see that my family hasn't suffered at the hands of your garrison."

"They haven't. Now, sit, madam. We're far from finished here." He lifted her off the bench—his hands hot around her waist—and set her on the bench, her knees as loose as a joint-doll's.

"And I should believe they are unharmed because . . . ?"

"Because I said so."

"I trust that information from Leod alone. I sent him to see to their safety when you came crashing through my gate, and I refuse to take your word—"

"Bring me this Leod person," de Monteneau said to one of his eager pages, then scanned the crowd as he sat on the table, one boot on the bench beside her. "Dougal, your security report, if you please. Assure the lady Talia that her castle remains intact."

A tall, self-assured man strode from the crowd and stopped in front of Talia. He removed his leather helm cap, even dipped his knee toward her, in what could only be mock courtesy, because he was, of course, just another invader, though he wore a smile that one could almost trust.

"Dougal of Provence, my lady," he said. "Carrisford Castle is as Lord Alex received it from Rufus."

"Hardly a soothing recommendation, Dougal of Provence." She sent the rest of her anger toward Alex. "A castle is only as safe as its ability to protect its people. You'll pardon me if I am not convinced."

Rufus would have backhanded her and sent her sprawling, de Monteneau only called up another tall, unhesitating sergeant for still another report.

"The food stores?"

"Intact, my lord."

"The village."

"Untouched."

"The wells."

"Pristine."

And on it went. A litany of her castle's inventory, as she forced herself to hold her tongue, to control her growing panic, disbelieving her new guardian's assurances that anything was well, let alone all of it.

Yet de Monteneau seemed far more intelligent than Rufus or any of the others, doubtless aware that sparing the castle would only add to his coffers.

Which made him all the more dangerous. The sort who would keep careful watch on everything she did.

"My lady! My lady!"

"Leod!" The agile old man boxed and protested every step as he was led by the elbows through the crowd. "Take care with him!"

"Are you all right, my lady?" Leod climbed up onto the dais, threw himself between Talia and de Monteneau, and glared up at the towering warrior.

"I'm quite fine, Leod." She stood and put herself between Leod and His Lordship. "How are the children? Brenna can be difficult during these raids."

"Oh, they all be fine, my lady. The young ones slept through it all." Which, finally, soothed her fears, because Leod was a lion when it came to protecting her family.

De Monteneau rose and stood directly behind her, a wall of heat and smoke and leather, surpassingly tall. "There's your proof, madam," he said softly.

Leod glared up at de Monteneau, his hand at

his dagger. "And who be you, sir? Who is he, my lady?"

Who, indeed?

"It's all right, Leod. This is Alexander de Monteneau. He's the new lord of Carrisford."

Leod gave a good snort. "Is he, now?"

Knowing Leod's stubborn, squint-eyed challenge all too well, Talia turned him on his heels. "Now please go back and stay with the children."

"You're sure you'll be all right, my lady? He's a big one, he is," Leod said, loud enough for all to hear. "Bigger'n any of the others."

And quicker.

And wiser.

And far, far more handsome. A stray thought that went fluttering through her chest.

"You gonna marry him?" Leod whispered.

Dear God! Had de Monteneau heard? Her ears filled with the slamming of her pulse.

Not that it mattered; she'd marry the man over her dead body.

"Please go, Leod. Hurry." Talia watched Leod dodge through the crowd, leaving her with a dark crimson blush, unable to look at de Monteneau.

But he seemed not to have heard Leod's ridiculous question. "We're done here for now, Dougal. Settle the men into the barracks, and I'll see you back here at daybreak."

De Monteneau turned to his men, gave a nodded salute, and they broke into another bellowed cheer that hung in the rafters as the hall emptied.

"So. Am I finally free to go as well, my lord guardian?"

He eyed her for a very long time, then relaxed, as though the battle was won and he believed he was settling into her castle for good. "You're free to show me to the keep."

The family quarters? "The keep, my lord? Tonight? Why? It's late and—"

"And I want to see to my chamber."

Talia's heart stopped. "Your chamber? In the keep? But Rufus housed himself in the Red Tower—"

"I am not Rufus." He bent to her, his gaze steely cold and dangerous. "You'll do well remembering that, Lady Talia. Now, take me to the keep."

He hooked Talia's elbow and pulled her through the great hall and out the door.

Toward the keep. Her home.

Her heart.

"I'm sorry, my lord," Talia said, trying to disengage her elbow from his grip. But he only pulled her against his side and kept walking. "You see, there's no chamber made up for you at the moment. My own chamber is—"

"Available, madam?"

Where the devil was all this unseemly blushing

coming from all of a sudden? Every word the man spoke seemed to take on wholly improper textures.

He was steel and leather and a soft kind of heat that forced its way through the seams of her gown.

Talia stopped beside the well and turned on him. "My chamber is *not* available to you, my lord. You can take the . . . uh . . . the solar."

In the shifting shadows of the courtyard, she could see the hardening of his jaw.

"You'll soon learn, madam, that I'll take whatever I please, whenever, whether you will it or not."

Chapter 4

Deceptive woman. Her every word, every breath as distracting as her scent.

She flounced past him, stopping long enough to scratch a scruffy hound behind the ears and murmur an encouragement that set the beast's entire body wagging, then laid him out, legs up, on his back.

"Good lad, Rollo." And then the woman took off across the bailey, trailing the enchanted hound in her wake. "The keep is this way, my lord."

Feeling too much like the hound himself, Alex caught up with his ward in two strides, only to become a part of her growing entourage.

"What shall I do with the feast, my lady? There's food everywhere in the kitchen."

Feast? What bloody feast?

The woman stopped and studied Alex for the briefest moment before she turned slightly from him and whispered something to the anxious young man, never shifting her eyes from his own, as though he would allow the woman her secrets.

"Oh, aye! Consider it done, my lady. Thank you!" Then the young man sped away, his apron strings flying.

She started off again, but Alex caught her arm. "Feast, madam?"

Her eyes tracked his, stars of mutinous brightness in the moonlight. "Venison, a turnip custard, a lumbarde, sorrel soup . . ."

"I didn't ask the menu. What sort of feast? Why?"

She sighed as though he could never understand. "Your arrival interrupted what was sure to become another of Rufus's drunken brawls, my lord."

More than a drunken brawl, to be sure. "So what did you just tell the boy?"

"That he could distribute the food to anyone who was hungry. A common malady here at Carrisford, my lord." She stood with her shapely hip against her palm, daring him to reverse her order, so obviously certain that he would do just that.

So utterly incorrect. Better to keep her off-balance. "Now to the keep, madam."

She drew up her mouth into a confused frown,

then nodded and ducked through an archway into a small inner ward that was moonlit and smith-iron blue, bordered by the three-storied stone keep itself, and flanked by timber-picketed walks along the wall towers.

The woman was stopped by three more of her frantic people, efficiently answered their questions, then led Alex past a well house and a neat, rain-glinted garden before starting up a short, wooden-roofed staircase that ended abruptly at a thick, closed door.

"Jasper!" The lady rattled the latch. "'Tis me, Lady Talia!"

The door opened a crack to still another elderly, wiry bearded man, this one wearing an ancient helmet. The remains of her army, perhaps?

"Thank the good Lord, my lady!" The old soldier threw open the door and pulled the woman inside, only to give her what must have been a bone-cracking embrace. "Leod said you were safe, but there's nothing like seein' for m'self! Were many killed this time?"

This time. Such a telling phrase.

"None, Jasper," she said, throwing Alex a disdainful, disbelieving glare as he followed her inside the guardroom. "At least none according to His Lordship, here." She tsked. "My new guardian."

Jasper glowered at Alex, tucking his frown up

into his moustache and brushing a light powdering of grey off his sleeves and his thin shoulders. "The devil, you say?"

"He might well turn out to be the devil, Jasper," the woman said, taking off the old man's helmet and handing it to him. "But just now he'd like to see his chamber."

Jasper snorted. "His what?"

"Yes, Jasper. His Lordship will be staying here, in the keep."

A very pointed statement, rife with secret meanings.

"But the *children*, my lady! Rufus never even . . . I mean, all the others—"

"Yes, I know, Jasper. But the solar will have to do for tonight. We'll make His Lordship comfortable, won't we? If you'll follow me, my lord."

She flashed Alex a completely false smile as she grabbed an oil lamp off the neat worktable and started up the circle of stairs, muttering under her breath—doubtless cursing him and all his kin.

She'd already opened the door by the time he reached the landing and was breezing into the room, lighting a lamp on a table beside a brazier.

" 'Tis a fine room, my lord guardian," she said, suddenly more the overly generous hostess and less the she-dragon of but a few moments ago. "Plenty of light during the day. Windows to the inner ward."

Tapestried walls and a cluster of chairs, a worktable, a settle by the cold brazier. No bed, but that was easily taken care of.

Certainly better than the tent and cot he was used to.

His home, for the moment.

His castle.

His ward.

"I hope you're pleased, my lord?"

Pleased? Bloody hell, the woman pleased him dangerously well; that softly impatient hand shaping her hip, her hem revealing an equally impatient tapping foot, the discrepant flowers sagging from her girdling belt, her inexhaustible resolve.

"It will do, madam." Would have to do, for the time being, for his purposes.

"Good, my lord, then I'll see that you get a—" She stopped short as a great pounding suddenly rolled down from the wooden stairs. A sound that drew a sharp but deeply concerned frown from the woman.

He nodded toward the thundering sound. "What would that be, madam? Prisoners?"

Fear flickered across her fine features, softening them for an instant. "My private apartments are above."

"Then you have bats, madam."

And then they came swooping down the stairs, pounding footsteps and giggling voices and then a useless bellow from far above.

"Come back here, young ladies! This minute! Do you hear me?"

But the chaos only increased, until it spilled into the solar along with two girls, then Leod, who hadn't a chance of catching up with them.

"Taliaaaaaaa!" The girls sped past him to his irritated ward, encircled her with their arms.

"Is he gone?"

"Are you married, yet?"

Married?

"Did you have to kiss Rufus?"

Kiss de Graffe?

"Does this mean you're going to have a baby now?"

A baby? Holy Christ!

"What the bloody hell is going on here, madam?" His bellow stopped everything. Gained him two pairs of startled eyes and another pair flashing over the heads of the girls.

"My lord, please refrain from cursing in front of the girls."

Her family? Sisters? Far too old to be of her own body. Golden-haired, clinging fiercely to her, hiding in her skirts now.

"Who's he, Talia? Who are you, sir?"

"Talia, there's a man in here."

"Yes, Fiona."

"Where's Rufus?"

Why the devil would the woman be kissing that bastard de Graffe? And why was she looking at him as though she had just been caught in some magnificent falsehood.

"Explain, madam."

She ignored him, bent to the girls. "Rufus is gone."

"For good, Talia?"

"Please, please say for good."

Another glance at Alex, before she said, "Rufus won't be coming back."

She was bloody well right about that.

"Yayyy!!" The girls clasped hands and jumped around in a circle until the woman took hold of their wrists and held them apart.

"Settle yourselves, please. My lord, this is Brenna." She raised the hand of the eldest. "And this is Fiona. My sisters. Ladies, this is Lord Alexander de Monteneau."

They turned to him as a pair, inspecting him from head to boot, still holding fast to Talia's hands.

"A new one, Talia?" Fiona said, leaning hard against the woman, her teeth catching up her lower lip. "Is he going to stay, do you think?"

"Are you going to marry him, Talia?"

Marry him?

"Brenna, please. Take Fiona and go to bed."

But the pair didn't seem to be finished with him. "He's big! Lots bigger than Rufus!"

"To bed, Fiona! Take them, please, Leod."

Alex could only stare at the woman and wonder about all this marriage talk. And babies and kissing. What the holy hell had been going on before he'd arrived?

She cast him a short, angry glance, then shuffled the two girls toward Leod and the door. "Upstairs with you both. Now!"

"But Talia, what happened to Rufus?"

She sighed and closed her eyes for a moment, then said to Alex, "I'll have a bed sent here to you, my lord guardian. If you need anything further, my chamber is on the next landing, and Jasper is below."

She turned to leave, but he took hold of her arm. She stopped and looked up patiently into his eyes.

"Madam, you haven't answered my question—"

She frowned, glanced at each of the girls, then shook her head at him. "Please, my lord, the morning will have to be soon enough."

And then she was gone. Without a by-your-leave!

The bewildering woman and the giggling girls and the frowning old man, and all those drooping flowers still tucked into her circlet and her belt.

Bleeding blazes! Nothing had gone as he had imagined, beyond the bloodless battle and the simple transition of power. He'd expected to find an acquiescent and overwhelmed young woman; not an intelligent, too clever, passionate beauty who could so easily distract him from his intentions.

A woman wholly entangled in her family; one she loved more dearly than her own life.

The sort of love he'd lost long, long ago.

He wouldn't dare hang me, Alex. Kings don't do that.

But, oh, my brother, Henry hadn't been just any king. What was the life of a ten-year-old hostage when it could satisfy his royal fit of outrage? After all, he'd murdered his own brother to gain the throne of England, and with it Normandy.

It should have been me he hanged, Gil, not you.

Bloody hell, it should have been their cunning bastard of a father. A man who had gladly offered two of his young sons as fodder for his dishonorable deeds.

The sort of love that he'd learned to keep clear of.

"Your bed, my lord. As my lady ordered." Jasper entered abruptly with three other men, as though the woman had magical communications with her people.

God knew the kind of enchantment she was capable of working on his men.

"There in the corner, Jasper. I'll be back." Alex started out the door.

"Would you like bathwater as well, my lord?"

Great God, that sounded good. Leisurely and

steaming. But later. Just now, he had a castle to secure.

"Bathwater, yes."

With any luck it would be well chilled by the time he returned—cold enough to divert his thoughts from the compelling woman who lived on the landing above.

Are you going to marry him? A bizarre question. Asked not only by the woman's sisters, but he was sure that he'd heard the same question from old Leod in the great hall.

He crossed the courtyard, his mind sorting through the work ahead of him, the rest of him wondering why the devil the idea of Rufus laying a finger on the woman, let alone kissing her, should set his nerves on end.

"I think you should have married Lord Alex right away, Talia!" Brenna breezed into the girls' chamber, twirled around the room in her night-gown.

Fiona joined her whirling dance. "He's bushels more handsome than Rufus!"

"And taller and grander!"

"And nicer."

Nicer? A minute in de Monteneau's presence, and the girls were enchanted. Not quite the response that would keep them safe from his influence. And nothing of the fear they'd had of Rufus and the others.

"Quiet your voices; you'll wake the girls." Talia bent over Lissa and tucked the soft woolen blanket around her shoulders, then kissed Gemma on the top of her tousled red head, grateful that they could sleep through most anything.

"You'll marry him sooner or later, Talia. Just like what happened with the others."

"I never married a one of them, Brenna, if you recall."

"But this one's different, I think." Brenna dashed to the casement window and pushed open the drapes, then the shutter. "Did you see his dreamy eyes?"

Dark as a moonless midnight and just as dangerous.

"I don't want to hear another word about marriage or kissing, Brenna. Not about Rufus, and certainly not about my new warder."

Marriage was off the bargaining table this time around.

And she was in the process of making sure there wouldn't be a next.

Lord, she was so tired of it all, the war and the unrest, and the loss. Being tossed from one man to another as though she were but a ball of cording.

"Now, to bed with you both."

It took her a quarter of an hour to settle them into the bed they shared, still another to describe in detail every minute leading up to the marriage ceremony which, thank the Lord, never happened.

"Did Lord Alex take you by the hair when he

found you, the way Rufus did?" Fiona took a sudden death grip on Talia's hand, worry in her eyes.

De Monteneau's hands were too strong and rough to be as gentle as they seemed, to be trusted.

"No, Fiona, Lord Alex didn't hurt me." And he'd never have the chance to.

"There, I told you, Brenna!"

A rap sounded on the door, followed by a whispered, rasping voice. "My lady! Be you there?"

At Talia's "come," Quigley and Leod and Jasper all came scrambling into the room.

"Shhhh . . ." she murmured, pointing to Brenna and Fiona. "To sleep, young ladies."

And then she funneled the tangle of muttering men out into the dim vestibule, her heart pounding in dread.

"What is it, Quigley?"

"His Lordship's men have been pokin' around the granary in the village."

"Aye, my lady," Jasper said, "and we didn't have time to move all of the booty from the last run."

Talia took a steadying breath. "What exactly was left in the granary? Do you remember? The barrels of dried fruit . . . that spice box . . ."

Leod smacked his forehead. "Hell, that tapestry and the plate chest, too, from the earl of Hampton's sumptuary wagon. We almost lost Wilson getting that."

Aye, and if she was ever caught with the great earl's chest of silver plate . . . It was theft, pure and simple—a hanging crime.

But she'd been so distracted by the new work in the tower cellars and with the threat of her wedding to Rufus, she'd lost track of the contraband.

"How well is it all disguised, Quigley?" she asked, weary to her soul.

"Well enough, my lady, if they don't poke around too closely."

Doubtless De Monteneau would do more than poke.

"And the excavation work in the cellars, Jasper? Did you get a chance to check on any of it?"

"All but the barbican gate and the baketower. But I'll see to them right away, now that I know the girls are safe with you."

"Just make sure the work is undetectable. We'll have to leave off any digging for a few days while we study de Monteneau's comings and goings. Meanwhile I'll try to distract His Lordship from his snooping."

Quigley grabbed her hands between his cold and leathery ones. "Do be careful of him, lass."

"Don't worry, Quig. Now go on back to the granary and be sure it's all hidden. And take care."

"I'll go with him, too!" Leod said, hitching up his sagging sword belt.

They all ought to be safely in their beds, but

they seemed to thrive on chaos. And there seemed always to be plenty of that.

"All right then. Keep an eye on things, but please don't challenge anyone about anything."

"Well, ya heard 'Er Ladyship, men!" And off they hurried down the winding stairs, hobbling like ducks, grabbling at each other.

Talia went back to settling her chattering sisters into their bed, wondering how best to keep de Monteneau from uncovering her secrets.

Directness. Yes, that was the way. Up front and unflinching.

When the girls finally fell asleep, Talia left quietly and stopped by her own chamber to change into dry slippers, and her heart spilled over with relief when she saw the full jug of wine and the pair of cups sitting beside the fire that had long since died.

The wilting flowers on the pillow, the greenery winding up the bedposts.

Her bridal bed.

Her *never-to-be-used* bridal bed.

And de Monteneau had just better get used to the idea.

I have the right and the purpose to do whatever I please with your wardship, madam.

Damn the man! Talia took the dozen steps from her chamber down to the solar, gave the door a single rap with her knuckles, then shoved it open with her shoulder, prepared to stand her ground.

But not in the least prepared for the dazzling sight of de Monteneau, standing tall and entirely naked beside a bathtub, his arms raised with a towel against his long, dark hair.

His eyes clear and piercing her through.

The broad, darkness of his chest.

The sleek, shadowy arrow that led to the trim of his waist.

And his hips.

And the rest. All of it—not at rest.

Startling, dark. So . . . weighty-looking. Lovely and begging the touch of her hands.

"May I help you, madam?"

She swallowed. Gulped. She really ought to look him in the face, but there would be trouble there.

Besides, this was just a stolen glimpse. An irreproducible miracle.

No, this was out-and-out staring.

"Help me? No. I mean, yes . . . my lord." *Still staring. And he is still magnificent.* She purposely bit the end of her tongue, and the flinching pain flicked her gaze upward. Found his eyes, and focused there. "I mean, that is . . ."

"Yes, madam?"

Oh, oh, what a stunning wedding night *that* would have been. With him. The weight of him, his scent. His low, silken voice stealing across her skin.

A foolish, girlish thought.

But the *only* thought she could conjure, beyond something about a wedding . . . A night with him. Ah, yes.

"I don't care what you say, my lord guardian, I will not marry you."

The man had the gall to smile. At least it looked like a smile. A glint of white hinting at his amusement, at her expense, though he stood so completely, so utterly naked, his towel at his side, without a care toward her staring or her opinion.

Bronze and big, so *exquisitely* big. That shadowed mystery at the joining of his thighs stirring on its own, as though something lived there apart from the man himself.

A breathtaking sight that she could get very, very used to seeing if she ever had the misfortune to have to marry him.

If.

"Then, my lady, you'd best not enter my chamber again without knocking first."

Look away, Talia!

"I . . . I knocked loudly enough!" She finally found the sense to turn away from him and all that self-assured maleness, to study her mother's tapestry, to idly straighten it. The ripening orchards and the alabaster tower, the rearing unicorn and its silky, jutting horn.

"Aye, and then, madam, you entered without my permission. I advise against the practice."

"Is that a threat, my lord?" Holy Mother, she was baiting him and stealing sideways glances at him through her lashes.

"Consider it fair warning."

Not fair in the least, but she would heed it from now on. "Speaking of warnings, my lord, that's exactly the reason I came."

De Monteneau's stride was measured as he approached, making her turn toward him in self-defense as he tucked away the end of the towel, now wrapped carelessly around his hips.

Precariously.

"You burst into my room in the middle of my bath, in the middle of the night, to forbid me to marry you?"

"No. That's not the reason I came." He was just a few steps from her, an enormous, quizzical bear, studying his supper. "But, yes, actually. You can't. Ever."

"Can't marry you?" He raked his fingers through his hair, shedding light little drops on her face and across her neck, like sharing a spring shower.

"That's absolutely right, my lord. You can't marry me."

"Ah, but my dear Lady Talia," he said deliberately and so nearby, she could feel the heat pouring off his bare chest, his arms, seeping through her kirtle. His steamy kind of spice. "I *can.*"

"But you won't, my lord. I forbid it."

He laughed softly and from deep in his chest, narrowed his dark eyes, sending a thrilling glint through the slits. "Just like the rents on your lands and your knight's fees, my lady, I am free to dispose of or collect for you or from you whatever I choose. Be it a marriage between us or selling off your herds of sheep and cattle."

Barely able to breathe for the power of his dizzying nearness, Talia slipped from him to the safety of the opposite side of the table. "You're too late."

She'd never seen quite so thunderous a look. "For your *marriage*?"

"For my sheep and cattle, de Monteneau. My warder before Rufus sold them off. And the lambs. And everything else he could put his claws into."

Somehow, he'd distracted her long enough for her not to have noticed that he'd backed her around the table onto the casement cushion, giving her no choice but to sit.

"'Tisn't quite morning yet, madam, but it's time that you answer my earlier question."

"Which question was that, my lord?" This interrogation had gotten completely out of hand. She'd come only to distract him from the evidence in the cellars and from pillaging her granary, and now he seemed bent upon pillaging her.

He put his bare foot on the casement step, pinning her knees between the seat and his rock-hard calf.

"Exactly what were you doing just before my attack on your castle?"

"Me?" She felt stalked and hunted. "Why would you care about that? You were after Rufus, not me."

He studied her for a very long time, scrubbed at the line of his jaw with the back of his fingers, his midnight-dark, two-day beard making a raspy, homey sound that made her want to reach out and stroke him herself.

"I was, indeed, after Rufus de Graffe. A lazy bastard of rebel, a sharp pain in Stephen's royal backside. I also knew that his castle—"

"*My* castle—"

"That *Carrisford*," he said, without breaking his cadence, "would be simple enough to seize. But I couldn't possibly have expected the gates to be wide-open and the guards drunk, now, could I?"

Talia fanned the sultry air between them with her hand. "Imagine the luck, my lord."

"And I certainly never expected merely to stroll in through the gatehouse, unchallenged." He sifted his fingers slowly through her hair and came away with the stem of a wilted gentian, which he twirled between his fingers. "Now tell me, madam, what were you doing before I came?"

Dear God, she didn't want him to know this

about her. A rag doll bride, handed off again and again, her life at the whimsy of a bastard like Rufus.

The deed nearly accomplished this time but for his arrival.

Her savior.

It shouldn't matter in the least that he knew about the wedding he had interrupted, and yet she felt a dreadful embarrassment begin to blossom in her chest, fueled by her thrumming heart.

"Well, if I recall, I was . . ." She swallowed hard, gulping some of his soap-scented air. And noticing, for the first time, that the estate rolls were spread out on the table across the room, sending her heart in a completely different direction. "I was . . . we were preparing for a feast. The feast of St. Albans. Now, my lord, if you'd—"

His smile grew slowly, utterly feral. The pleasure of the catch. "What a lovely liar you are, Lady Talia."

"How dare you call me that!" She spread her fingers against his bare chest and shoved, trying to slip past him, but he had her well pinned against the cushion, and bedazzled by the imprint of his heat on her palm.

"You've been asked a half dozen times by your people if you were married. Why? What were you doing just before I arrived, and Rufus fled like the coward he is?"

"I was . . . well." If she could only look away

from his eyes, from that dangerous darkness there. "It doesn't matter anymore, my lord."

"It matters considerably that you tell me everything, madam. Or should I send for your sisters, or for old Jasper or Leod or that cagey Quigley fellow?"

She didn't need that worry, de Monteneau scouring the castle and village, interrogating the people she loved. "Leave them out of this."

"What were you doing?"

It really should be a simple thing to tell him. It meant nothing in the long run, and he was bound to find out soon enough, by asking anyone.

"We were . . . That is, Rufus and I were about to . . ."

"You and Rufus . . . ?" He barked this, then straightened to stare at her. "You were about to what?"

Tired of wrestling with this misplaced shame, Talia stood in that small space between his chest and the casement seat. "If you must know, de Monteneau, Rufus and I were about to be married when you seized the castle. That said, my lord, I want your men to stay out of my granary."

Alex caught himself from stumbling backward, fought the force of his heart ramming up against his chest.

Bloody hell! The feast, the greenery draping the great hall. The truth had been there all along, but he'd been too busy to put it together.

"You were . . . married tonight, madam? To de Graffe?"

She huffed. "Nearly married, my lord. There *is* a difference. Now, good night."

Chapter 5

_____ ⌒⊙⌒ _____

"**N**early?" He caught her before she could slip past him. "What the bleeding blazes does that mean, madam? Were you nearly married, or left not quite married?"

His heart was pounding louder still. Not that it mattered in the whole of his scheme. Carrisford Castle belonged to him now, by the king's decree, whether the woman had married de Graffe or not. A rebel's castle was fair game to seize, wardship or no.

But, damnation, she was _his_, to give or to take or to leave be.

"_Not_ married, my lord." She tipped her prideful little chin toward him. "You interrupted the wedding ceremony with your attack."

Interrupted. Incomplete. The stunning relief

dizzied him, startled him with the intensity.

As startling as the directness of her gaze had been when she'd walked in on him with that magnificently honest appraisal of hers. So damned honest that he'd become instantly aroused, pike hard, and it had taken—was still taking—every ounce of restraint not to reel her back against the cushion, spread her lovely thighs, and claim the rest of her.

And now this incomprehensible announcement.

"Interrupted exactly when, madam? Did you manage to leave the chapel steps and make it to the altar?" So much seemed suddenly to hinge on that particular detail. It was a legal matter only; but the outcome had great potential value.

"Why?"

"Tell me."

"I don't see how it matters." But she harrumphed and pressed her rosy lips together, then slipped away from him to the table. "If I recall rightly, my lord, Father John said, 'Bless, O Lord this—'"

She turned, folded her arms under her breasts, and stared at him, as though that was enough information to satisfy him.

"This *what*, madam?"

"This nothing, my lord. There *was* nothing after that, because you arrived with your horde and—"

Alex had been holding his breath, fearing that the woman had been left half-married, loose-ended, in some legal limbo. But now the full force of his relief blew out of his chest like a hot wind, replaced by an even stronger need to be absolutely certain.

"Madam, you are sure that the priest stopped there and then? Asked nothing about the groom taking the bride?"

"Nothing."

"No blessing pronounced?"

"No."

"You gave no consent to anything?"

"I am not married to Rufus." Her cheeks were pink and lovely with anger. "Believe me, my lord, I would know it if I were."

"De Graffe settled nothing on you? No gift of cloth or plate?"

"I was neither given away, nor was my hand covered, my lord. And the only gift that Rufus gave to me during my near wedding was the sight of his ungainly backside scrambling into the nearest cellar. My wardship remains free and clear of any legal encumbrance, if that's your concern." Sparks seemed to flare from her eyes as she bore down on him with a leveled finger. "Mark me well, my lord, I am intimately familiar with the vagaries of wardship. And betrothals. And I want nothing to do with yours."

He'd let her back him against the table with her little tirade, let her poke her hot little finger into his bare chest, her brows winged with fury.

Yes, but a fury from what source?

She hardly seemed the type to be attracted to a brute like de Graffe, let alone defend him. Despite the wilted flowers in her hair and the obvious plans for celebration after the appalling deed had been done. The drunken feasting that would have followed, the parade of disreputable celebrants snaking up the stairs into this very keep, on its way to profane her marriage bed with the devil's blessing.

Alex imagined de Graffe wallowing in Talia's bed, defiling her tender flesh, and felt a bolt of jealous heat.

Bloody hell. He grabbed his robe and shoved his arms into the sleeves. "Do accept my pardon, madam, for setting your marriage plans on end."

"I don't accept your apology for interrupting my wedding to Rufus, my lord, because I don't want it." She turned from him and went to the brazier, taking some of her lightness with her. "But what I do demand is that you keep control of your men as you promised me you would."

"Meaning what?" To a man, his army was the model of restraint, the bad apples weeded out long before they could cross him.

"I mean that my people have little enough to

keep them from starving, especially with winter approaching. How dare you send your men to search the village for the very grain that feeds them?"

"What exactly are you saying?" He'd ordered that the village be left completely alone.

She waggled that finger at him again. "That your men were stealing grain from the village granary. Obviously pillaging for the mere entertainment of it, because as you will discover in the morning, there's nothing left in the village to steal."

He belted the robe and went to the table of rolls. "I gave my men explicit instructions that pillaging would be met with swift punishment."

She glowered down at the estate rolls, lifted one and studied the seal at the bottom. "I see you've already started to work on the records. What's a few sheaves of barley from the village granary, when you can strip the land itself. All five thousand acres."

"Madam, if you learn nothing else about me, you will learn that I don't pillage, that I have no need for plunder. And that I keep my word."

Her gaze was as intent as her probing questions, her lips wine-tinted and moist enough to make him crave a taste. "Then what have you to say about the granary?"

Bloody hell. "Damn the granary, madam. I

don't know why the devil my men were there tonight, but I shall inquire about it in the morning and let you know. My word on it, madam."

She puffed out a laugh. "We'll see, my lord. But since you're number seven, I can't imagine that you'll be the first to break the mold."

The woman was a tangle of scented riddles, meant to ensnare him. "Seven? Seven what?"

"Surely your good king must have told you?"

"I'll hear it from you, madam."

She sniffed and fixed her crystalline blue gaze on his mouth and then his eyes. "You're my seventh guardian in two years, de Monteneau, which puts me in a position to—"

He caught her arm, stared into her face to guard against her dancing diversion. "What did you say, madam?"

"I said that I'm in a position to—"

"Nay, you said that I'm your seventh guardian. What the hell do you mean by that?" Stephen had said nothing of the history of Carrisford; only that it sheltered a rebel baron who must be routed out.

Oh, and you can keep the woman as well, Alex, if you like. Administer the wardship as you see fit.

He didn't see much that fit at all.

Except her thighs around his waist. There, she'd fit him far too well.

"I've had six warders before you, my lord de Monteneau, each one more vile than the next."

"Which makes me the vilest of all."

She opened her mouth, then caught her comment between her teeth and her lower lip, before she said, "I'll reserve judgment, my lord, and pray every day that you're not half so vile as Rufus."

But here was still another relief—that she truly had no tender feelings for the man she had nearly married.

"So this marriage to Rufus wasn't your idea?"

"Hardly."

"He forced you?" Alex waited for her confirmation, felt a stinging need to believe there had been nothing at all between them.

"He was my guardian. I was his ward. He gave me no choice." She was hiding something else from him, something darker and deeper.

"He threatened you?"

She seemed to gather her words carefully, closely, observing his every move. "Rufus didn't have to overtly threaten me. His cruelty was well-known to me. I knew exactly what he was capable of, and he knew whom I loved and how much, and so I . . . capitulated."

Capitulated. He didn't want to imagine what that meant, didn't like the inference.

"And number five, madam? Your guardian before Rufus? Who was he?"

She took a deep breath, glanced down at her fingers, then up at him. "Aymon de Saville."

Now there was a bastard. A man who would sell his mother to the devil for the right price. "Saville held your wardship for how long?"

"For four very long months. Our crops never got into the field this spring. The livestock was slaughtered for his troops, without a thought to husbandry."

His heart was sinking, wondering what he'd find in the morning. "And before Saville?"

"Count Roderick of Ayre, and his brother's eldest son before that. Roderick stuck a knife through the heart of his very own nephew . . . on the eve of . . ." She stumbled and stopped, her shoulders sagged.

And no wonder. Hers was a catalog of loathsome creatures who had power over her by virtue of taking it by force. Himself included.

And now she looked ashamed, those streaks of crimson blushing her cheeks and brow again. He felt every inch the rogue for pursuing. "On the eve of what, madam?"

Talia didn't want to admit to another near wedding. Her life spinning out of control. Or that her would-be bridegroom—nasty bugger that he was—was murdered by his own uncle as they both sat celebrating the coming nuptials in the great hall.

"It was on the eve of St. Cassian's Day. A day I remember well because before my father was killed, we would always celebrate the peach harvest, which, of course, had failed completely that year."

De Monteneau leaned casually against the table, crossing his powerful arms against his chest, his tone pensive, as though he were truly interested. "Yours is a royal wardship, Lady Talia; your first guardian following your father's death would have been appointed by King Stephen himself."

"Lord Cowan was his name. A pleasant enough man. Harmless, and it seems everyone knew it." Elderly and in need of a bride who would give him an heir. She'd refused him repeatedly, but the old blighter had been making arrangements, and she would have gone along with it.

"What happened to Cowan?"

"He was my guardian barely three months when one of Maud's armies came ransacking through the valley, overrunning the castle, leaving Lord Cowan dead and Lord Murdock in his place. My second guardian, in case you hadn't been counting. And now I'm reduced to being shuffled from victor to victor, no matter his allegiance. To Maud then Stephen then Maud again, and so on until now it's back to Stephen and so it will go."

Except that now she'd taken hold of the situation. It wouldn't ever happen again.

His frown darkened as though she'd called his

manhood into question. "I have no intention of losing Carrisford to anyone, madam."

Hardly comforting, with her estate rolls spread out on the table like a tidy meal. "Do you read, my lord?"

"French and Latin. And you?" His voice was suddenly softly probing, like friendly hearth talk.

"My father always said that he could hear me thinking through my ears and insisted that the chaplain teach me. To keep me occupied and out of his hair."

"And did it work? Did you stay out of his way?"

"No."

He laughed lightly, the threat gone from his manner as quickly as it had come. "Ah, then you understand the estate rolls?"

The sly dog; he'd gotten that information without any cost to him. "I do."

He lifted a roll and unscrolled the first three pages. "Are they up to date?"

"As far as I know."

"Reliable?"

"Meticulously accounting for their greed seemed important to each of my guardians. It's all there for you."

Hopefully, my own stores are well hidden in the columns of figures, or listed nowhere at all.

"That being said, de Monteneau, it's past time that we come to an agreement about your conduct while you're here at Carrisford."

"*My* conduct, madam?" He straightened, nearly to the rafters.

She'd never have dared make such a statement to any of the others, but this man seemed to thrive on order, and so she planned to offer him just that.

"Firstly, my lord, you will keep your door locked when you are bathing or in a state of undress."

He took a slow step toward her, then pointed toward the door, his black hair mussed and nearly charming. "Madam, if you recall, you are the one who walked in on me."

That very stunning recollection made her cheeks burn. All that sleek bronze skin, the dark mysteries of the man. The shape and the size of him.

"Completely by accident, my lord." She looked down and studied her fingertips for fear of catching the man's eye and lighting another blush. "You are living in my family quarters, my lord, not with your soldiers. This is our solar. My sisters are not used to a man living here. Therefore, you will comport yourself accordingly."

"Will I?" The man grew treacherously calm all of a sudden, as though he were absorbing her words one by one, to use each later as weapons against her.

"You will also keep your men away from the village. It is mine, and of no interest to you and your soldiers. Which goes doubly for the women of the village. They are off-limits to you and your men."

"Off-limits?" He actually snorted.

"Completely. And so are my stores of food and the remaining livestock in the fields. I will conduct my own manor court, among my own people, without your interference."

The longer she went on, the more quiet he grew, a storm collecting just beyond the mountains.

"You will not commandeer my villeins for your labors. That includes the laundress, the carpenter, the hayward, the cobbler, and anyone else who isn't among your own personal entourage. Should you require laborers, then you will negotiate hours and wages with me."

He was silent and staring for a very long time before he crooked a midnight eyebrow. "Anything else, my lady?" A dark and low question that moved the air with its chill and made her wonder if she'd gone a bit too far.

"Yes, my lord. That you will keep me informed of the war's progress, so that I can be prepared should this bloody, uncertain war come this way again."

He just stood there, unblinking, growing taller, his brow darker with every indrawn breath.

Feeling that she ought to run for her chamber, Talia put herself between the man and the door. "So, if you have no questions for me, then I'll bid you a good night, my lord."

Alex let the woman go, let her trail her hem across the scuffed tiles and out the door, let her believe that she could spout orders to him and that he would simply comply.

Or that he would risk everything he'd built his life upon on a scrap of feminine temper.

The woman would just have to learn differently.

He dried his hair, dressed, pulled on his boots, then took the double turn of stairs to her chamber on the landing above his.

Surprise had always served him well. So he lifted the latch on her door and strode right in.

But the surprise was all his this time.

She was standing in the middle of the chamber, half-turned toward the door, her kirtle in her hand. There was nothing between him and her soft flesh, those glorious legs, but her linen shift.

All the while the brazier flared wildly behind her, silhouetting her too perfectly.

Touché, madam.

"You should keep your door locked, my lady. With a lust-driven lord housed just a few steps away, you never know what might happen."

She chewed on that for a moment, then arched an eyebrow. "Ah, then we're even, my lord, aren't we?"

"Not nearly, my lady." He enjoyed the crimson that rose from her gaping bodice, the whetted peaks of her breasts. He shut the door behind him and opened his mouth to begin his own list of orders, but then noticed the room.

Wilting flowers had been woven into sagging greens, draping the bed hangings and winding down the poles. Pale petals were scattered across the plank floor and the counterpane. A small cask of wine and two cups perched on a chest at the foot of the bed.

An unsettling picture, framed by a half-clothed woman glowering at him from over her pale, finely formed shoulder, her hair free of its moorings.

"What's all this?" Although he already knew at the core of him as he lifted a branching of laurel draped over the doorway. A leaf came off in his hand.

" 'Tis a bride bed, my lord. A wedding bower. Or it would have been, if you hadn't come when you did."

A damned disruptive thought that made his gut churn. Bloody hell, if he'd arrived two minutes later . . .

A marriage interrupted.

A wedding night never completed.

And it pleased him deeply.

"But I did come, didn't I?"

She took a deep, uneven breath. "I'll admit, my lord, that in this one matter at least, I'm very grateful that you have such perfect timing." She turned from him, hitching her shift back onto her shoulder. "You've never married?"

"No." It was an unbalancing question. One that he bloody well shouldn't have answered so blithely, so quickly, not with her outrageous orders still clinging to him, unchallenged. But she had an unsubtle way about her, an honesty that he could only admire, no matter the trouble it might cause between them.

Unusual in a woman. Compelling in this one, standing now with her back to him as she laced up the front of her linen shift.

"Why haven't you, my lord? You're certainly old enough."

A knight without land hadn't much choice in the matter. Though now that he had Carrisford Castle and the king's support . . .

"Circumstance, madam." She didn't need to know anything more.

"And children?" She went to the bed and unhooked a green garland from the drape. "How many have you fathered?"

"I have no children."

"None that you know about, at least." She draped the garland over a chair back and returned to the bed for another.

"You presume entirely too much." He found himself standing beside her in the next breath, outraged to the marrow at her accusation, lifting her chin with his fingers, forcing her to look up into his eyes. "I've fathered no bastards."

"But you're a soldier, after all. It's all a part of the plundering, isn't it? Planting your seed—"

"Enough, madam. I've come here to disabuse you of the notion that you will set the rules for this matter between us. That I would obey them."

"You are my guardian, not my lord and master. Nor will you ever be."

"And you, Lady Talia, are about to learn *my* rules."

He allowed her to slip out of the circle of his arms. "Oh, and what might your rules be?"

"There's but one for you to remember."

"And that is?"

"Simply that I make all the rules and that you will obey them."

She laughed lightly and swept the flower petals off the counterpane. "That's two rules, my lord. I'd be happy to lease you my chaplain. He's very good with figures."

"I rule Carrisford in your name, madam," he said, following her fluttering trail of petals.

She straightened and leveled a glare at him. "In that case, you will rule with honor and compassion, my lord guardian. And due respect for the lives of my people."

"Bloody hell, woman! For the last time, I will administer your guardianship as I see fit, without your opinion or your interference."

"And I will never marry you. Ply me with flowers or threaten me with a hanging, I'll refuse."

Good Christ, if things were different, he just might. . . .

But things weren't different. Could never be. He had precise and intricate plans, careful strategies.

And he was exhausted.

Too tempted to tarry here with her beneath the counterpane. To tangle himself in that curtain of hair.

He drew in a long breath, doing his best not to take in too much of her meadowy scent. "Make no mistake, madam, we'll finish this tomorrow. Sleep well."

Talia watched the man leave, felt him go, like stealing the heat from the sun. But she called after him anyway through the closed door.

"And may you be visited by bedbugs, my lord."

Mother Mary, she wouldn't have dared speak to Rufus this way, or with any of the others.

Where the devil had all this brazen courage come from and where would it take her? She'd learned the hard way to keep her opinions to herself and her actions secret from the men who ruled her life with their edicts and their wars.

But this one was different.

The scented heat of him. Clean. Male. Powerful.

And, oh, so very provoking.

Chapter 6

⁂

"**W**hat do you think His Lordship means, my lady? Havin' me separate out all the horses that Rufus left behind and lead them into the village?"

Talia looked beyond Jasper to the line of house-holders that trailed along the trestle table in the hall. She was trying to catalog the most egregious incidents, trying to make sense of them.

He was a clever devil, this de Monteneau, hiding his sins against her so well.

She'd managed to stay clear of him this morning, though his men were gathering to break their fast, each of them looking clean and jolly and . . . well . . . almost civilized.

Aye, that was what had been missing from Carrisford for all these years. Order. Organization. Control.

Her own, most of all. She felt that palpably this morning. For despite last night's raid, despite the changing of her prison guard yet again and having to put her larger plans on hold for the moment, she felt more in control than she had since her father was killed. Her guardian's equal.

"I don't know what de Monteneau means, Jasper, but do as he says with Rufus's horses. We'll sort it out later."

"The man's a bloody marvel in the smithy." An unusual show of admiration from Leod.

"He is that, my lady!" Jasper added. "Forged an iron shoe his very self, then shod that great snortin' beast of a horse of his."

Wouldn't he just. "I suppose he cooks and weaves as well? How many horses did Rufus leave, Jasper?"

"Well over a dozen, my lady. Maybe two."

No doubt the leavings, the lame, the wormy and the foundering. Hopefully better than nothing.

"For the moment, put the horses in the common pasture and keep watch over them until you hear from me."

Jasper leaned in to her and whispered loudly enough out of the corner of his mouth so that all around them could hear. "He's a fine-looking fellow, he is."

She had to ask, "Who is?"

"His Lordship."

Great Mother of God. "Meaning?" Though Talia was more than certain what Jasper meant even before he raised one of his shaggy eyebrows.

"Seems a right kind of bloke for a husband, don't you think?"

Leod smacked Jasper's shoulder. "Bite your tongue, you old goat!"

Talia caught the end of Jasper's beard and tugged him close by. "I think you'd better go move those horses, Jasper, before His Lordship changes his mind."

Jasper's ready smile sagged, the old man's soft heart forever broidered on his sleeve. "Ya know I'm only askin' after you, my lady."

Talia would have grabbed him back for a hug, but he was swallowed up by three other men who took his place.

"We're frightfully low on barley, my lady," Alroy said. "And none in the village."

"And the quay's lost its east shoring."

Ha! Finally, something to report to de Monteneau. "How did it happen, Leod?"

"Blind Philip's wife saw it ripped out by Rufus's men trying to escape in a currack."

Blast it. Not de Monteneau at all. "And the fulling mill, Matthew?" Always a prime target.

"It's fine, my lady. Though we're still in dire need of wool, what with our sheep gone."

"Aye, Matthew, if only a flock of sheep would

wander by, or a caravan of the king's woolens for the winter." A quarter hour later, she was left with Leod, the rest of the problems having apparently taken care of themselves.

"Leod, have you seen Quigley this morning?"

"Not since last night, my lady. We left him in the village and come home."

Quigley often took chances where he shouldn't. "He didn't say anything about—"

"Holding court, madam?"

She ought to have known that de Monteneau was nearby; the air around her eddied and crackled, lifting the hair on her nape, sending Leod hobbling off.

And blast it all, if that wasn't a telltale blush blooming right out of her chemise.

Talia spared de Monteneau a brief glance but was met with the distracting memory of the man standing naked in the light of the fire—an unwelcome artifact of the night before.

"Good morning, my lord."

He took a possessive moment and cast his arrogant gaze around the growing crowd in the hall. "It will be, madam, after I talk to your steward."

"Why him?" Had Quigley been found out?

A muscle firmed and flexed in his jaw. "The name of your steward?"

"His name is Quigley. But whatever you need to say to him, you will say to me first."

"Very well, madam." He took a cocky stance,

one boot on the bench beside her. "When was the last time the cesspit in the barbican tower was cleaned out?"

"Well . . . I don't know. Why?"

"Because it's offensive to my men, and therefore to me. When was it last cleaned?"

Talia had made a point of never entering the barbican towers. "If the cesspit offends you, my lord, you have my leave to clean it."

"Do I now?" That muscle in his jaw was working hard, the deep midnight of his eyes becoming darker.

Before she could decide whether to respond or to ignore him or to haul off and kick him in the shins, a young voice rose above the crowd, parting it.

"A message, my lord. From the king."

A stony coldness shuttered de Monteneau's eyes, directed toward the lanky lad standing at attention beside him. "When, boy?"

"Came just now to the guardhouse. I brought it straight away, my lord."

De Monteneau snatched the sealed document. "Does the messenger await a reply?"

"No, my lord. He's gone, my lord. Thank you, my lord." The young man had dropped a terrified, trembling bow with each "my lord," bent upon scurrying out of his lord's reach. But when he turned to go, Talia realized that the dark red stain on his tunic sleeve was blood.

"Just a moment." Talia caught his wrist then studied the stain. "Is this yours?"

His dark eyes flew open. "Of course it's my tunic, my lady. Bought it in London a few months past."

She tried to smile him out of his terror. "Is this your blood, I mean? Are you wounded?"

The young man shot his questioning gaze to de Monteneau and received an even deeper scowl. "Uhm . . . well . . ." He looked stricken, caught between flight and paralysis.

"Answer her, boy." It was a cold, lifeless command.

"Yes, ma'am. My blood."

She gentled her voice. "Here, then, let me see." She gingerly raised the wide sleeve past the wound. "How did this happen?"

"Last night, my lady. I was helping to take the guardtower."

"No injuries, de Monteneau?" Talia lifted her eyes to the frown she knew she'd find. "What about this boy's wound? Ragged and dangerous and completely untended. Or don't your young soldiers count for anything? How many others do you have lying about mortally wounded?"

"Away with you, lad," he barked, "to the barber."

Talia planted herself between them. "No, my lord. I'll dress the wound myself. Sit."

She backed the startled boy to the bench, and he

sat down with a plunk, watching in terror as she started rolling up his sleeve to his shoulder. She'd brought her medicines with her this morning, certain that she'd find something exactly like this.

And just as certain that de Monteneau wouldn't approve. "I have a company surgeon, madam."

"Aye, my lord, but where is he just now? Tending to your horses, I suppose?" Talia sat down beside the boy and studied the wound. Not life-threatening, at least not yet, but sore enough to make him suck air between his teeth when she dabbed gently at it with a rag dipped in a tincture of agrimony and vervain.

"If you please, kind lady, I . . . I can wait for His Lordship's surgeon." The boy kept his eyes trained on de Monteneau and tried to stand.

"You should have thought of that last eve, lad. Now hold still. I'll do my best not to let it hurt." Talia kept him in place with one hand to his shoulder and dabbed at the wound again. "Now, you'd please me a great deal if you tell me your name."

"Kyle, ma'am."

"You're doing just fine, Kyle."

At last a shy smile from the boy and a sigh that seemed to melt him. "And 'tis feeling a lot better."

De Monteneau leaned the heel of one hand hard on the table. "Madam, I insist that you—"

"Excuse me, my lady, but when you're done there, could you please give look to my finger when you're finished?" It was the huge man who'd put out the fire in the stable and had promised not to harm Figgis. "Burned right through my glove. Hurts like a damned conflagration."

"Damnation, Simon!" De Monteneau grabbed the soldier's hand and scowled at the angry red blister that must have broken recently. "Why didn't you see Hartman about this?"

"Didn't hurt till this morning, and he's with the horses like the lady said. I thought since she was tending to Kyle here, she wouldn't mind tending to me."

"I don't mind at all, sir." In fact, it pleased her to no end to see de Monteneau's will thwarted. And the boy grinning at her. Perhaps she'd even be able to resurrect the old garrison infirmary.

"According to the lady herself, Simon, she's got far better things to do than to play nursemaid to—"

"Every wound on the battlefield is a danger, my lord. You know that. Is there anyone else in your company the worse for last night's attack? I'd be happy to look at them."

Why the devil was it more disturbing when the man grew quiet rather than blustering?

"Fine, then play nursemaid all you wish, madam. I've a castle to secure."

Talia resisted the utterly childish urge to stick out her tongue at de Monteneau as he walked away toward the dais, leaving Simon unfazed by the man's bluster.

"And I'd be doubly happy if you'd give a look at my squire Keenan and the knot on his head."

"Of course, Simon." And so went the next hour, with Talia sorting through the reports trickling in from her household staff and tending to a never-ending parade of de Monteneau's ever-more-slightly wounded men, who afterward offered their seemingly genuine gratitude for every poultice and salve, until Quigley was at last standing in front of her, a fidgety cast to his old grey eyes. That telltale blend of fear and triumph that had allowed him to serve her and her father so faithfully and well.

He waited till the last patient was gone from her makeshift infirmary, then whispered softly, "Three barrels of lamp oil, my lady. A bundle of saddle leather, a bag of arrowheads, a chest of sawyer's tools, two wheels of cheese, three sacks of beans." He flashed her a wild half smile. "And more."

"How? From where?"

Quigley said nothing more, only nodded slightly in de Monteneau's direction.

Sweet Mother of God! Not a passing caravan, not a stray delivery cart, but right out from under His Lordship's arrogant nose.

"Quig, you shouldn't have taken the chance."

"Oh, but the opportunity, my lady . . ."

"Except that de Monteneau seems the sort of man who keeps records of all he owns." Well, there was nothing to be done about it now but see the lot safely stored.

Talia started packing up her medicinals, keeping one eye trained on her new guardian, watching for some indication that he might have already learned of the theft, trying to ignore the lifting of her pulse when he smiled at something Dougal said. "How did you manage it, Quig? And when?"

"The last of His Lordship's carts were having trouble coming through the brindle cut early this dawn. A few of us offered to help. 'Twas a simple thing to relieve the carts of a few items in the process."

"Dear God, Quigley. That's too close." Yet Talia couldn't help but smile back at the dear old man. "I trust that you used your usual ingenuity in covering His Lordship's loss?"

Quigley waved a dismissive hand. "His men won't notice till they're unpacking the goods here at the castle. Maybe not even then."

"You've stashed it all where?"

"In the west sheepfold. I'll try to bring up the oil and the sawyer's tools this afternoon."

"And the salt pork, too. Excellent work, Quig." Though he terrified her at times.

"I was taught by the best, my lady." He bowed in her direction.

Aye, but she'd become the best highway robber in the kingdom out of dire necessity, not from any desire for infamy or revenge or greed.

Just as she'd had to learn to read mason's marks and stone arches and timbered cellars. Necessity.

"And now I'm off to the village before de Monteneau gets a chance. I'll signal if there's a problem with bringing in the goods from the sheepfold. Now, you'd best go check with His Lordship. He had a question for you. Something about the cesspit in the guardtower."

Quigley scrunched up his weathered face. "Am I at his service, then?"

"I've already told him I'd lease him a shovel and pail. You can take it from there."

Quigley shifted on his feet, looking unusually hesitant. "One more thing, my lady. A delicate question for you. Not that you have to answer, of course."

"Go ahead, Quigley." Talia tucked a bag of dried agrimony into her medicine chest. "You've known me since I was a babe; you can ask me anything."

More feet shuffling. "Well then, will you be marrying this one? Seems a cleaner sort—"

"Any question but that one, Quigley." She kissed him on his bristly cheek. "Now, go see if you can head him off while I see to the village."

Talia watched Quigley tuck himself into the periphery of de Monteneau's crowd, and hoped that His Lordship's meeting with his council would keep him occupied well into the afternoon. Taking one last look at the compellingly handsome man so intently involved with his men, she slipped out of the hall.

She made a brief detour to her chamber for her cloak and more medicines, to the kitchen to heap a large basket with bread and salted meat, before starting for the barbican with its new garrison of orderly watchmen walking the parapets, the sun glinting off their armor.

"Good morning, my lady," came a series of greetings as she approached the guardtower. Polite bows, hands to hearts, unexpectedly courtly smiles.

Respectful in the extreme. Rufus's men had always made her feel uneasy with their leering whenever she passed through the gates—as though they would jump down and drag her into their lairs, or slam the gate shut behind her—de Monteneau's men seemed . . . safe.

Protective. As though they believed they were on her side, and that she was on theirs.

As though their lord demanded something different from them, and they gave it readily.

If she could only believe such a thing was possible. That Alexander de Monteneau was different than all the others.

That he could actually protect her family and defend Carrisford and its people from the war, stave off starvation and the cold. And all of his soldiers were as loyal and as invincible as they appeared to be.

Peace and protection, the children running and laughing freely through the village and the castle gates.

A husband to love and respect, for her to cherish and honor in return.

Then she wouldn't have to . . .

But all those fanciful feelings of hope and security fled a moment later. She hadn't seen the familiar shape in the gatehouse passage until she was out of the glare of the sun and almost upon him.

De Monteneau.

The most astounding thing was that he'd somehow slipped ahead of her and now leaned easily against the portcullis channel, looking as patient as a wolf about to pounce.

"Ah, my lady, I see that I'm just in time for my tour of the village."

She sniffed at the grandness of the man's arrogance, at her plans gone awry, and strode right past him, knowing that he would follow.

"As you proved last night so well, my lord, you do have impeccable timing."

He followed after her like a swirling summer storm, his cloak wrapping around the backs of her legs, his astonishing warmth clinging to her ankles.

"Timing, my dear, is all in the eyes of the beholder."

Chapter 7

~~⁀o‿o⁀~~

Alex had rarely seen such a breathtaking contradiction of expressions so quickly brought under control. From enchanting, openmouthed surprise at seeing him, to horror to suspicion to absolute determination, and now to this lovely flushing that grew from out of the neckline of her chemise—all in one splendidly smooth sweep across her lovely features.

So very telling.

"I haven't time for touring just now, my lord. I have food to deliver, and the miller's wife is near to her time." She jutted her stubborn chin toward some distant horizon.

"Then I'll carry your basket and speak with the miller while you're busy with his wife." He reached for the basket, but she shifted it to the opposite hand. He damned well wasn't going to lose track of his elusive ward again. Not after losing the staunchest of his soldiers to her tending.

He'd looked up from the table full of his advisors to where the woman had been standing only moments before and felt a sudden unease.

He didn't like the idea of her wandering about unsupervised, hatching her little plots against him. He'd planned to keep her well within his sights through the day—despite the distracting glint of the morning sunlight on her hair—but she'd vanished from the hall.

He'd checked the kitchen, her quarters, even his own chamber, then had remembered her concern over the village. And Gordon's comment that it had been deserted last night.

"You may follow me, if you please, my lord. But know that I have work to do that should have been done last night."

She went tromping across the drawbridge, heading down the steep incline in a stride far longer than her slightness might suggest, her heaping basket swinging freely among the weighty folds of her cloak.

He caught up with her easily and suffered her snort of derision with a cool-headedness he hadn't known he possessed. The more he learned about his ward, the more valuable she would become to his future.

The small village spread out at the base of the

castle, neat and trim, though there was a leanness about it that made him think of a wounded animal balanced carefully on the edge of existence.

"There. Do you see, my lord?" She stopped short at the top of the lane before it descended into the village and made a great show of taking in the sights, blaming him for every leaf out of place. "The result of more than two years of guardians who had no regard for anything but their own greed. Six years of a petty war between two royal marauders, each claiming to know what's best for their subjects."

Let her damn him for something not of his making, let her bait him. He'd not rise to it. Or to the heady call of her hair, caught back in a thick plait, the boldest strands making a halo of soft curls around her face.

He inhaled a head-clearing breath but managed only to draw in more of her, mint and yew and gentian. The stunning intimacy of her bride's bed.

"Tell me what was destroyed in last night's attack, madam, and I'll have it restored before sunset."

She raised a frown at him, shielding her eyes from the sun with her hand. "I don't expect you to understand, my lord. You bring your wars here where they're not wanted."

"The war goes where it's needed."

"What purpose did it have in coming here?" She knelt and scooped up a piece of charred wood. "To the threshold of a family of weavers, my lord?"

He could see the remains of the cottage, the outline of its foundation, the brown, overgrown garden beyond. "When did this happen?"

Her voice lost its bravado, a pain too recent. "They were burned out when Lord Murdock decided he wanted Carrisford for himself."

He'd seen many burned-out villages, but only from the perimeter, and only to pass them by. He knelt beside her and sifted a heat-twisted nail out of the rubble. "Where's the family?"

"Brenna is the only one left—the older girl you met last eve." She stood sharply, her brow fretting deeply, her eyes red-rimmed.

"I thought she was your sister."

"Orphaned. I took her in because she hadn't anyplace to go. You see, we've been sacked, looted, razed, starved, murdered, and frozen to the bone so often that I would have lost count long ago if I hadn't recorded every outrage."

"And what of *this* time, madam?" He stood and wrapped his arms through the handle of her basket, their arms touching, drawing her closer to him, making his point as clearly as he knew how. "What offenses of mine against your village have you recorded? You looked quite busy earlier today."

"I . . . well—" She clutched the basket tighter.

"As you might have noticed, I've had no time to inspect the village for myself."

He pulled her even closer, her nose an inch from his own, her minty breath mixing with his across his jaw, threatening to unbank the lawless fire glowing in his belly. A simple thing to cross the distance between them, to taste her, to satisfy this distracting craving for her. "And you have not a single loss to record against me, have you?"

She furrowed an angry brow at him, "I haven't seen all of the village yet. Now let go."

It was only when she started off again that he realized the street was still deserted, and so was the wide, open square with its spokes of narrow lanes. Just as Gordon had reported last night. No hearth smoke, no children or dogs or grazing livestock.

"Madam, your village lacks people. Where is everyone? Are they in the fields, bringing in the harvest?"

She gave an ungainly snort of pure derision. "What harvest do you mean, my lord? The fields were never sown, remember? And it's October, long past harvesttime."

"No harvest at all?" He was no kind of farmer, but, Christ, that didn't sound right. "But Carrisford does have a village full of people. Where the devil have you stashed them all?"

But she'd already strode away from him again, through the oddly deserted square and into a two-storied barn. Before he could discover exactly where she'd disappeared to in the dusty, shadowed darkness, a bell began to ring somewhere high in the rafters above. A deep, throaty tolling that filled his chest and the building, thrumming against the walls, rolling up the length of the valley.

He followed the tolling through the nearly empty barn and finally found his ward up a flight of stairs, her fingers wrapped around the thick bell rope, her face tilted upward, catching the sunlight in bright, moted stripes across her rosy cheeks.

What the devil?

"Is this the village church?" he shouted.

She shook her head. "The granary, though as you probably noted, it does lack grain."

He hated her secrets, the large ones and the little dodgy ones that she placed in front of him to slow him, as though they could. Half-truths that told him much about her.

"Why the bell then?"

She waited while the tolling faded to nearly nothing, doubtless measuring him for the story she would tell. " 'Tis a make-do pele tower. The villagers left last eve at the first sign of your assault."

Ah, so that was the bell he'd heard last night as he'd ridden through the courtyard. An alarm. "Do you mean that the entire village has been in hiding all this time? In the woods, all night?"

She shrugged lightly. "They're used to it, my lord. And where else would they go to be safe?"

"Into the castle, madam. Behind stone walls and thick doors."

She laughed and wrapped the thick rope around her hand and then her wrist. "Into the arms of another overlord like Rufus? Oh, no, my lord, we learned the folly of that strategy after the second assault. Everyone scattering to the winds is far safer than seeking shelter in the lord's castle—whoever that lord might be."

She still didn't understand or was purposely ignoring the fact that *he* now made the rules here. "*I'm* the lord now."

"Aye, but the villagers will still take to the hills the next time Carrisford is overtaken."

"Damnation, woman, there won't be a next time."

That seemed to amuse her, drew a smile to the corners of her mouth. "Perhaps you're right, my lord guardian."

Bloody hell, he hated that word and the indicting way she said it. He wrapped his fingers around hers on the bell rope, took a handful of her sleeve to keep her close. "Madam, if there is ever trouble on my watch, you will instruct the villagers to come to the castle for their safety, not flee to the woods. Do you understand me?"

She fixed him with an unflinching gaze, one steeped in doubt and sorrow and a dangerous kind of determination. "Quite perfectly, my lord."

She leaned toward him and hung her weight into three quick pulls that drew his hand and hers through the steady rhythm, the rise and the fall and the fading ring, that reminded him of simpler days.

Of summer and the sea.

When she tried to pull away, he held fast to her hand, this clever, fearless woman and her conspiring bells. "What did that mean?"

"Which?" Her blue eyes widened in an almost believable show of innocence. He'd have to remember that.

"This second alarm you just rang."

She huffed at him and blew a stray strand of hair off her temple. "The same as before, my lord. I want to make sure everyone heard that it was safe to return."

Not the same signal at all. Quicker, sharper, struck with deliberation and defiance.

"Don't ever take me for a fool, madam," he said, chancing the softness of her hair as he tucked the loose strand behind the ridge of her ear. Chancing the downy graze of his knuckles across her cheek.

Never expecting her little gasp. The erotic pleasure of it. Or her own obvious surprise.

"Believe me, my lord, you seem like anything but a fool to me." She yanked her hand out of his, then brushed off her skirts and picked up her basket. "Thank you for escorting me to my village, my lord, but I have a great deal of work to do." She started down the stairs.

"Then you'll do it with me." He followed her through the granary, wishing he knew more about the workings of a village. About harvest yields and lambing.

"Surely your soldiers need you."

"The trick to running a disciplined garrison is to engage the most skilled officers and to trust them." He caught her arm and turned her, braving all that illuminating indignation.

"And do you trust them, my lord? Are they as skilled as they seemed to be last night?"

"I've the best trained, most loyal men in the kingdom, Lady Talia. We've never lost a contest, no matter how great the odds."

"You've never had to defend a castle, my lord. Never one like Carrisford. I pray that you're not too disappointed when you lose her."

With that odd pronouncement still ringing in his ears, she started away into a narrow lane that had been deserted only moments ago, and now she hurried to greet the bedraggled people who were beginning to slip back in from the country-side.

Moments later, she was helping an elderly woman over the threshold of a sagging cottage, leaving her with a loaf of bread and a kiss on the cheek.

She gave three more loaves and a cut of salted pork to a large, threadbare, thin-limbed family; dressed a boy's scraped elbow, chased and caught a piglet for a woman whose arms were filled with two children; dashed from one crisis to another, however minor, tending to every illness and sorrow with her good works.

Unwilling just to stand idly by and watch the woman trying to patch up her tattered village, Alex helped two men prop up the rear wall of a cottage and secure the flagging roof, repaired the rope on the well bucket, and, a half hour later, found Talia hurrying toward the market square, her basket nearly empty and her hair springing from its plait.

A small knot of women were gathered there, careworn, but chattering like geese. Their chatter stopped abruptly as soon as they saw Talia, and then erupted again as they swarmed around her, hugging and kissing her.

"Oh, my lady! We're so glad to see you!"

"Auch! We feared you were surely going to have to marry that Rufus! But they came in time!"

Alex caught Talia's eye as she looked up at him from the short distance across the square, and damn if he didn't find her more dazzling than ever. If the blue of her cornflower gaze didn't rouse him like a callow lad.

"Rumor was they came *just* in time!"

"I prayed and prayed it wouldn't happen to you this time 'round, my lady! And it didn't, praise the Almighty."

"Ooo, and didn't I hear that your new guardian is a . . . a . . . well, then!" The woman had followed Talia's gaze and stopped abruptly and gaped at Alex, which made the rest of the women turn in his direction, bunching themselves around Lady Talia as though they feared that he would abduct her.

"Is that him, my lady?" one of the women asked, as though he couldn't hear or see.

"Is it, Lady Talia? Is he the new lord?"

Alex had never felt so much like a bullock on the auction block. He felt Talia's openly appraising gaze tracking over him, from his eyes to the soles of his boots and every place in between, heated and perilously familiar. So like the night before.

"Will you be marrying this one, my lady?"

This one? Had she been pledged to another man before de Graffe?

"*I* certainly would, Lady Talia!"

His enchanting ward turned her head then and said something to the women under her breath which made them all turn and stare at him and then giggle and coo.

An excluding sound that sent them off in a dozen directions.

He caught the back of Talia's cloak before she

could slip away from him. "What's all this marriage business, madam? I thought that was done."

"Something that you, my lord, needn't trouble yourself about."

Blasted woman and her little secrets. "I damn well plan to trouble myself about—"

"Talia! Talia! Taaaaaalia!" The little voice came streaming toward them from behind, another squeakier voice screaming high atop it.

Talia shot Alex a frown and bent down just in time to scoop up the little girl who threw herself into her embrace.

"Oh, my, my, what is it, Lissa, my sweet?"

"It's Radish! Gemma's bunny! He's . . . he's . . . got all tied up!" The choking sob was far larger than the little girl and shook her like the winter wind.

His ward smoothed back the unruly blond curls and dropped a line of kisses across the fretted forehead. "Tied up where? Who would do such a thing to poor old Radish?"

The woman glared up at Alex over the top of the girl's head, as though he'd had something to do with tying up a scruffy old rabbit.

"You gotta come help Radish, Talia. Please!" A younger, red-haired little girl raced past him, grabbed the woman's skirt, and climbed into her arms. "Please, Talia!"

"Dear Gemma! Show me, then, girls. Your pardon, my lord. Important business." The woman was off in the next breath, the two village children nearly dragging her through the lane toward the quay.

Bloody hell, what was next? He ought to be settling his garrison into the castle, not following the deceptive woman around the village, joining a nursery parade. But he refused to lose sight of her.

Understanding one's opponent was the first step in conquering him.

Her, in this case.

A fact that did little to soothe him.

"There he is, Talia! Do you see!" Gemma was pointing frantically to a forlorn-looking bundle of rope bound up in the mud at the foot of an abandoned piling, a good hundred feet from the shore.

"How do you know Radish is there?"

"His nose! Don't you see it?"

Ah, yes. A dark nose, long-whiskered snout, and a pair of familiar eyes.

"The poor thing! How'd this happen?" Talia got as close to the mud line as she could without sliding into the low-tide muck.

"We have to get him out of there, Talia, before the water comes again!"

The tide was coming in, lapping at the first piling sticking out of the glossy mud. Hoping that poor old Radish hadn't already died in the moonlight tide, she bent down to take off her boots, then felt a familiar shadow cross her shoulders and fall upon her hands.

De Monteneau. She'd hoped that she had bored him back to his garrison with her village prattle. But he was standing there beside her, bigger than ever, and shaking his head at the approaching tidal water.

"There's a rabbit out there?"

"There is, sir! In the tangle of rope." Gemma ran behind Talia and grabbed the man's hand and started tugging. "He must be scared. Can you save him? Please, sir?"

De Monteneau glanced at Talia and looked as though he were about to pronounce the fate of such an unlucky beast, but Talia shook her head, and he stopped. "How the devil did he get inside all that rope?"

Gemma offered as good an explanation as any. "He was probably looking for a nest to lay his baby bunnies."

"Babies?" De Monteneau's scowl deepened.

"Doubtful, my lord," Talia said, wishing the man would leave off his speculation, "Radish is a male."

Gemma tugged on the man's hand again. "Can you save him for me?"

By the look of the shifting muscle in the man's jaw, rescuing pet rabbits was obviously far beyond the lord's purview. "His Lordship's too busy for this sort of thing, Gemma. I'll do it, sweet."

Talia reached down again to slip off her boot, but the man grabbed her around the wrist, his eyes flashing.

"No you won't, madam."

"I'm going to at least try," she whispered harshly, "Radish is a pet."

"I don't care if he's a papal legate sent on a holy mission to appoint a new archbishop," he said between his teeth. "You're not going out into that treacherous muck."

"And I'm not leaving the poor thing to die right there in front of Gemma."

The huge man grunted at her, then straightened, his fingers still a trap around her wrist. Then he nodded sharply toward the piling. "I'll go get the bloody thing."

"Oh, no!" Lissa squealed and threw her arms around the man's leg. "Is Radish hurt, sir? Do you see blood on him?"

Talia bit back a contrary smile as she rescued de Monteneau from Lissa's vise and held her against her skirts. "His Lordship was merely cursing, weren't you, my lord?"

He showed strong white teeth through his frown, as he sat down on a rock and yanked off his boots. "Aye, lass, I was only cursing."

Lissa broke away from Talia and waggled a

gently chastising little finger at him. "You shouldn't curse, sir. You won't go to heaven if you do. And I think you ought to go to heaven when you die."

Gemma joined her in front of de Monteneau. " 'Specially if you're going to rescue Radish."

"Thank you, ladies," he said evenly. And then the enormous man stood, squared his oh-so-broad shoulders, and slogged into the mud as though into battle. First, to his ankles in the slick stuff, then to the middle of his very fine calves, then nearly to his knees.

And Talia realized with a feathery fluttering in her chest: *Gracious, Mother of God, Alexander de Monteneau is rescuing Gemma's rabbit.*

How utterly amazing.

Oh, but what did he know of rescuing families and villages and tattered old castles?

"He's brave, isn't he, Talia," Gemma said, clinging to Talia's skirt with both fists, leaning toward the rescue, "our new lord."

"He is that, sweet." And game. And gallant.

She blinked away *thoughtful* and *kind*. They got in the way of all his more virulent faults: thunderous arrogance and the stubborn, self-righteousness of a bred-in-the-bone warrior.

She watched him reach down to his knee and yank his foot out of the mud to make another step.

Please God, after all this, let Radish be alive.

"Is Radish all right, sir?" Gemma shouted,

straining at Talia's skirts, nearly toppling them all into the muck as de Monteneau bent to the tangle with his knife.

Talia's stomach took a tumble when he didn't answer, picturing him lifting a limp rabbit from the ropes, costing the girls their hearts.

"Come, come, Radish, old chum. Rest yourself," she heard him say, as though he were calming his champion destrier before a battle.

"Is he all right?"

"Is he?" The girls were up to their ankles and hems in the mud.

"Well," he said, holding up the very wet and bedraggled Radish by the scruff, "I've seen worse-looking rabbits."

She could swear that de Monteneau almost smiled when Radish danced a little rabbit jig.

"He's alive!" Lissa threw her arms around Gemma. "Radish is alive!"

The girls stayed on the bank only because Talia held them there while de Monteneau slogged back toward them, one sucking step after the other, cradling the terrified rabbit in his arms.

And her heart began skipping oddly.

"Hoorrrayyy!" The girls threw themselves around de Monteneau's mud-coated legs when he reached the bank. "Thank you, sir! Thank you!"

He settled Radish into Gemma's arms, his smile soft. "One pet rabbit, miss. Delivered safely."

He was covered in mud from stem to stern. As were the girls now.

And Talia wanted to grin like a fool.

How foolish, indeed.

Gemma tugged at his sleeve, and he knelt to her level. "You're best lord we've ever had, sir! Are you going to marry our Talia?"

His dark eyes found Talia's instantly, his suspicions unspoken.

Lissa grabbed Talia's hand. "Talia, is he going to marry you? 'Cause I'd like him to be part of our family. Wouldn't you? Wouldn't that be the best ever?"

"Lissa, please." The last thing she needed was to remind de Monteneau of his warder's rights. She had other, more lasting plans that couldn't possibly include marriage. To anyone.

Even if he was the best of all, it was beside the point. She couldn't let him matter in her final plans.

And yet, if his men were truly invincible as he claimed, if he could safeguard the people she loved, shield them all against the killing and the famine.

"These are Lissa and Gemma, my sisters."

"More sisters?"

"And that's Radish," she said, pointing to the rabbit being nuzzled by two very grateful little girls.

"We've met."

"Thank you for saving Radish!" Gemma planted a kiss on de Monteneau's mud-streaked cheek and Lissa planted a noisier one on the opposite cheek before they both danced away to coddle the rabbit.

De Monteneau looked completely stunned as he stood, touching his jaw as though he'd been struck.

"You did a very heroic thing, my lord."

He blew a dismissive snort and then looked down the spattered front of his studded-leather hauberk, at the thick coating of mud on his leggings, now beginning to harden like thick plate armor.

A golem, right out of legend. Complete with hands of clay and a face of stone.

Talia touched her mouth with three fingers and bit her tongue, but couldn't help the little giggle that slipped out, which only brought on a deeper scowl.

"I'm sorry, but you're very muddy." She also couldn't help brushing at the heavy clumps that had spattered across the front of him, couldn't help admire the hard-muscled feel of his chest when she ought to be sending him on his way, on some fool's errand. Hopefully Quigley had been warned off from entering the village with his ill-gotten goods by the second set of bells, waiting for the all clear.

"Are you hiding any more sisters from me?"

"No."

"No brothers tucked away in the brambles, ready to ambush me."

"If I had a brother, he would be your ward, not me. And we'd all be much happier."

"Carrisford would belong to him, my dear, and you and I would never have met."

That made her heart stumble, caught up a breath in her chest. "Truly."

"However, madam, you and I are inextricably bound at the moment. And to that end, we will finish our tour of the village."

Talia sighed, hoping he heard boredom and not impatience to be away from him. Not her fear that Quigley hadn't heard her warning.

Or the very sobering notion that he was so un-balancing, so unlike her other guardians had been.

"It's just a village, sir; nothing you haven't seen before. Carrisford is plainer than plain. You have other castles; you must have at least as many villages of your own."

"I have but one castle—this one."

"But you're a baron, de Monteneau. Surely you've held castles for the king before mine."

"I'm a soldier, madam." He left her for his boots standing against the rock. "I've had no time to bother with holdings until now."

So he was new to this, too. "What's so special

about Carrisford? Or did you just suddenly fancy a wardship and mine was available?"

"The tour, madam—" He stopped abruptly and turned toward the sudden burst of shouting.

"My lord! Here, my lord! A message for you!" The clamor came from the same squire who had so irritated de Monteneau earlier. Kyle. He sped along the bayfront, came skidding to a stop directly in front of the scowling golem, and looked him up and down before screwing up his face.

"Whatever happened to you, my lord? You fall off the quay or something?"

"You'll speak when you're spoken to, boy. What message now?"

The lad quailed and bowed his head, mumbling, "From Sir Dougal. He wanted you to know that the rest of your caravan has arrived and it seems to have been robbed."

Oh, great Heaven. Quigley, stay hidden. Please.

"Robbed?" The lighter side of the man vanished as though it had never been, leaving only the warrior.

"Sir Dougal thought you'd want to know."

Talia felt a chill when de Monteneau shifted his darkly suspicious gaze toward her.

"Indeed." Then he bellowed suddenly. "Now away, boy!"

Kyle raised a spray of pebbles in his wake.

"Must you be so unkind to Kyle?"

"Excuse me, madam," he said, slapping off the mud and yanking on his boots. "I'll have to take that tour later. It seems I've a robbery on my hands."

"Can't trust your own men?" She could only hope.

He went still, then said deliberately, "That's just it, my lady. I trust *them* completely."

He strode away, leaving a threat as clear as a shot from a catapult through the front door of the keep.

So he didn't trust *her*. Well, then, she would just have to redirect his suspicion and offer Quigley to him to help with his findings.

Better yet, she'd offer herself.

As bailiff, of course. Only that.

Will you marry him, Talia?

Absolutely not.

He's the best one yet.

She couldn't let that matter.

Couldn't allow herself the luxury of letting down her guard for a moment. Not even out here on this beautiful spit of land that gave a panoramic view of everything that was dear to her.

The quay and its boats. The tiny, sloping village with its ramshackle cottages and the plots of land behind them, the old barns and the abandoned workshops.

The cross in the square and its spoke of lanes.

The common fields and their empty rows, the hills and orchards and the forest beyond.

And standing above the remarkably peaceful setting was the castle itself.

Ancient and stout. Thick walls of stone, six limestone towers, battlements of timber here and stone there. Rickety in places, solid in others.

Home. Her father's legacy.

Too big for the ocean bluff, looking sadly awkward and out of place now, embarrassed at the attention it received from those who came to it without love.

No longer a center of strength and protection for everyone for miles around, but a magnet for greed and violence.

A tempting prize.

A corpse. A mistake that would kill them all if she didn't do something about it.

A devastating truth that she'd come to realize only recently—if not for the castle itself, no one would pay a moment's attention to the little village in the snug valley that rolled peacefully down into the sea. The war would pass them by unnoticed. Her family could live safely there, they and all the people who depended on her.

Her heart still lugged with the weight of her awful decision. To purposely raze her dear Carrisford to the ground, to reduce it to a heap of stones, to nothing but a memory.

They'd begun undermining two of the tower cellars a month ago, shoring as they went, weakening the walls just enough so that a final, fiery conflagration would make the castle unsalvageable.

Working around de Monteneau would be far more difficult than it had been with Rufus. But it was the only way.

She and Jasper would start again in a day or two, after they had learned de Monteneau's routine.

"C'n we go put Radish in his basket, Talia? He needs a nap."

"I know how he feels."

Talia watched the girls run off, her heart in her throat, wishing that there was another way, praying that they would all make it through another winter.

And another lord.

One who was too vigilant.

Too rational.

Too . . . willing to rescue a rabbit named Radish.

Chapter 8

That was a very heroic thing you did, my lord.

Hardly, madam. He'd felt the sting of heroism, and rescuing a pet rabbit from drowning wasn't it.

He'd felt her smile, her amazement as he slogged out into the mud. Hell's hounds, he couldn't very well have let the woman do it herself.

Though she seemed capable, and utterly determined to take care of everything for leagues. A woman whose heart was too big for her own good.

He heard the now familiar drumming of running footsteps coming up behind him. Tiny footsteps, tiny feet. And all that squealing.

"Lord Alex, Lord Alex!" They dashed around

him, her sisters, stopping him at the foot of the incline below the drawbridge, their joy making him feel old and used up.

"Have you lost another rabbit?"

"No," Lissa said, grinning up at him, "we just wanted to say thank you again."

And then they went speeding off up the incline, leaving an unexpected emptiness inside him and a compelling urge to turn back and find Talia.

But he reined in his far-ranging thoughts, and entered the cart-cluttered bailey, on the lookout for Dougal among them, and his precise inventory. He came around the back of a wagon, and was nearly toppled over by the boy.

"Sorry, my lord," he called as he went speeding toward the great hall.

No, he didn't need to burden himself with concern over a family. They would tangle and tie him and shift his perspective from the real prize. He would marry for the greatest profit and beget legitimate sons.

Not like his father, who had strewn his seed all over the kingdom, leaving a chain of bastards in his wake.

Bastards like Alex himself.

And the boy. Kyle. His own bastard half brother, sent to Alex against all his protests by the king, to be trained up as a squire.

He's your brother, Alex, Stephen had said, as though that gave the boy a legitimate place in his life. He'd agreed to the responsibility, only because he couldn't refuse the king's wishes and because the boy wasn't aware of their relationship. That Kyle doubtless wondered the reason his lord couldn't bear to look upon him was immaterial.

He needed no reminders of his own illegitimacy, only his unflagging desire to rid himself of the blight on his name by any means possible. He would simply keep his distance from his ward and her family, and from the boy.

"Alex, there you are!" Dougal saw him as soon as he entered the courtyard. "It's not like you to disappear."

"Business in the village."

"Ah, with your new ward?" Mischief glittered in the man's eyes, then he seemed to notice the mud. "Good God, Alex, what the hell happened to you?"

"Never mind. What's all this about my caravan being robbed?"

"Foley noticed the loss as he was unloading." Dougal threw back a wagon's oiled-canvas covering. "Here. A missing barrel. You can see the load's shifted slightly, but there had been a barrel there."

"A barrel of what?"

"Salt pork."

"Is that all that's missing?"

"Three barrels actually. Saddle leather, a butt of arrowheads, beans, tools, and a few other items, all stolen from three separate wagons."

"Doesn't sound like pilfering among the troops." Alex carefully inspected the corner of the wagon where the barrel had been removed but found nothing out of the ordinary. "When could this possibly have happened, Dougal? We've been on the move for two weeks."

"Probably somewhere between here and Lincoln, when Foley packed the wagons. You know his precise accounts—nothing escapes him."

"Or you, Dougal. But the barrel of salt pork obviously did." Though why take a chance of discovery by stealing from three different wagons? "It's not much, just damned odd." Damned suspicious. "See that the stores are under lock and key."

"Aye, my lord, and accounted for every evening."

He'd never given much thought to the upkeep of a castle, to accounts and stores and such. He'd been on the move all his life—from one sagging, dirt-floored hovel to another, then, after Gil's death, always one step ahead of Henry's sheriffs, then a squire, then soldier, with little more than a small pavilion, his armor, and a few chests to his name—all of it fitting into a single cart.

He looked up at the battered pickets of the outer bailey, at the prize he'd just captured.

Now his home. His castle.

Though he only held it in *her* name, until the time was ripe to make his move to the next one. A better castle, that better fit his strategies. A respected title, hard-fought and -won and bestowed upon him with all pomp and honor.

"What are you going to do with her, Alex?"

"Do with her?" Had Dougal been reading his mind?

"The lady Talia."

"The profitable thing, Dougal."

Legitimacy, no matter the cost.

"But it's dangerous, my lady," Quigley said from behind the little cart. "Right under His Lordship's nose."

"It can't be helped, Quigley." Talia tugged on the goat's harness, while Quigley shoved the beast from the rear. "The goods aren't safe in the village right now, not with His Lordship's men everywhere. If one of the cotters was caught with contraband, heaven knows what His Lordship would do. Or what he might learn about our little enterprise."

"But carting the goods into the castle courtyard, flaunting them, my lady?"

"It isn't much. And we need the tools. We'll store the rest in the cellars directly below the great hall until it's safe to move everything out through the sally port and into one of the caves. He'll never notice, Quigley, believe me. He's new at this, he told me so himself." And, caked in mud

and impatience, he had disarmed her completely
with his confession.

Quigley strained against the cart as it moved up
the incline. "He's smarter than Rufus—"

"This fine goat is smarter than Rufus. You've
repacked and camouflaged everything?"

"Aye, as always. But it's too late now, the deed
is nearly done."

Feeling utterly exposed, Talia started across the
drawbridge, then nearly jumped out of her skin
when one of de Monteneau's guards shouted,
"Giddrey, you and Mackie give Her Ladyship a
hand with that cart!"

And so very different from Rufus.

Feeling like a cheat, Talia smiled at the two
young men who raced out of the gate to help her
wheel de Monteneau's goods into her castle.
"You're very kind, Giddrey."

Quigley rolled his eyes at her and put his
weight into helping Giddrey push the cart
through the barbican, right into the outer bailey.

And right into de Monteneau's path, knocking
her heart off center.

"What have you got there, madam? Are you
smuggling your own army into the castle to oust
me?" He was standing there like a wall, the mud
flaked off and dried.

"I promise that these eggs pose no threat to
you, my lord." Feeling safely smug, Talia pulled

aside the heavy canvas and lifted a fine egg from a basketful. "They're for tonight's dinner."

"At least the village hens are still laying, despite last night's fracas."

"Like the rest of us, my lord, they've learned to persevere." Eager not to tempt the man's curiosity any further, Talia replaced the egg and the canvas and dipped him a curtsy. "Come along, Quigley, Cook will be wondering if we're not under siege again."

"Your lady will follow you in a moment, Quigley."

Quigley cast a glance at de Monteneau, who'd wrapped a firm hand around Talia's upper arm, then gave a yank on the goat's lead and was on his way toward the cooktower with His Lordship's salted and purloined pork.

Yes, right under his nose.

His very attractive nose, which at the moment he was glaring down. "The armory is an utter disgrace, madam. The arms are nearly rusted beyond use."

"You should have seen it before Rufus came— he'd actually made some progress. De Saville was the worst. Lazy as grass, because he was well supplied by your king."

De Monteneau's brow creased. "According to my armorer there are very few supplies in the blacksmith's shed for making repairs."

"Ah, is that what you've brought in your caravan?" Talia inspected a pile of supplies, lifting the lid of a crate on the top. "Weapons? Because if you plan to keep Carrisford, you must be well prepared to hold out against a siege."

"I'm well aware of the process of besieging a garrison. I've commanded a few myself."

"Aye, my lord, but only from the outside of a castle, I'll wager."

"Meaning?"

"Have you ever been caught inside a castle during a months-long siege?"

He scowled. "No, I haven't."

"Then you obviously have never wondered where your family's next meal was coming from, or how they will last the winter without the wood to warm them. Never been hungry or cold."

Darkness overtook his features. "A good commander worries about his men as though they were family."

"Then you'd best start worrying immediately, my lord, because our siege stores are disastrously low. They have been so for ages. If one begins, it's best just to open the gates and invite the army inside."

He leaned a lazy elbow against a wagon wheel, studying her face, searching again. "Since you have so much information in that beautiful head of yours, madam, you'll sit beside me tonight and every night afterward until we've compared the account rolls with the contents of the cellars and have made plans to redress the situation."

Beautiful? Oh, my, is that what he'd said? Beautiful.

And something about inviting her to sit beside him.

At supper?

No, at the account rolls. Helping him compare ... oh, blazes, the cellars! The excavation work! How could she stay ahead of the man, when she so easily stumbled over his every word?

"I'm afraid I can't help you. The rolls are my guardians' private estate records. I haven't any idea how they were kept or what any of their scribbling might mean."

"You'll sit beside me anyway."

The very idea made her heart skip around and that flush start to tingle across her chest.

"Perhaps."

But she did.

Sat beside him, and across the table from him, and paced with him—through a whole, long night in the solar, which he'd overtaken with his overwhelming presence. Plain soldier's blankets on his bed, his armor ready, his suit of chain mail waiting for him to jump into at the first sign of battle, his boots beside the door, the whole of him stretched out in his chair, heels stuck into the planked floor.

"You say there are three wells in the castle itself?" he asked Talia as he crossed his arms behind his head and studied the low rafters.

"One in the inner bailey, one near the cook-tower, and another in the cellar below the keep."

"Their condition?"

"Clean, with plentiful good water. We're very lucky."

He righted himself and tapped his finger against the weighted roll. "And yet according to the last records, there should be sixteen butts of wine, but as far as my steward could see, the wine is nearly gone."

"I wouldn't doubt it. Aymon had a taste for wine. Rufus's men seemed to prefer ale from the village. They never left any to store."

"It says here we've got but a bushel of beans. How many should we have?"

"Seven, at the least. As we have eleven hams, but should have seventy, or more."

"Seventy? Bloody hell." He threw himself from his chair and went to the casement, staring out at the night. "How the devil do we get more hams?"

"Well, since there are two hams per hog, my lord, we'd need thirty-five hogs, to start with. But most of the hogs have been slaughtered. Husbandry was never high on any of my guardians' lists of intentions."

But Alexander de Monteneau was proving a dangerously different kind of guardian. More than dangerous, because she'd begun to wonder if he might be the man who was strong enough to fight off the war.

Not that she should be thinking in that direction. A warder was a warder, not to be trusted.

Yet it was difficult not to notice his admirable qualities when they were so apparent: intelligence, forthright honesty, plain civility.

Like just now, as he poured her a cider, a smile gathered around the corners of his mouth.

Rufus had never served her anything but grief.

And Aymon had actually tossed a cup of cider at her in the midst of a drunken brawl in the great hall. Never mind that he'd been aiming for Father John.

"Will you, madam?"

He was sitting on the edge of the table beside her, supporting his weight on his arm, leaning palpably close, his gaze steady and challenging.

Will you, madam?

"No. Absolutely not, my lord." She could not possibly marry him. "No."

"No?" He raised one of his wicked brows, staring at her as though she had just grown another nose.

"*Absolutely* no." She jabbed her fingertip into the table. "I told you when you first came storming through my castle gates that I could not, that I would never agree to marry you."

Now he stared at her as though she were a complete lunatic, and had pushed his patience. "Not that I would need to ask your permission in the matter of your marriage, but that wasn't the subject of my question."

"Oh." Blazes! She stumbled quickly backward through their conversation, but found nothing to straighten her path, or to help stave off the bothersome blush that was boiling once again in her chest, flitting like a butterfly inside her stomach.

"Well, my lord. I'm just taking every opportunity to remind you of my resolve against such a union between us."

The blighter only leaned closer. "And as your legal guardian, my Lady Talia, I am merely offering you this wedge of apple."

It glistened between his fingers, freshly cut with his dagger and sweetly moist.

Delicious.

Inviting.

A drop of juice dangled off the end of his thumb. Close enough to just lick it off.

Great blazing heavens! She couldn't very well go around wishing to taste the wild fantasy of his thumb or that spicy scent of him.

Or wondering at the simple fact that he was offering her a bite of apple.

Rather than stammer out a no-thank-you, she reached out and slipped the wedge of apple from between his fingers.

Surely not batting her lashes at him.

Or at that insufferably arrogant smile of his.

Which wasn't really a smile but some kind of victory.

Because, as he'd assured her, he was a man who would settle for nothing less.

"Now, tell me about this matter of husbandry, madam," he said, settling his largeness into his chair and dropping his heels onto the bench beside her. "I am at a loss."

So possessively familiar.

So breathtaking.

He's the best one yet, Talia.

And the worst of all. Because in this short span of a day, she could feel her guard slipping, was beginning to wonder if she could dare hope that he was the man who could save her people from the war and starvation.

That kind of hope could bring ruin upon them all.

"Holy Mother of Jesus, my lady, you plan to start up *what* again?" Jasper's wiry grey hair was standing on end in the pale lamplight, his back braced against the center post in the baketower cellar.

"Nothing's changed, Jasper." Talia rolled out the mason's chart and weighted it atop a barrel, keeping her eyes on the cellar door, certain that her nosy guardian would sniff out her mischief. "Carrisford must come down, the sooner the better. The village can't take much more of this war."

"But he's a fine, strong, bull of a warrior, my lady. Surely, you saw him at work in the training lists these past days."

"I've been busy with my own work, Jasper." She'd purposely avoided the fighting, had only heard the clanging of blades, the shouting, then the muttered groans from his men as she patched their cuts and polticed their bruises.

"You should see them all—those knights of his know their business like none I ever seen in all my days of defending this old castle."

"You were my father's mason, Jasper. You know little about the strength of a fighting force." And besides, it wasn't possible to stop the tide of an invading army. Not even a man like Alex.

"Please stop to think, my lady!"

"I can't afford to take the chance on de Monteneau and his garrison. It's never worked before."

"But the danger, my lady—"

"That's exactly what I mean to eliminate, Jasper; the constant danger." The dying and the hunger.

"By setting Carrisford ablaze?" He crossed himself and rolled his eyes to the low ceiling.

"By razing my family's beloved home to its very foundations. Yes, Jasper. It's the only way."

He came to stand at her elbow. "I think you're mad to do this now, my lady."

"Aye, and sad and outraged that we've been reduced to destroying the home I love."

"But, my lady, Carrisford is your home. And mine."

"And it's killing us all one by one. I love you too much to allow that. So are you with me, Jasper, or not?" She turned to him, knowing that he'd never desert her. "Because I'll brook no more discussion on the subject."

His thin shoulders sagged along with his moustache. "'Course I am, my lady. I can't have you pulling it all down on top of your head afore it's ready."

"Thank you, Jasper. I wish it could all be different."

But she was fast running out of time and had long ago run out of options.

Chapter 9

❦❦❦

"Keep your eye on the quintain, Harkness." Alex cringed as the young squire hit the target off center again. "Duck, lad—oh, bloody hell."

As predictable as the path of the moon, the heavy leather ball swung fast around the pole, whacked into the lad's back, and knocked him to the ground.

"Up you come, boy!" Alex reached him nearly before he landed, grabbed hold of his leather-armored forearm, and sat him upright, trying to judge the extent of the damage.

Gordon ran a grueling training program, but Alex insisted on working with the new squires himself. A solid foundation in warfare would keep them alive in the thick of battle. One lifesaving skill built upon the next, reinforcing the one before.

But this dizzy young man hadn't yet learned that the laws of nature couldn't be broken without consequence.

"Didn't . . . see it, my lord!"

"You're not supposed to see it, Harkness; you're supposed to know in your gut that it's coming for you. Because it will. Be glad it was only a leather ball, lad. In combat it would have been the deadly end of a sword, and you and I wouldn't be having this conversation."

"Aye, my lord." The boy staggered and sagged, still gasping for air.

"To the end of the line with you, lad." Alex stood him upright, then told the other squires who had gathered around them, "Take him, lads! He'll be fine as soon as he catches his breath. Who's next?"

Alex looked back toward the list, motioned to the next more-than-eager combatant, who charged forward full bore, but a bit crazily.

A trajectory Alex would have easily dodged, except that at the very moment when he should have been stepping aside, he caught a glimpse of his bewitching ward coming down the stairs, carrying a large basket of apples.

The gilded ends of her hair were caught up by the sea wind, her cheeks were the dusky pink of sunset, and her eyes the wide blue of an April sky.

And there were suddenly stars and blackness

everywhere. Brilliant bursts of them on this afternoon which had turned to darkest night.

But such a sweet-smelling night.

And her mouth. Oh, good Christ, it was sweet and soft and damp.

Her hand against his cheek was soothing and insistent. "My lord, wake up!"

A most odd way to make love, patting his face and combing her fingers through his hair. But damned fine, still.

Finer even were her whispers against his ear, so hot, pleading. "Please, my lord."

If he could only bring her closer to him.

If he could just cup that round, firm bottom in his hands again. So warm. And he did so want to see it, feel it, bare. All of her . . .

"My lord, you can't—stop that!"

Ow! Blazes, the woman had slapped his hand. And now his head ached. Throbbed near his temple, so that opening his eyes didn't seem wise.

"Stand back, my lady."

Gordon? What the hell was he doing in their chamber? And not only Gordon, but the murmur of others nearby. "This'll bring him 'round."

If he could only open his eyes, he would—

"Bloody hell!" Alex woke with a clearheaded start when a shock of water hit him squarely in the chest. He scrambled to his feet, suffering a blinding rush of pain in the back of his head as he shook off the water and regretfully opened his eyes.

"He lives," his ward said softly. She was standing at his elbow, peering up at him, her eyes alight with real concern. They were surrounded by every soldier who'd been on the training field a moment before.

"What in Christ's name happened?"

"I'm sorry, my lord." A squire threw himself at Alex's feet, groveling. "To my soul, I'm sorry. It was my fault. I lost control of my mount—"

"Never mind, boy." He remembered now. Clearly. The squire's wild charge and the woman distracting him, just when he ought to have been—

"That's a nasty wound you have, my lord," she said, wrapping her fingers firmly around his wrist and tugging at him. "Come, I'll tend to it."

"You'll leave me be." She was the very cause of his troubles—all of them. He touched the throbbing knot on the back of his head if only to prove to the woman that he didn't need her tending. But the place was sore enough to churn his stomach, and his fingers came away bloodied.

She left her sultry whisper against his ear, a riot of nonsense. "Come, before we lose you again and your men grow even more concerned."

Bleeding hell, they already looked as though they were attending his funeral. He managed a nod toward Gordon.

"Seems Lady Talia wants another go at my

head, in private. Carry on, Gordon. Less speed and more rein, boy," he added as he strode purposefully, painfully past the terrified young squire who'd plowed him down, hoping the kid wouldn't throw himself on his sword.

Refusing to let the woman guide him off the field like an invalid old soldier, Alex led her up the stairs, every step bringing pinpointed stars to the backs of his eyes.

"In here, my lord," she said, in that voice that made him want to follow her as she slipped past him.

"What is this place?" It smelled of pungent green and spicy sweet, its tabletops and shelves neatly lined with small pots and baskets. The rafters bristled with shocks of dried herbs.

"I've reclaimed the old garrison infirmary. Sit here on the stool, in the light."

"Reclaimed it?" He sat gingerly, liking the feel of her hand on his shoulder, the natural pressure of her reassurance. No wonder his men had flocked to her with every scrape. "What has the room been in the meantime?"

"God knows." She shrugged and went to the wall of shelves, taking down a large vial before turning back to him. "A gambling room, an alehouse. Even worse, I suspect. The room was a disaster until you—" She caught her lower lip with her teeth and turned away to the table.

He watched her every move, wondering where he'd gotten the idea that her mouth was velvet-soft, sweet, and warm. "Until I what?"

"Well, until you arrived."

"Why reclaim the infirmary now? Are we that much more prone to injuries?"

She laughed as she poured a cup of water into a bowl. "No, my lord. It's just because I . . . uhm . . . because your men are . . . because you're different."

This pleased him to hear, puffed up his chest with guilty pride. "Different in what way?" He'd never seen her quite so shy, not even that first night when she'd walked in on him just out of the bath.

"In most every way." She leveled a finger at him. "It's not gratitude, mind you. You're still just another invader. I mean only that the past week has been . . . well, a moment's relief. And I'm deeply glad for it, after two years of unending worry about the children and the villagers, not to mention the harassment and cruelty." She sighed heavily and put a bucket between his feet.

First a compliment and then another wound. "So you continue to believe I've only brought you a moment's relief?" That stitch of guilt settled between his shoulders, because he did plan to leave her. Though not until he was certain of her safety with a guardian who would protect her.

She waved away his question with a flick of her

hand. "You can't think that you're going to stay here long, my lord. Nobody ever does. They come and they go."

The guilt became a sizzling leap of jealousy and a flagrant need to defend his motives as well as his means.

"Well, damnation, woman, it's been a week, and no sign of a siege. No army creeping over the battlements. And should it happen, I'll take care of it."

Because an intact castle was far more valuable when he offered the Lady Talia and her wardship to the highest bidder.

Auction the wardship, Alex. Or offer it in exchange. Or marry the lady yourself.

Stephen had been overflowing with grand advice upon honoring Alex for his loyalty. But Alex wanted more than this meatless bone. Moving on to something better was his plan, finding a richer heiress than Carrisford's.

Richer than the extraordinary woman who was standing at his side, frowning down at him as her hip rested firmly against his shoulder.

"Still, it's just a matter of time, my lord."

"How do you know? Have you taken the time to see my men in the training lists?" He knew she hadn't, had watched for her too often, craving her admiration.

"I was on my way to do just that, my lord, when you went down. I don't know what to make of that."

"You distracted me."

"*I* did? How? I thought I was very quiet as I approached. I didn't mean to cause you trouble, my lord."

"It's *Alex*, dammit." He stood, furious that she could so easily dismiss his efforts.

"What?"

He started to scrub his fingers through his hair, but drew back when he touched the sticky knot. "Do have the decency to use my Christian name between us. You make me feel like an old man."

She prissed up her lips, hardly hiding her smile. "You're not that old. Are you?" At the moment he felt aged, and stirred by her teasing. "Now sit back down, my lor . . . my Alex. Uhm . . . Alex."

My Alex. God, he liked the sound of that.

Her Alex. A rowdy thrill shot through him, blazing out of his chest and through his groin, racing toward the top of his head, where the searing, dizzying sensation turned instantly to an entirely different kind of throbbing.

"Ouch." He sat, still aroused, still craving more of her than he could ever have.

Then she disabled him completely as she slipped her delicious fingers lightly along his nape, and lifted his hair. "Now, bend over the bucket please."

He snorted, which hurt. "I've had plenty of wounds in my life, stitched up on the battlefield. I won't vomit with your tending."

"I'm sure you won't. But I don't want bloody water all over my clean floor . . . Alex."

"Very well." Feeling coddled and chided, he dutifully put his head in his hands, resting his elbows on his knees. But instinct shot him to his feet the moment he heard running footsteps coming toward them along the corridor.

It was the boy, Kyle, standing in the doorway flushed and breathless, a message rolled up in his offered fist.

"Great heavens, my lord, what happened to you now?" The boy went instantly pale.

"Not to worry, Kyle," Talia said. "Fortunately, His Lordship's head is harder than steel."

"What have you got there, boy?" Alex grabbed the scroll out of his hand, suffering an uncomfortable bit of shame for his gruffness toward the boy who knew nothing about their blood connection, who never would.

"From King Stephen, my lord. No reply." Kyle gave one last look of horror at Alex, then sped out the door.

Alex didn't have to look at the woman to know she was frowning at him as he slit open the royal seal with his dagger, that she'd crossed her arms over her chest and was tapping her foot.

"Did he poison your horse?"

"Who? The king?" Though he knew very well who she was talking about—this woman and her very large heart.

"Kyle," she said. "You treat him as though he's wronged you."

"It's none of your business, madam." It was simpler to change the subject. Not nearly as simple to reason out the message. "I'll be damned. It seems that Chester has submitted to Stephen."

She harrumphed and gave a stir to something on the hob. "Who's this Chester?"

"Ranulf, the second earl of Chester. Gloucester's own son-in-law. Bloody hell. What the devil does this mean?"

"I'm sure I wouldn't know."

And he doubted she cared. "It seems, now that Stephen has captured Faringdon, he's broken Maud's communication between Bristol and her strongholds in the Thames valley."

"So . . ."

"So, madam, to keep you abreast of the war, as you demanded of me. Chester seems to think he can run to the side that seems to be winning."

"Which is . . . ?"

"Stephen, of course. A major victory, if Chester can be trusted. His holdings rival that of the king's."

"As long as they keep it to themselves," she said, laying her hand on his shoulder. "Now, hold the bucket on your knees." And then she ever so gently cradled his forehead in her warm, capable hand. "I'm sorry, but this will sting some."

But it didn't. The tincture was soothing, minty

and cool as she sluiced it over the back of his head. And her hand was an oasis.

"What is it?" Nothing like the tending he'd suffered on the battlefield.

"I'm cleaning the wound so I can see to work. Are you all right?"

More than all right, dazzled, tempted. "What the devil did I hit out there?"

"The quintain pole first, and then one of the supporting stones at the base. I saw you go down. Heard your head hit like a melon."

And then she must have come running. Is that when she'd kissed him? She couldn't have.

"With any luck you won't need a stitch." She worked quickly and efficiently, melodically humming, finally finishing with a flourish.

And a smile that made him want to grin. "There you are, my . . . Alex."

My Alex. He liked that tongue slip of hers. Liked it fine, and he let the guilty pleasure thrum around in his chest as she buffed a towel over his wet hair.

"Your opinion?"

"Well," she said, drying her hands on a towel, "you've got a nasty cut in your scalp, but it will heal cleanly as long as you keep this ointment on it. Now drink this down. It'll take away that headache."

His head did ache, but not enough to keep him from noticing other aches, in other places. Deep ones. Long, lusty ones. The drink was bitter, indeed. Far worse than all her probing. Sobering.

"There. You can go back to your training now. Only please keep your mind on your work. It's dangerous out there, and I need you to be well—"

"That's a change. I'd have wagered anything that you'd prefer me dead."

She smiled, revealing a dimple he'd never seen before. "Not just yet, my mmm . . . Alex. I'm getting used to this moment's peace you've brought me."

My mmmm Alex. He couldn't stop looking at her mouth, the full shape of it, the dewy color of roses, the scent of persimmon. A now familiar need filled up his chest and spilled into his groin.

He had to know if he'd been dreaming. "Did you by any chance . . . kiss me?"

Her eyes grew wide, worried. She hooked her finger in the neck of her shift and laughed just a little. "Did I do what? Kiss you?"

"Well, did you?"

She huffed and jammed her fists into her hips, a high blush rising on her cheeks. "When would I have done that?"

"Out on the training field just now, madam. After I went down. Did you kiss me?"

"And why would I do a thing like that? Kiss you in front of all those men? I certainly didn't."

An interesting denial. That she might have

dared, had they been alone. He damned well would have kissed her back, then.

And been devilishly sorry for it ever afterward.

"I . . . uh . . . well, I apologize, madam. I wasn't in my right mind. I must have imagined—"

"You very well did imagine it. I didn't kiss you. Though you—" She shifted her eyes to her fingers, then shrugged and set the basin on the table. "Never mind."

"Though I *what*?"

"Ohhh, nothing." She had a tantalizing secret caught up in the bow of her mouth. "As you say, you weren't in your right mind at the time. I knew that when you . . ."

"When I what?"

"Your hands. You did get a bit familiar for a moment."

"With my hands." He remembered that. Her bottom had been quite real. And round. And warm.

"You must have thought I was someone else."

He'd known exactly who she was. He'd just not been aware that they weren't alone.

"My deepest apologies, madam."

"No harm done. I doubt that anyone saw. And besides, it's nothing that hasn't happened before.

"*What's* happened before? You've been groped?" Fondled by another man?

Kissed . . . and bedded?

"I don't hold a wounded soldier to the same standards as a fully conscious one."

"Answer me, madam. What of Rufus? Did he molest you?"

"I was most often quicker than Rufus—because he was usually well into his cups."

"Usually?" An ominous word. "Did the bastard ever catch you?"

He watched her shrug in the way she did when she was tossing off a cruelty as part of her ordinary burden. "Twice, he inflicted his version of a kiss."

This was the last thing he wanted to hear, for it conjured sundering images of Talia in the arms of another man. Soft and pliable, other hands on her soft flesh. Not Rufus or that damned Aymon, but a better man.

A husband whom Alex himself would choose for her, for her own good.

"May I help you with anything else, my . . ." She sighed and rolled her eyes. "I mean, Alex."

Bloody hell. "Nothing, madam. You've done more than—"

"Talia. Please."

"Talia. Yes. Well . . . thank you for repairing my thick head."

"Please don't let there be a next time."

He loved her sternness. "I shall do my best."

"I'm certain you will."

He shouldn't preen, shouldn't go around wallowing in that chest-swelling pride every time she tossed out a compliment. "Thank you."

"In fact," she said, smiling as she hooked a basket from one of the rafters, "I'd wager that you don't kiss like he did, either."

Bloody, bleeding hell.

She brushed past him with the basket and disappeared through the door.

Alex remained rooted firmly to the stone floor, though he wanted to follow on her heels, to pull her back inside her scented infirmary and sample her.

Instead, he gripped the edge of the table and bit down on the edges of his tongue, long enough to put a great distance between them, a distance that would—he hoped—keep him from attempting to prove her dangerous theory.

Did you kiss me?

Dear Lord, she hadn't meant to. But Alex had been out cold at the time, and kissing him had seemed the most natural thing in the world.

And now here she was in the middle of that same afternoon, stealing a glance at the lists.

Brazenly gaping at him again, just as she had that first night.

Alex was nearly as naked now as he'd been then, bare to the waist, but for a leather jerkin, boots, and a pair of long breeches. Bronze-muscled and broad-shouldered as he effortlessly wielded his great broadsword against Gordon's obviously lesser skill.

The pair of combatants were surrounded by cheering knights and awestruck squires.

Alex broke away from the fight, then reached out and shook Gordon's hand.

Then each of the men found another opponent and began their battles again, and then once again in their inscrutable warrior's dance, until the entire field was teeming with pairs of sweating, striving swordsmen, the echoing clang of iron blades and all that shouting.

Skilled fighters, to a man.

Well trained by a powerful warrior who had arrogantly promised that he could protect her and the people she loved as no man had been able to do.

Ah, but could he protect her from herself?

Chapter 10

"The last cart's coming this way, my lady,"
Leod whispered, as he and Jasper hobbled over the top of the embankment and into the
midnight shadows to hunch beside Talia and
Quigley.

"Only one carter?" Talia listened for the cart
wheels to hit the slick shale pathway, wishing she
could have talked her three rickety old warriors
into giving up this business and staying home
tonight. But they always followed her anyway.
"No guards bringing up the rear, Jasper?"

"Naw," Jasper said, lying back against the
scrubby berm, "nothing but an outrider light on
the cart and a bit o' off-color verse. The last cart of
twelve, by my calculations."

The moon was high and full, giving off more

157

light than was safe. A half dozen pairs of eyes blinked at her from the brush and brambles.

Her own fine, brave warriors.

The whole operation would take but a half minute, and the driver would never know that he'd been robbed until he reached wherever he was heading. They'd gone far afield, following word of a caravan of grain and beans that was headed to Gloucester and Maud's forces there.

"He's turned out to be quite a worthy man, ain't he, my lady?" Leod said out of the blue, hunched as he tightened the lacing around his leggings. "His Lordship."

"Right level thinkin'," Jasper said, his eyes glinting at Talia from beneath his wiry brows.

"Aye, an' he tells a wicked jest," Quigley added.

"The patience of Job himself."

"That's enough."

"So when's the wedding, lass?" Leod asked. "You haven't said."

"And I won't say, Leod." That's just what she needed right now: three more matchmakers when her thoughts were already tangled tightly around the same subject.

Around Alex and his ever-growing catalog of traits she'd come to admire.

To believe in, when she shouldn't.

The other wagons had finally lumbered around the bend, out of sight and hearing of the last cart.

The carter would soon be isolated completely, ripe for the picking.

"All right, everyone. Let's go." Talia stood and gathered her cloak around her as Quigley and Leod and the others moved into place with Jasper.

But a too-familiar whisper from directly behind her stopped her. "What can I do, Talia?"

"Brenna!" Talia grabbed the startled girl out of the bushes and held her by the forearms. "What the devil are you doing here?"

"I came to help, Talia."

"Are you completely mad, girl?" She dropped with Brenna to her knees as the first glow of the carter's outrider light reached the rugged wall of the cut.

"I'm old enou—"

Talia clamped her hand over Brenna's mouth and whispered, "Be still! Else you'll give us away, and we'll all be caught and hanged. You, me, Quig and Jasper and Leod and the girls, and a lot of other innocent people. Do you want that, Brenna?"

Brenna shook her head frantically, her eyes wide and glistening in stark terror.

"Good. Will you stay right here? And do absolutely nothing?"

Brenna nodded just as fiercely, and Talia's heart melted. "Oh, sweet, I do love you for wanting to help."

Brenna's chin wobbled as she whispered, "I'm sorry, Talia."

Talia kissed Brenna on the forehead, then ducked away to help set the trap for the unwary carter, praying that her warning had stuck with the girl.

All was ready a moment later: a few natural-looking obstacles placed at odd angles along the narrow track, which would cause the carter to pick his way along.

The band faded expertly into the shadows and waited.

"What's this? Whoa, there." The driver stopped the plodding horse as he crested the cut, then stood in the foot well and peered into the pool of light. "Well, we'll just take it slow, Daisy, girl. And easy."

And so he did—as most carters always did—concentrating so hard on the track in front of him that he never noticed the noiseless pilfering going on at the back of the cart.

Then her little band of robbers hid silently in the underbrush until the carter was well down the hill with his off-color ditties, and out of hearing.

"I think I've got a barrel of dried apples, my lady."

"Beeswax here."

"A roll of vellum."

"And there's at least twenty-five sacks of barley from the earlier wagons."

Talia turned back to Brenna, who was still kneeling, stiff as a statue.

"Was I quiet enough?" she whispered eagerly.

"Perfectly. Thank you, sweet." Feeling old and weary to the bone, Talia sighed as she recalled the thrill of her first raid. And suddenly wondering if her unorthodox plans weren't full of great gaping holes. Razing her castle, making the village a smaller, insignificant target, living off what they could steal and store, managing the estate from the old manor house.

"Let's get these goods to the blackthorn cave. Thank you, everyone. Looks like we might have a tolerable winter, if we can keep this up."

Sneaking back into the castle with Brenna in tow proved more daunting than usual. The sally port door that she'd left unlatched dozens of times was shut tightly.

"I'm sorry, Talia. I closed it when I slipped out. Sorry. It was my first time."

"You put a lot of people in danger—"

"But Talia, I want to help."

"Then you'll have to be willing to do as you're told. This isn't a lark."

She hung her head. "I know. We need food. But everyone keeps stealing it from us."

Great heavens, Brenna was growing up right before her eyes. "Well, we'll talk about your helping the next time."

Her eyes glistened. "Really? Do you mean it?"

"If we make it safely back inside. Which means convincing His Lordship's guards to let us pass through the postern door, when they didn't see us leave in the first place."

But the guards were as gracious and polite as usual. They didn't question her, only helped them over the cobbles into the barbican.

"Stick to me and the shadows, Brenna. And follow my lead if we're caught." Not wanting to look furtive, Talia laced her elbow through Brenna's and started off through the darkened courtyard.

She dodged around the well and past a tinker's cart and had made it to within three steps of the family quarters, before she plowed into a familiar chest.

Broad and male and growling when he stared down the length of her cloak, one eyebrow cocked in suspicion. "Where have you been, madam?"

She clutched Brenna closer and prayed that the girl had an ounce of deceit in her blood.

"Chasing after Brenna, Alex." Talia fixed the man with a deep glower and prayed she'd play the game. "It seems she has a beau in the village. She went missing, and I caught her sneaking out to meet him."

Alex frowned at the girl and took a stance of authority. "Is this true, Brenna?"

Brenna trembled and shrank behind Talia.

Come on, sweet. Please. Lie to the huge man. Give him the best you've got.

"Were you out meeting a boy?" he asked again sternly, admirably patient in the face of such girlish rebellion.

"Well, I . . . uh . . ." Brenna tossed a terrified glance at Talia and then like a miracle, a full-bodied fib flew out of the girl, heartworn gestures and all. "I do love him, my lord. We were to meet on the quay and watch the moon set."

Good girl.

"To watch the moon set, girl?" Alex bristled with outrage. "And you believed this boy?"

"Well . . . I . . ."

"Exactly what I told her, my lord. That she should never have trusted the boy and his pretty words." She covered Brenna's hair with her cloak hood. "Now off you go to your bed, Brenna."

"Yes. I'm sorry." Brenna bobbed a curtsy toward His Lordship and was gone up the stairs and into the tower in a flash, leaving Alex staring down at Talia.

"Don't worry, madam, I'll rout out the boy's name and find him in the morning—"

"Please don't, Alex. I'll take care of it. He's a good lad—"

"You know him?"

"Aye, and he's just a bit starry-eyed and stupid at the moment." The last thing she needed was to have His Lordship starting an inquiry through the village, searching for a boy who didn't exist. Though there was something dramatically dear about his concern for Brenna's honor and safety. "I'm sure you remember those wildly uncontrollable feelings. Your first love. Not a clear thought in your head."

His half smile thrilled her, sent her heart reeling as he stepped closer and reached out, tangling his strong fingers in her hair, spending such a long, wonderful time sifting through the strands at her temple that she leaned into his fondling like a wanton.

"You have a leaf in your hair, Talia."

He lifted it out with a gentle tugging that made her close her eyes and sigh and imagine that marriage to the man might not be so very horrible.

"A remnant of a long day. Thank you."

"My pleasure."

And mine. She felt his gaze on her face as he let the leaf drift to the ground.

A grandly domestic and protective feeling, one that made her wonder again if Alex might actually be the only man to keep them all safe, if she could abandon her plans and just trust him.

"You be sure to tell Brenna's eager lad," he whispered just above her ear, "that if it happens again, he'll have me to answer to."

Talia drew in a breath of him, then swallowed roughly when she remembered that he'd almost caught her at her thieving, "Aye, Alex, I'll do that."

Then she brushed quickly past him, holding

back her sigh of hope and dread and relief until she'd shut her chamber door.

Shut it hard against the troubling changes in him, in herself. Because she didn't dare examine the truth of him, didn't want to hope because she'd already used up her lot of miracles.

Alex had waited outside at the bottom of the stairs for the sound of Talia's footsteps to make it past his chamber and all the way to hers. It was safer that way—for both of them.

Because he was having trouble keeping his hands off her scented softness, a hell of a trouble keeping sight of his goals in the light of her gaze.

Far better to wait out the next few hours in the great hall, playing chess with Simon than to risk stalking past his own solitary bed and slipping beneath her coverlet, finding her warm and ready for him.

He made a circuit of the battlements to cool his brain and was hurrying out into the bailey when he ran smack into something, somebody, who grunted and stumbled backward before gasping.

"My lord! I'm sorry!"

The boy. Kyle. His own father's eyes stared back at him from a face freckled with innocence.

"Never mind, boy."

"Aye, sir. I'm sorry."

Alex waved him away and then realized that the boy's tunic was crumpled, or hunched, or . . .

wrong somehow. He grabbed the boy by the scruff and brought him into the hard light of the fire basket.

"What in God's name have you been up to?" The wool was bunched, the shoulder caught up on itself.

"What do you mean, sir?" The boy stood stock-still, his long, gangling limbs drawn up like a string puppet's. "I haven't been doing nothing."

Feeling like a bully, Alex released the boy and looked closer at the odd garment. "What the devil's wrong with your tunic?"

"Oh, this." The breathy admission was followed by a loud gulp. The boy scrunched up his face as he plucked the shoulder and stared down at the mess. "It isn't very good, is it?"

"Good?"

"The stitching here. Off center, I know. And kind of clumpy."

"Did you do this, lad?"

"Me?" An unfettered laugh broke from the boy, a sound that sank deeply into Alex's gut. Brother to brother. Gilbert's laughter. "Oh, sir, I'd soon be skewered to the bone if I tried this myself. Fiona mended it for me."

"Good lord, what did the tunic look like before the mending?"

"Torn at the seam back here. I caught it on a nail in the stable. What do you think I should I do, my lord? She was so proud of her stitching, I don't want to hurt her feelings. And she worked so hard."

The boy's eyes were as large in his quandary as his heart seemed to be. The sprawling feelings that this brotherly exchange roused in Alex angered him.

"You'll just have to wear it as is, lad."

The boy nodded and patted the bunched-up wool as though it were a badge of honor. "That's just what Lady Talia suggested, too."

"You asked her about your tunic?"

Kyle offered him a rueful smile. "She saw for herself." He cast a moon-calf gaze toward the family tower. "She's a very fine lady, don't you think?"

"It doesn't matter what I think, boy." It mattered only that he didn't think about her at all.

"All the men like her."

They would, the way she cosseted them and bandaged their bruises.

A soldier could become soft here, could lose his edge, his direction—could almost come to believe that he had a legitimate connection to this scraggly lad.

"To your pallet, boy."

"Aye, sir." The boy didn't move, save for chewing on the inside of his cheek. "But I was wondering, sir, if you could tell me when I might do a mite of squiring for you? Or for one of the other knights?"

It wasn't their mutual father that the boy reminded him of, it was Gilbert. His true brother. His fallen hero. The bright blue eyes, the raven darkness of his hair—the eager, quirking smile.

He wouldn't dare hang me, Alex. The loss washed over him again, unbalanced the ground beneath him.

"You'll know that it's time, boy, when I tell you, when you've earned it. Now, be off with you."

Alex watched the boy speed away toward the barracks, his long legs, so loosely strung, his arms ungainly. He remembered that awkward place in his own life, where nothing fit and everything hurt, when he hadn't known where to go or what step to take next or when he'd eat next.

He damn well knew his place now, and Carrisford certainly wasn't it.

Talia spent the next two days supervising the stone-by-stone destruction of her home, taking inventory of the contraband hidden across her estate all the while fighting off the horrible feeling that she was losing ground.

Because, like the cunning warrior he was, Alexander de Monteneau conducted an unrelenting campaign against her: every day, every hour, in small, astonishing ways.

"Oh, Talia, Talia! Look what he gave me!" Lissa

dodged her way through the tables in the great hall, a dark bundle of fur tucked under her arm, trailing Gemma and Fiona in her wake.

"Now Lissa has her very own bunny!" Gemma said.

"He said his name is Licorice." Lissa cuddled the rabbit against her cheek in an ecstasy of love.

She'd never seen the girls so carefree, and the sound of their laughter made her heart and her hopes lift and soar. And all this unfettered joy had been made possible only because Alex had come through the gates of her castle.

And he'd stayed. Steadfastly.

He'd brought her such a simple and seductive peace, with his disciplined army and his efficiency, the calming influence he had on her householders and the villagers and her family.

His captivating smile.

Perhaps . . . yes, perhaps.

"Lissa," Talia said, swallowing the lump in her throat as she set a ewer on the table, "do you mean that this amazing bunny told you his own name?"

"Noooo, Talia! *He* did!" Lissa spun around and pointed back toward the door, to the broad-shouldered shape just entering the great hall.

Alex was striding easily toward them, his saddlepack draped over his shoulder.

"Ah, another daring rescue, my lord?" Talia

asked, her pulse racing for no reason at all, except that the provoking man seemed to become more handsome with every hour.

"Hardly daring, my lady. I found old Licorice in my horse's stall, cowering behind the manger."

Lissa was at his elbow, gazing up at him, the light of pure adoration in her eyes. "Thank you, my lord. I'll love him forever."

And didn't the man smile patiently back at Lissa as he ran his fingers over the rabbit's ears. "Do keep him out of the stables."

"He'll go everywhere with me and Gemma and Radish."

Talia didn't know what to make of the scene, the girls so completely enthralled with their toweringly tall new hero, her own stomach alive with butterflies.

"Fiona, I think Licorice and Radish need a large basket to live in together. Would you mind taking the girls to Quigley? He'll know where to find one."

Fiona grinned. "Right away, Talia!" The girls ran out of the great hall with Fiona, the three of them chattering and laughing.

"Do they ever stop, Talia?" Alex asked, settling the bag on the table.

"Only when they're sleeping, I'm afraid. They like you, Alex. You're in their every bedtime prayer." She hadn't meant to admit that to him, but he looked nonplussed, then shyly pleased.

"Well, they are the first then, in all the world." A confession that instantly shortened the distance she'd been striving to keep between them, tested it.

"Actually, you're in mine as well." He'd crept into them, and into her dreams, into her days.

"Am I?" The lout lifted a skeptical brow. "God help me, woman!"

"Selfishly, of course. Because, well"—she felt more than a little vulnerable—"I really ought to confess something to you."

"Confess at your own risk, Talia. I'm no priest to keep your confidences."

She liked his smile, the easiness of it, and the even easier way he followed her into the crowded, fragrant kitchen, past the elevated caldrons of stew and the bread ovens and then up and up the baketower stairs and into the deserted spice pantry.

"It's only that despite our differences, Alex, I have been meaning to thank you for making the castle and the village safe again for the children." She stopped in front of the tall herb chest, turned and leaned against it, wondering why her heart had started thudding against her ribs.

And if it was safe to be alone with him like this. In an intensely aromatic room, motes of dust and spice and bits of day riding the bright rays of sunlight slicing through the pair of arrow loops, striping his shoulders as he approached.

" 'Tis my job, madam. To secure Carrisford and keep it that way."

Yes, and he had. Splendidly. She'd thought, impossibly.

"It's just that my sisters have been confined to the family ward for so long. But little girls need fresh air and sunshine and a place to run. And now you've given that back to them. I thank you."

It occurred to her that he'd changed in the last few moments, or she had. Or both of them. Because he seemed to be all around her, his hands spread out on the chest door on either side of her head, his breath so like a kiss.

In fact, he could kiss her, and she wouldn't complain at all. She might even like it.

She would definitely like it. Love it.

"Go ahead, Alex. You might as well."

"Might as well what, Talia?" He brushed her name along her jaw, against her cheek, his mouth so close to hers, she could turn and collect his kiss.

She let out a long sigh. "You might as well give it a try. It's only a matter of time."

"Before what?"

He smelled of male and leather, roused and breathing deeply. "Before the inevitable happens, though I did tell you that it wouldn't ever."

He lifted a brow and then went back to nuzzling. "What are you talking about?"

"I'm trying to tell you that—"

Mother Mary, she'd decided! Somewhere in the back of her mind, sometime ago, she'd decided to trust him.

With everything and everyone she loved.

Oh, yes! The rightest thing she'd done in a long, long time.

"That . . . ?" he asked, prompting her with a nudge against her nose.

Great heavens, it all seemed so perfectly clear to her now, her stubborn foolishness and his excellence.

"You must remember, Alex, that I very firmly told you, when you first came to Carrisford—and many, many times since—that I would never agree to marry you."

His eyes tracked hers, held her gaze for the longest time, before he made a low, derisive grunt that was steeped in amusement. "You've made that very clear, madam."

"Aye, but now I've been . . ." He suddenly looked tremendously tall, as powerful as she was helpless against him, without him.

Her perfect protector.

"You've been what, madam?"

She obviously wasn't making herself clear. Not that she could be faulted for it—with the man hovering like this, raking his fingers through the hair at her temples, tilting her head up to him.

If he'd only just haul off and kiss her, the subject would be broached and racing forward. He would understand that she'd like nothing better than to marry him.

"I've been thinking, Alex. . . ."

"God help us all." His brow was quirked, amused and seemingly ready for anything. "About what?"

Mother Mary, this was coming to be a dreadfully immodest proposal. "I really shouldn't be so forward, Alex, but . . . uhm, this is business after all—"

"Business?"

"I'm only thinking of what's best for my family and my people."

"Best in what way?" He lifted her chin with his knuckle as though looking into her eyes would help to unmuddy her thoughts. "What are you talking about?"

"The best possible future for everyone, given . . ."

"Given what?"

"Well, the war and the troubles that have come with it." Peace and honor and his powerful arms, his fine sense of humor. "So I've changed my mind."

He was looking at her as though she had grown a horn out of the middle of her forehead. "About . . . ?"

"You."

He straightened, a smile stuck into the shadows at the corners of his eyes. "I've noticed that somewhat. You haven't thrown a cabbage at me in days."

Proposing marriage to a strapping man like Alex wasn't as easy as it seemed. "This will sound very forward, Alex, but I've changed my mind about marriage."

"In what way?"

"Very specifically, about you."

"Me?"

"So now . . . after all my chiding and warnings—my answer is *yes*."

He shook his head lightly, his black hair drifting against his brow. "Your answer to what, Talia?"

It would certainly help if the man wasn't being quite so dense. "I'm telling you that if you choose to insist upon a marriage to me, Alex, I won't object."

Not in the least.

"Marriage?" He narrowed his eyes at her, canting his head as though he'd never heard the word before.

"Yes."

"To you?"

"It was inevitable, as I said. It always has been. But this time, a marriage might really be for the best."

"This time?"

Alex had heard that term, dozens of times since he arrived, from everyone he'd met.

He stood away from her, already cursing this wayward need for her that he'd so stupidly acted upon. "What the devil do you mean by 'this time'? Are you talking about Rufus?"

"About Aymon and Count Roderick before him—only I was to marry Roderick's son, that time. The terms had just been decided when Aymon showed up outside the gates."

He wanted not to have heard this, wanted the hot stuffiness to leave his chest. "Are you telling me that you were to marry Aymon de Saville as well?"

She nodded, as though this was a simple thing. "Aye, and Roderick's son as well. And his nephew's second cousin just before that. All six of my previous guardians, in fact. One way or the other."

Bloody hell. He took her hand and sat her down at a table, on a short bench before bending to her.

"Please, Talia. What the devil does 'one way or the other' mean?" Besides this unnamed churning in his gut.

She tilted her head, apparently puzzled. "Marriages arranged for me. I thought you understood, Alex."

"I damned well *don't* understand! Explain to me how you came to be nearly married to three men."

She laced her fingers and rested her hands on

the table. "Well, six men, actually. I've almost been married six times in two years."

He lost his breath, had to drag it back inside him before he could speak. "Six, Talia?" Great God.

She sighed, her brow fretting. "Six near weddings, stopped somewhere between the betrothal and the actual wedding. Which has been the one single blessing of having Carrisford regularly besieged and overrun—no time to complete the marriage contract or the ceremony."

The ceremony be damned! What of groping hands and lustful cravings? The romance before the wedding?

"Bloody hell, woman, how close have you come to the marriage bed?"

"Only as far as the church steps—with Rufus. The rings had nearly been blessed, as I told you before. Your arrival was the closest call of any. If you hadn't come . . ." Talia pinched a little frown between her lips, then shook her head. "I can't imagine."

Nor could he.

Damnation, no wonder she had always assumed that he would marry her at the first opportunity and that she had objected so fiercely to the prospect. "You were forced each of these times?"

"I was agreeable the first time," she said, counting off the tips of her fingers as she stood and paced away from him, "terrified the second, bartered the third, blackmailed the fourth, tricked the fifth time, and . . . well"—she turned back to him, her eyes watery and her words unsteady— "Rufus threatened to marry off my Brenna to his unspeakable marshal if I didn't agree."

"The bloody bastard."

"And then you came along, Alex." Her voice softened to honey. "With your orderly army and your knightly courtesy toward everyone, and your amazing willingness to wade into a field of mud to rescue a rabbit. Not to say that you're not stone-headed and blustery and difficult to predict." She smiled brightly at him as she went to the cabinet door and opened it. "But you've governed with honor and compassion. You've respected the lives of my people. You've trained up your army to be the most fiercesome force in the kingdom, so that they're ready to protect Carrisford against anyone who might try to take us."

"Talia, I—"

"You've been the best of guardians, Alex." She paused in her astonishing speech, clutching a bundle of rosemary in her hands. "I can only imagine that you will be the very best of husbands."

And then she was gone.

Bloody, bleeding hell.

Chapter 11

"The very best of husbands?"

Bloody hell! The woman had been coerced into a despicable marriage by every one of those bastards who had been charged with protecting her.

Yet, what were his plans for the lady? As diabolical as any of the others had been. To sell her to the highest bidder. To profit from her.

To be there at the wedding, making sure the transaction was completed. Arranging a profitable marriage to his ward had seemed simple. An exchange for a more strategic castle. Logical. Intelligent.

The very best of husbands.

He winced and glanced at the door, feeling the compelling warmth of her shadow, her sweet, curling scent, which seemed to have seeped into his blood.

Damnation, he didn't need this. These great clouds of guilt. The temptation. She wasn't in his plans. Carrisford was nearly indefensible in its present condition. Hell, in any condition. To have its walls breached six times in two years was a bloody poor record.

He needed a better castle, larger, with a prestige all its own. He needed to marry into an honorable title to erase the shame of his father's name, to find a far more suitable heiress than the lady Talia of Carrisford.

Wanting to outpace his culpability in this disreputable game of kings and castles and the trappings of dominion, to shrug off this highly discrepant speculation that he might even consider settling for less, Alex left the scented room and stomped out toward the lists.

All the better to give and to receive a good battering.

He got as far as the barbican and met Leod coming through the main gate, pulling a cart full of kindling.

" 'Tis a lovely day, my lord."

"Aye, Leod," he said through his teeth, stopping for a moment to warm his hands over a fire basket.

"A bit chilly though," Leod said as he joined

Alex at the fire, turning to warm his backside. "Has my lady been giving you trouble, then?"

"How do you mean trouble?"

"She's always been an opinionated little thing."

Alex blew out his cheeks. "Then you've known her for a long time, have you?"

"Since she was but a glint in her good father's eye."

Alex looked up and around the timbered pickets, wondering what Talia's father had done to protect Carrisford and his herd of daughters.

"Why do you stay here, Leod? You and Jasper and Quigley?"

"She's our lady, isn't she?, my lord." Leod gave a goes-without-saying snort that Alex could only envy for its undiluted intensity. "We'd each one of us gladly lay down our lives for her."

For some hell-borne reason, he felt the backs of his eyes begin to sting. An old, unfriendly feeling.

"You'd be doing yourself a favor if you stayed, too, my lord."

His heart thudded once, then stopped. "Meaning what, Leod?"

"Well, they don't get any better than our Talia. Not anywhere near better."

Alex glanced up at the late-afternoon greyness, feeling less than adequate at the moment. "A good day to you, Leod. Keep yourself warm, else the woman will have my head."

He left the barbican to the sound of Leod's rumbling laughter, cleared his head with a huge breath, and continued to the lists, the pale sunlight illuminating everything that was wrong with the castle.

Hell, there was nothing right about it. And not nearly enough for him.

Carrisford.

Its threadbare wardship.

Its extraordinary lady.

Christ, he would have to confess his plans to her—tonight—if he could track her down. He owed her that much, after her confession and everything that she'd been through.

Her honesty and her untimely expectations.

He kept himself busy at the lists until supper, then took his meal in the guardtower, hiding from her like the coward he was, unwilling to chance a casual meeting with Talia while he kept his secret from her.

He waited until he knew she'd have put her sisters to bed, till the lights darkened in the family ward, then changed out of his hauberk and climbed the stairs to the landing in front of her chamber.

The points of his speech now an orderly cascade of logic, he knocked hard, rattling the latch and the hinges and bringing her to throw open the panel.

"What is it, Alex?" Large beautiful, luminous

eyes, thickly lashed, so liquid he could barely think. "Are we under attack again?"

Holy Christ. Her nightgown was loosely draped across her shoulders, flowing and light. Her wild hair, unfettered and lit from behind by a low brazier. She was clutching a soft cloth against her chest.

"What's happened, Alex?" He heard her question, saw the worry on her brow, but he hadn't a thought in his head or a word on his tongue.

But oh, there was lust in his loins. Raw and unrighteous. Boiling his brain.

"Come inside, then." She took him by the hand and boldly pulled him through the doorway. "The draft is frightful out there."

The soft slip of her fingers lacing through his righted his thoughts immediately, drove him away from her and deeper into the chamber.

Just tell her.

"I missed you at supper," she said softly.

Domesticity. Tantalizing bits of it.

"I'm sorry. I had dealings at the guardhouse."

Just say it. Tell her that he had no plans to marry her himself.

Quite the opposite, in fact, madam. I plan to arrange a suitable marriage for you—to another man.

There. Short and to the point. Anything to stop her from constantly making her incorrect assumptions and bringing up the subject of a marriage between them.

Anything to push away this impossible yearning for her, for the family that he'd never had, the deep itch to stay.

"Since we're not under attack, how can I help you?"

By not being quite so lovely.

He loved losing himself in her gaze, but couldn't bring himself to look there just yet. He caught his hand around the bedpost.

"It's just that I wanted you to know that—" Christ, this ought to be simpler, ought to fit more lightly against his tongue, because this was exactly the direction he wanted his life to take.

"To know what, Alex?" She seemed overly patient, as though she'd already forgiven him for leading her to believe that he would marry her.

"It's just that you needn't worry about marriage or . . . that sort of thing."

"What do you mean, Alex?"

Feeling bereft and thoroughly dishonest, he spun around to face her. "It's just that . . . I don't . . ." Oh, hell, this was going well. Struck the breath from him. "You see, Talia, I . . . won't be . . . actually, I can't marry you."

She blinked once at him, then set her mouth in a line. "Can't, Alex?"

He wanted more from her than this high-chested, breathless staring. Relief or joy or indignation. Anything.

"What I meant to say, Talia . . . to clear this up between us before it goes any further, is . . . that I have no plans to marry you."

"Oh." A flat sound. And flattening. And still she stared at him, not helping him at all.

"Talia, what I'm trying to get at"—and what ached so much to say—"is that I don't intend to marry you myself—"

"I heard you the first time."

"And, Talia, that I will be, as is my right as your guardian"—*and doubtless my deepest regret*—"looking for . . . a suitable husband for you."

Husband. Talia felt her heart rattle and drop into her knees, a weight so heavy it loosened them, caught a gasp in her throat.

"A husband?" She swallowed to keep her voice steady, to keep from crying out, chiding herself for her girlish hopes that anything could possibly be different. That she could have possibly hoped for—

Him. This large man, taking up so much of the air and the light, his dark hair made darker by the shadows, his gaze fixed on her, the muscles in his jaw flexing.

"I should have said earlier, Talia, that I—"

"That you what, Alex? That you were planning all along to sell me to the highest bidder?"

He squared his shoulders and took a wide-spaced stance of authority, once again the cold-hearted warrior. "It means that I have the right and the privilege to dispose of your wardship as I see fit."

"Rights and privileges that ought to be mine, except that I'm a woman." He looked so coldly determined, not at all like a man who would rescue Gemma's bunny.

"The king granted me your wardship—a great honor, Talia, one that I had no intention of refusing." He briefly shifted his fierce gaze from her face and it returned, resolved. "But I never planned to remain here."

"So I'm on the marriage block again." Back to dismantling her castle.

"Talia—" He reached for her hand, but she whirled away from him, putting a chair between them.

"Well, why wouldn't I be? Not to worry. I'm quite used to it, my lord guardian."

That's what she got for trusting the man. She was back where she started, with only one future, one possible path to follow.

"It's a matter of business, Talia. That's all. The sum of my intentions. I have plans that cannot possibly—have never—included Carrisford."

"Well, good. A man needs plans, doesn't he?" Would he be shocked to discover that she had plans, too? Already in the works, and invisible to him because he'd never have believed her capable of such a grand scheme.

"Carrisford is too small for me."

"It's not the Tower of London, my lord, but it certainly isn't a damp-rotted old hill fort." Good enough for her father, and her grandfather.

For me.

"I was born without a title, Talia. I have gained none in all these years."

"Ah. Power and glory. I understand how important and arousing they can be to men."

"You can't possibly."

"Why is that, my lord? Because I'm not a man? Because it's my lot to sit here helplessly in my tower and pray that whoever does have power over me will make honorable and constructive decisions for me? It hasn't happened yet. Can you imagine how powerless that makes *me* feel?"

"Talia, it's critical that a man wrest power wherever and however he can." He was very close to her, another source of heat opposite the brazier. "I've spent my entire life moving toward one goal, and that is to acquire the right holdings and the right titles and the right heiress for my—"

"For your bed?" She nodded at him, pleased to see his distress, because it made it so much easier to dismiss him. "You see, my lord, I do understand. When do you mean to arrange this . . . marriage of mine?"

"As soon as possible."

"Of course."

"Talia—"

"Nay, you needn't explain any further, Alex. My fault. I had no right to expect better from you." She raised her hand against his chest to stop him, though the heat of him burned through to her marrow. "Men have their needs, and women pay dearly for them, my lord, one way or another."

"This is not how I ever meant it to be between us, Talia." His mouth took on a sternness, his manner a thankful distance.

"If you're going to sell me to the next man who comes along, then we obviously have only a business relationship between us. Lord to lady. Merchant to chattel."

"Don't be cynical, madam."

"You've left me little alternative." She tugged her bed drape closed. "Now, my lord, if you have no other pronouncements, please leave me. I'm tired and sick to my soul, and there's so much more to be done before another winter sets in. I don't want to lose anyone else this year."

"Talia, please—"

"Good night, my lord."

She knew he stood behind her, unmoving. "I made no long-term promises to you."

"Except to protect my family." She turned back to him, pressing harder on him than she had ever dared of another man. "And if you mean a word of that promise, you will allow me an opinion about who this husband will be, the man I will wed and bed."

The corners of his mouth paled, tightened the muscles in his jaw. "An opinion?"

"Out of respect for me. And my sisters. And the children who will come of this marriage."

He became a wall of flint, chilly and impassable. "You'll marry who I say, madam. When I say. And without comment."

She wanted to tell him that none of his blustering mattered anymore, because in a very short time he wasn't going to have a castle to sell.

"I'll say whatever I please, Alex. You've just lost the right to ask civility of me."

"You'll damn well do what I tell you, Talia. The king is coming, and I'll not have you—"

"The king?" She drew back from him, breathless at this announcement. "What do you mean, he's 'coming'?" Kings brought war and rebellion.

"The earl of Chester is promising to restore the king's lands in the north. Stephen doesn't trust him, wants to see for himself."

"So he's coming here to Carrisford? Why?"

She didn't trust Alex's shrug. A visit from a king must mean the world to him, to his bloody plans.

"We're on the way to where he's going."

A dark and desperate fact of war that chilled her to the bone. "He'll bring his army, won't he?"

She felt his gaze on her, testing her temper when it was already set hard against him. "He's a king, Talia. And kings don't travel lightly."

How foolish to have allowed herself to be lulled into thinking that Alex would marry her and solve all her problems. It would be business only between them from now on.

"How do we provision such a horde, Alex? We haven't enough stores for winter."

He sighed, lifted his palm toward her. "Talia—"

"And what if this self-serving Chester is only laying a trap for the king? And suddenly we have a full-scale war sweeping through the valley? What then?"

"Then we'll defend against it."

"We're not ready."

"We will be, madam."

She caught a laugh in her throat, fearing that it would make her sound mad.

Your castle will have fallen into the sea by then, my lord guardian.

"Well, my lord . . . *Alex.* I'm weary to the marrow, so if you've said all that you need to say, then I wish you a good night. And the best of dreams."

He stood there for a very long time, staring at her, studying her face, his mouth working on some other pronouncement—one that would surely leave her aching.

He looked away to her bed, then back at her. "My deepest apologies, Talia. Good night."

She watched him leave, clutching her arms against the cold he left behind.

What a horribly ironic state of affairs: the only

man she'd ever consider marrying was the only one who refused to consider it. The only man she could possibly trust to keep them safe from the war.

De Monteneau was correct, of course. He had the right to sell her to whomever he pleased, to marry her off to his cousin or the king's chandler or to his saddlepack for that matter.

She'd gotten used to the man's presence—that was all. To his smile and his good nature. She'd felt gratitude toward him, and a tantalizing bit of hope.

But not love. Love was for simpletons, and she was wiser than that.

Wise enough to have realized long ago that de Monteneau hadn't been merely biding his time before marrying her himself.

That he had other plans for his life, better brides to consider, with larger coffers and consequential titles to wed.

Business.

She could hardly grudge him his motives; she was in business herself.

And she had a castle to raze.

Chapter 12

"The king is coming here to Carrisford, my lord? When? Does the message say?"

"He'll be here in two weeks, Quigley." Alex went to the guardhouse window, wondering absurdly how long it would take to find a bridegroom for Talia. He ought to be paying attention to Dougal and the rest of his staff, which now included Talia's old steward. "He and I will be consulting together on the plans for the spring campaign."

"'At's a right splendid honor, my lord," Quigley said, whistling his appreciation as he lowered himself onto the bench beside Dougal.

Alex held back the persistent yawn that had threatened all morning. A tangible sign of his restless night, wrestling with his final image of Talia.

Her quiet, disdainful anger at him. His altogether ridiculous guilt over a business decision.

"As far as the king's lodgings, my lord," Dougal said, "do we make ready for his lady queen as well?"

Simon groaned and pinched at the bridge of his nose. "Please God, not that useless boy of his."

"Just Stephen," Alex said, "and a few of his advisors. Fifty all told." Not a crippling burden on Carrisford's precious stores because Stephen would supply his own, madam, he said to the absent woman who would demand that very answer.

Just as she had demanded a say in the choosing of a husband. Bloody hell! He'd wrestled the lot of them all night, as well.

Thick men and tall ones.

Warriors and earls.

Young men and the elderly.

The fair and the wise.

All of them looking at Talia with lust in their eyes and vileness in their black hearts.

Damnation! He slapped his gloves against his thigh, realizing that he had been watching for her in the courtyard below. Anticipating a sighting. The graceful flow of her skirts around her ankles.

"You asked for a detailed map of the castle and its village, my lord. Are you going to be needing that before the king arrives?"

"Aye, Jasper."

Good God, he just realized: Conrad would doubtless be with Stephen.

A reasonable man. A friend. Unmarried.

The perfect sort of bridegroom.

Then why did the thought of it drop the ground from under his feet?

"Dougal will help you with the map."

A bargaining tool to show off Carrisford Castle in its best light.

Not that he wanted to trick Conrad or any other potential bridegroom into thinking that he would be wedding himself to a rich fortune and a flawless castle. The truth would be immediately obvious.

As obvious as the startling beauty of the lady to be wedded in the bargain.

Though he found himself searching for Talia, he didn't see her at all that day, though he'd sensed her vanilla fragrance trailing through the bailey, and felt the lavishness of her goodwill upon the spirits of his men in the lists and her presence in the great hall during the evening meal.

Hell, he was watching for her as though he was a stripling lad waiting for a glimpse of his first love, his pulse racing, his heart crashing around inside his chest when he thought he'd caught sight of her.

But he hadn't.

It wasn't until late afternoon the next day that

he saw her again. He was in the gristmill, and felt her, quite suddenly, in the doorway, so businesslike with her mouth set and rosy, and her cloak and her overloaded basket, her fine face laced with curls poking from the edge of her linen cap.

"What are you doing here in the mill, Alex?" As though she believed she had any right to question him about his activities.

"I might ask the same of you, madam," he said over the clatter of his heart, the slowing, surge of hot fluids through his veins that shook his fingers as he set the quill into the horn.

"A good afternoon to you, lass." Quigley grinned fondly at the woman over the top of his map; Dougal looked simply besotted with her, as most of his men did.

"My thanks for the infusion after last eve's supper," Dougal said, climbing to his feet. "Settled my rocky stomach right away."

"You're most welcome, Dougal, anytime. You know where to find me."

Hell's hoarfrost, *Alex* certainly had no luck finding her last night, he'd prowled the battlements and the family ward, the kitchen and the great hall.

"But I'm most interested in knowing what you three are doing in the mill. It's idle."

"Idle for months it seems, madam. Why is

that?" Alex turned away from her disarming gaze and studied the complex of gears.

"I tried to explain to His Lordship how it's been lately, my lady." Quigley hobbled over to her side, and she enfolded his gnarled old hand inside hers.

"Yes, I know, Quigley. You see, my lord, to be of any use, a gristmill needs grain," she said, as though he hadn't an intelligent thought in his head. "And we have none in the village granary. Please tell me you have found a stray cache of wheat or barley somewhere."

"That isn't my point, madam." Though it was definitely a problem: He hadn't seen any grain but the stores he'd brought himself, and the village would need a sturdy supply come winter. "Will you leave us, Dougal, Quigley?"

His seneschal was too interested in the conversation, Quigley too protective of his lady, and Alex had much more than gristmills to discuss with the woman.

"Straightaway, my lord." Dougal rolled up the half-finished map of the village.

"Be kind to the man, my lady." Quigley patted Talia on the shoulder, gaining only a glower from her as he hurried out with Dougal.

When she turned back to Alex, her frown was making tiny puckers of the inner edges of her brows.

"What was Dougal doing, my lord? With the parchment, all those lines and forms."

His guilt returned full force, but he shoved it aside. "A map of the village, and an inventory. Including this mill. Which does work."

"Aye, it does quite well, when the water's diverted to the wheel. When we have grain." She plunked her basket down on the table. The sun slanted into the mill through the high windows, glinting bits of gold along the strands of her hair. "But why do you need a map? And what has all this to do with the king's visit?"

Not that she had the right to know any of his commerce, but the woman seemed to take comfort in the truth, and he could afford to dole it out to her. "The map is so that I can locate each of Carrisford's assets."

She perched a hip on the edge of a stack of worn millstones. "You're very good, Alex. Creating the best possible impression of your ward and her merchandise."

Hardly deniable. "The more I know about Carrisford, the better for both of us, Talia."

She paused, cocked her head, and asked softly, "By the way, have you anyone in mind for me?"

"Possibly." Alex turned from the potent clarity of her gaze, to run his hand along the edge of the thick wooden gear. But she caught his arm and turned him easily, with the sizzling, featherweight of her touch.

"Possibly, Alex? *Possibly* who do you mean? An earl, a squire, a shepherd? Who?" She was glaring up at him with fierce blue eyes, unbowed. "If you've decided my fate already, I'd appreciate a hint."

His mind thick with images of Talia becoming another man's wife, Alex raked his fingers through his hair, needing a breath of air that didn't hold her sweetness, craving more of her than he could hold.

"Good God, Talia, I've only just started thinking about the matter."

"And *I* haven't stopped."

"I have far more on my mind than your groom."

"The king's visit, I know."

At least she'd changed the bloody subject to something he understood, something that didn't tighten his chest and rile his stomach. "Aye, the king's visit. As well as consulting with him on his spring campaign."

She crossed her arms under her lovely breasts, then stuck an impatient foot out from under her hem. "Oh, and what exactly does consulting with the king on a campaign mean?"

Pride, for one. "Trust in my military skills."

"I thought you said he was just passing through. Now you're going to help plot his wars?"

"Yes." Though he knew that scowl, now he was in his element. "It means planning battles, forecasting the number of archers and cavalry, deciding who will captain the vanguard, organizing supply lines."

"Why is the king coming all the way to Carrisford to plan this campaign, my lord, when he could do it anywhere else in the kingdom?"

"Because, Stephen is fairly certain that this is the direction . . ."

Hell. A trap. A sodding, silken web of a trap, and he'd walked right into it.

"So I was right." She was tapping her foot on the planking. "Because he is certain that the war will come this way in the spring."

"The king is a mortal man, Talia. He can't be absolutely sure of anything." Feeling older than the sea, Alex sat on the edge of the table. "Gloucester will doubtless rise in the west again—"

"And the sun in the east."

"It's my job, Talia. My duty to advise the king, to do my utmost to see that he wins the war." He understood her helplessness. He felt it, too. The empty places, and the days stretching out before him.

"Well, then, Alex," she said, flicking him an impatient frown after a long, heated study of his face, "I suggest that we get to work. Time is short for both of us."

She picked up her basket and stalked out of the mill without a backward glance at him.

Summarily dismissed as only Talia could do.

He'd have called her back, but he couldn't think of a single thing to say that would soothe her.

And she was just too tempting.

"Bloody kings and their bloody wars."

And thieving lords.

And Alex de Monteneau, with his false promises.

Weary of digging at the endless joints of mortar, Talia stowed the hammer and chisel, rolled up Jasper's mason's chart for the night, and stuck it behind a barrel. She threw her cloak over her shoulders, then climbed the stairs out of the east tower cellar only to find herself face-to-face with Alex on the landing.

Dear God, he knew! He was coming to accuse her of high crimes against him! Her heart took off like a hare, still she managed to say, "Good evening, Alex."

He narrowed his eyes at her, though there was a lilt to his voice. "I warn you, madam, that planning a coup against me or the king won't gain you anything but trouble."

"What exactly would a coup involve?" She started across the bailey, hoping he'd follow her far away from the cellar. "If I had the resources to start my own kingdom, I might give it a try."

He laughed long, and she liked the deeply rich sound of it, liked the feel of him striding beside her. "I do believe you would, madam."

He thought she was joking, that she had decided that it was all right just to stand by and let them murder her people.

"Tell me, what sort of castle are you looking for, Alex? Very large, I suppose." His frown pleased her, egged her on. "For that matter, what kind of an heiress are you looking for? Beautiful, of course."

"Not necessarily."

"Well endowered?"

"She would have to be."

"Bearing a hefty title from a powerful father who died in service to the king?"

He cleared his throat. Or was that a growl? "I prefer not to talk about it."

"I can probably advise you on both points, Alex. After all, I do have a castle. And I am an heiress."

"You've grown remarkably reasonable since last night, Talia," he said, opening the door to the keep and holding it open for her.

"Resigned to my fate," she said, feeling his gaze follow her as she walked past him, a light, lifting sensation that grazed her nape.

"You're not the resigning sort."

She'd done a fine job of distracting him from the excavation site; now if she could just keep him off-balance until the castle was ready to fall.

Dangerous business, but it might be fun to wield so much power.

"What I mean, Alex, is that I no longer have to worry that you're going to grab me by the hair and drag me off to the altar."

He caught her elbow, stopped her, forcing her to look up at him. "I would never have. You know that."

Pleased at the turn of his mood, she leaned back against the door to the solar, feeling loose-moraled and liking it a little too much. "Though you would sell me to just anyone."

"Damn it, Talia, I'm not selling you—"

"Bartering me, then." She lifted a shoulder in a rueful shrug and wound her finger around his cloak cords. "Perhaps you should post a sign out on the road, 'One bride available. Make offer.' "

"Talia—"

"Though I suppose it would take an educated man to read such a sign." She made a great show of considering the meaning of this, watching the frown deepening in his eyes. "A civilized man, one of accomplishment and learning. Which, I suppose, is better than some lowborn brute who has slaughtered his way into his fortune."

The man's nostrils actually flared. "Are you finished?"

"Yes."

"Then I suppose it's time to tell you that I . . . do have someone in mind for you."

Alex saw the chord that he struck in her; she came to a complete stop for the briefest moment, a flaw in the forward motion of time. Then she went back to brazenly fingering his cloak, her knee brushing his, driving him ever so mad.

"A hairy old ogre I expect," she said, fingers idling between the cords.

"A friend, actually. A good man." The best he could find. Because he couldn't bear the thought of leaving her with anything less.

Her brow fretted as she straightened, and sighed, a saucy courage in it. "Do I trust your definition of a good man, Alex? Because you have me entirely at your mercy. My future is only as safe as the breadth of your honor."

He was painfully aware of that. Another criterion to use in measuring his search for a buyer—

Hell, not a *buyer*, a marriage partner for his ward.

For the woman with the liquid blue eyes and the wide-open invitation for him to stay.

"Come." Fearing that he'd do something untoward here in the vestibule, Alex opened the door to his chamber and pulled her inside. "Believe what you will of me; Talia, I do have a few scruples."

"Aye, I know." It pleased him that she should think that of him, though the chiding way she offered it pricked his pride as she began to quiz him. "Do tell me about him, then. This paragon friend of yours. What's his name?"

Her transparent interest in this possible husband pinched sharply, assaulted his pride, made the man's name difficult to say. "His name is Conrad."

"Conrad." Said softly, as though she were tasting it for flavor and texture.

"The third son of one of Stephen's stewards in Rouen," he added, needing to steal her back for a moment, "recently knighted for his loyalty to the king."

She quirked him a smile and sat down on the blanket chest at the end of his bed. "Where did you meet him?"

"We squired together as young men. We've met often since then, and in the current war."

"What color is his hair?"

Bloody hell. "His hair?"

"Of course, Alex." She stood abruptly and went to the brazier, rubbed her palms together over the burgeoning flames. "I want to know what Conrad looks like, if I'm going to marry him. Is his hair blond?"

A woman's question to be sure, intimate, searching, and it angered him to the marrow. "I don't know, madam. It's medium, I guess. Brownish hair."

"Light brownish?"

"Perhaps. I don't remember."

"How can you not know the color of your friend's hair? Is it curly? Straight?"

"Maybe curly. Maybe not. I don't bloody

know!" Alex searched for details he'd never thought to catalog. "Blazes, woman. The last time I saw Conrad he'd just yanked off his blood-gouged helm, and his hair was matted against his head and dripping with sweat."

"What about his eyes? Are they kind?"

"I have no earthly idea, woman. I've never had the urge to pay that close attention to him. And if I had, he bloody well would have knocked me down."

She studied him in silence, chewing on the inside of her cheek as though impatient to be done with the matter.

No, *eager*. "How soon will I meet him, Alex?"

Aye, how soon? The whole affair had seemed a part of some distant future. Now the inexorability of it struck him in the center of his chest.

"Less than two weeks. Conrad will be here with the king's entourage."

She paled and her fine-fingered hands stilled inside the folds of her kirtle. "So soon?"

He felt compelled to soften the blow for her. "Not that Conrad will necessarily be in any financial position to acquire your wardship."

"Or even interested in a broken-down castle and a penniless, untitled heiress."

He found himself thinking that only a fool would pass her by. Or a man who had grander plans, who needed more than he could find in Carrisford.

"There's no guarantee in any case, Talia."

"None but your opinion that Conrad is a good man."

"He is that."

"Well, then, Alex, that is guarantee enough for me."

But it wasn't enough. Not nearly. He owed her far more than that, though he couldn't afford to worry about her future beyond the moment; he had a king to satisfy.

"Now, Talia," he said, hating this dance between them. "I would like to submit a request."

"You need my laborers," she said matter-of-factly, over her shoulder on her way to the door.

"Despite my men working every day to put the courtyard and the lists aright, the castle remains a disorderly mess. I need every sound body if Carrisford is going to be ready for the king."

"Of course, Alex." She stopped at the door and smiled as though she knew all his secrets. "Whatever you need, it's yours."

Leaving Alex with a single traitorous thought:

I need you, Talia.

Chapter 13

⚘

The amazing woman could have been a general leading the vanguard at the head of Stephen's army.

Alex paused to watch her from the picket walk, where he was binding timbers together with wet rawhide, pleased that the high October sun had already begun to dry and tighten the lashing, that the walls would be solid again.

In a little more than a week Stephen would arrive with his entourage, and there was still much to be done to impress the king and prove his own industry. He'd been granted the wardship and a dozen knights with the proviso that he would garrison a defensible fortification. Succeeding would well serve his plans for a more strategic castle.

Things were coming together far more quickly

than he could have hoped for, much of it with Talia's help.

And now, like a magical piper, she was leading a parade of happily dancing children across the courtyard just below him, each of them carrying bundles of sticks and heading for the baketower.

He loved her determination, loved the way she dived into her work and shepherded her people through every task.

What he didn't like at all—resented to the marrow—was that he was doing all of this for another man. Cleaning up after Rufus and the slovenly barons who had come before, restoring order to Carrisford so that he could raise a sizable profit from Talia's wardship and find a suitable heiress for himself.

He had a few already in mind, and a nod of support from Stephen—wealthy daughters of powerful barons, widows with valuable doweries, marriage bargains struck in ransom for the life of a captured knight.

And the ancient titles entailed to them. The possibilities were endless, the power enticing, driving the intricate design of his life.

Legitimacy.

If one made plans and worked them hard enough, even a bastard could achieve it.

A dozen sons to cleanse his line of its curse, each borne of his loins and his legally married wife.

Vast, enviable holdings to ennoble his name.

And absolute loyalty to a king who rewarded that loyalty with power.

His was a hard-forged plan, developed when he was cold and shivering in the gorse hedges on the edge of Henry's encampment, praying that he wouldn't be caught.

Praying for vengeance against his betraying father. In the name of his brother.

And here at Carrisford he felt unerringly sure of himself and his careful strategies, certain that he was in the right and ready—until Talia turned lightly as the children trooped into the tower, raised her hand against the sunlight, and looked right at him.

Looked and smiled.

His heart stopped, then bolted, sending bits of desire shooting through every part of him, drawing him to the edge of the picket.

Perhaps Conrad wasn't the right man for her.

After all, he wasn't her sort. He was, well . . . bloody hell, he *was* her sort.

Affable, intelligent. Even-tempered.

Jealous, old boy?

Aye. He was, hot with it. Sizzling. Jealous and overwhelmed with envy for Conrad, or whoever would win her in the end.

He seethed with the dizzying temptation of his golden-haired ward. And yet he couldn't let it matter.

Because she wasn't in his plans.

The day remained bright and beautiful, the air ringing with the satisfying sounds of hammers and shouting and in the afternoon Alex took his regular tour of the lists.

He stood at the railing, doing his best to watch without comment, because he was truly pleased with the progress of the squires. They looked bigger already, broader shouldered, more agile than even a week ago.

"Do please be careful if you're planning to go in there again, Alex."

Alex girded himself for the sight of her, the fresh scent of her, of lichen and autumn's gold. She was beautiful, her kirtle a messy accounting of the work she'd been doing in the forest, softly curling strands of hair framed her face.

"Not just now, Talia." Since he certainly didn't want her to know the truth, that she had the power to distract him from the most ordinary moment and lay him out flat, he sidestepped the issue. "We'll have another go-round with the estate records tonight. I want Stephen to know where I began this venture, as well as how far we've come."

"And Conrad, too, of course. The man who might be my husband. He'll want to know exactly what I'm worth."

That will be immediately apparent.

"Just now I'm far more concerned with the king's accounting. Especially in the armory." He would have continued, but he noticed the boy standing beside him, just beyond his reach.

"What is it?" Alex asked, without turning fully.

"Uhm, well, I was just wondering if . . . I mean, it wouldn't by any chance be *time*, would it, my lord?"

Good God, the boy had grown a half dozen inches in the last week alone. Which did nothing to help the fit of his mis-stitched tunic.

"Time, boy?" Alex asked, "What do you mean?"

But the boy wasn't listening anymore; Talia had turned him and was inspecting the sorry tunic.

"Dear me, Kyle. You're still wearing this sad old thing? How can you possibly work in it?"

Kyle shrugged, his great puppy eyes following her every move. "Dunno, my lady."

"Well, I do know. Loyalty, Kyle, and kindness. But at far too high a price. Come to me this evening; I'll give you another."

He clutched the baggy fabric in his thin fingers, his eyes wide and frantic. "But Fiona will—"

"Fiona will believe me when I tell her that you ripped your tunic beyond repairing when you fell out of the granary while repairing a roof tile."

"But, my lady, that isn't the truth."

"The real truth would **hurt** Fiona's feelings, and you'll only continue to **suffer** needlessly." The woman's logic was as convoluted as it was astounding. "Fiona will be so impressed by your daring, she'll forget all about the tunic and will hie herself off to the field for a fist of flowers. Which you must exclaim over as though they were the loveliest things you've ever seen."

"Oh, I will, my lady. You're sure?"

"Absolutely. Now, what was it you were asking His Lordship about?"

Kyle shifted his eyes up to Alex, then to his boots and started to inch away. "Nothing, my lady—"

She caught his lumpy sleeve in her fingers. "You asked him if it was time yet." Then she turned the inquiry directly on Alex. "Time for what, my lord?"

The boy muttered something unintelligible, but leave it to Talia to hear him with her mothering ears. "Time for you to begin your squire training? Is that what you said, Kyle?"

"Aye."

"Well, is it time, Lord Alex?" The boy's beautiful champion stood there, eyes ablaze with challenge, waiting for him to answer.

But he hadn't any answer. Except that to recognize the boy in any way seemed a betrayal of Gilbert—as though he were his legitimate brother. Blood of his blood.

There must be hundreds of his father's bastards running about the kingdom. Each one as expendable as the next.

I've sons and sons, my lord king, and sons to spare.
Sons to hold and sons to be hanged.

And this particular bastard was nobody's bloody business but his own.

He spared the boy a glance, risked the innocent eagerness, and realized that it would be simpler all around just to agree. "I suppose it is."

"Yaahoooooo!" The boy leaped into the air, a tangle of arms and legs. Then he grabbed Alex's hand to the wrist and shook it fiercely. A strong grip, earnest and from the heart. "Thank you, thank you, sir. I'll make you proud. I will. I will. I promise."

"Go on with you, boy." Feeling wholly unworthy of such gratitude, Alex waved him away. "To the lists. Tell Gordon to kit you out."

"With a sword, even?" The boy's mouth hung open in amazement.

"Go. Now. Before I change my mind."

The boy leaped over the fence in one bound and became a ruckus in the crowd of squires.

"There's a happy lad, Alex." She was smiling at the mob, at the boy.

"Cosseted, madam."

She laughed lightly, then fixed that tantalizing smile on him. "My dear Alex, you wouldn't know cosseting if it fell on you."

Trouble was that he did know cosseting. Craved it. Was patently aware of his yearning for the kind that Talia administered so freely.

"Tonight, Talia," he said, gruffly grabbing back the control that he'd lost.

"Aye, Alex—the king's accounting. By the way"—she tugged on his sleeve and he bent as close as he dared—"I did kiss you that day."

She kissed me. "What did you say?" He'd heard plainly, but the words made no sense.

"I just thought I'd confess to you that I *did* actually kiss you the day that you were clobbered in the lists."

There! He knew it. Still carried the imprint against his mouth, the taste of her. "Why?"

She dropped her shoulders and sighed, shaking her head. "I wish I knew, Alex. Then I'd know how to keep myself from doing it again sometime."

She patted his chest with the flat of her hand, flashed him a smile, and flounced off toward the guardhouse with her empty basket.

Trouble was that he wasn't sure he could stop himself the next time either.

"Producing two thousand arrowheads a day seems plenty to me, Alex."

"But a pittance, Talia." Try as he might, Alex hadn't been able to shake the woman's preposterous warning all day, and now the threat of her stopping in the midst of their meeting and kissing him was the only thing on his mind.

"Yes, but surely the king will be pleased with the progress you've made on the armory." She lounged back in his chair, the scroll in her lap, her eyes on him, as they'd been for most of the last hour.

"A good bowman can loose nearly a dozen arrows in a minute. If I've got fifty very good bowmen on the battlements, I'm only making four minutes of arrows per day. That's not a very impressive siege."

She touched her fingertip to the corner of her mouth, and he wondered, hoped, that she was giving her threat a heartfelt consideration. "Still, Alex, it's better than Rufus's rusting barrelsful."

"Not a valid excuse for an embattled king who expects me to protect his interests here."

"I thought *I* was your interest. Your bargaining chip."

He refused to take her bait. "It's all a part of the sum, Talia. You, your castle, the village, the fields, the quay, the bay, and the military interests of the king."

"I see."

He was damned sure she did, which pleased him as much as it irritated. "Did you clear out the cellar under the chapel tower?"

That seemed to surprise her, made her dampen her lips and then *tsk*. "Ah. It was on my schedule today, but we brought in wood for the winter, and that took much longer than I had expected. I don't think it got done, but I'll ask Quigley in the morning."

She smiled at him from under long, dark sable lashes, raising his pulse and his hopes.

He would have answered, but he caught sight of the boy standing in the doorway, clad in a fresh, new tunic, one that fit rightly.

"Begging your pardon, my lord. I just wanted to say thank you to Her Ladyship for sending the tunic."

"Come in, Kyle." Talia was already at the door, drawing him all the way into the chamber, then turned him. "Now, let me see."

"Fits fine, my lady." The boy's cheeks flamed as he bore up under Talia's inspection. "And you needn't spin a story for me, my lady, I truly took a fall—"

"What happened to your tunic, Kyle?" Fiona had come through the open doorway and planted herself in front of the boy. "Did all my stitches break?"

"No, uhm . . ." The boy looked askance at Talia, then tugged on the hem of his tunic. "I ruined it, Fiona. The whole thing."

"How?"

"Fell off my horse in the list."

Alex hadn't heard that; Gordon hadn't said anything about a fall. But the boy's cheek did look bruised, and he'd been favoring his right leg when Talia had dragged him inside the room.

"Oh, dear, Kyle." Fiona peered up at the new squire. "Did you hurt yourself?"

"Nahhh." The boy bravely waved off her concern. "Not much, really. Just tore up my sleeve at the quintain. My first time, you see."

"Taliaaaaah! Lord Alex!" Footfalls spiraled down the stairs, then Gemma burst into the room, Radish tucked under her arm. "Look what Fiona made for Licorice!"

She pointed grandly at the doorway and Lissa entered, holding Licorice under his front legs, a small, sagging green hat perched on the benighted creature's head.

"All dressed up to meet the king."

Alex found himself exclaiming his approval along with the others. Fiona beamed.

"What a handsome beast you are, Licorice," Talia said, lifting the rabbit out of Lissa's hands to nuzzle him, her voice like a warm cloud, a beacon pointing to the safe places among the shoals.

To all this cosseting.

"Talia, what else do you think I should put into the balm pot?" Brenna came streaming through the door carrying two small vials and a small kettle, and held them up to Talia. "Vanilla or rose?"

Talia sniffed lightly of the pot. "What have you put into the balm so far?"

"Beeswax, almond oil, and honey," Brenna said, putting the small kettle into the embers in his brazier, blithely taking over his chamber as the rest of the family had.

Talia uncorked one of the vials and touched her

little finger to its opening, sniffed and nodded. His favorite of Talia's scents: the bread ovens and the sweets. "Vanilla," she said, "definitely vanilla."

"That's what I thought, too." The young woman's eyes brightened when she caught sight of Kyle, and then shied to batting lashes. "Oh. Hello, Kyle."

Alex had the sudden, sobering thought that the fellow whom Brenna had gone to meet in the village just might have been his own half brother.

"Evening, Brenna," the boy croaked, making a great show of peering with interest into the steaming pot.

Bloody hell. His chamber was as crowded as a village faire, just as noisy, as full of gamboling and laughter.

Time to take control again.

But Talia already had Gemma in her arms, and was trying to herd Lissa toward the door. "Time for all of you to be abed. You too, Brenna, Fiona. Lord Alex and I still have lots of work to do."

Lissa reached up to Alex. "Carry me, please, Lord Alex. And Licorice, too."

The girl had an irresistible smile. Feeling sorry for the poor rabbit, he lifted the pair of them, surprised that Lissa weighed nothing at all, utterly ambushed by the feeling that she needed his protection.

That the lot of them did.

Talia felt her chest fill with adoration and horrible regrets as Alex led them all up the stairs, wondering why the simple sight of him carrying Lissa against his shoulder moved her to the brink of tears.

The little girls scrambled into bed and were dozing and asleep moments later.

"Please stay with them, Brenna, while I help Lord Alex with the records," Talia whispered, "and keep the rabbits inside the room."

"I will."

Alex was frowning fiercely at poor Kyle, who was standing at attention just inside the chamber.

"And you, boy," he said with unrepentant gruffness, "will leave the family ward immediately."

"Yes, my lord." Kyle bowed and scooted past them, disappearing in a clatter of bootheels.

Talia glared up at the man as she passed him on the landing and hurried down the stairs. She waited to speak her mind until they were back in his chamber, waited still further until he was settled in his chair, and wallowing deeply in another frown.

She stood in front of him.

"Tell me who that boy is to you, Alex." She leveled a finger at him. "And don't you dare ask *which* boy, because you know very well that I mean Kyle."

He leaned forward and poured ink into the horn well. "There's nothing to tell."

"Ballocks."

He flicked a brow at her, cocking his head as though he'd never heard a lady curse. "What did you say?"

"You heard me fine, Alex. I said ballocks. I don't believe you."

"And you heard *me*. I've nothing to tell you about the boy, other than that you coddle him."

"And *you* revile him."

"I do not revile him. I have no opinion at all. Now sit, please, we've got—"

"Alex, the very fact that you can have no opinion of that decent young man who lives only to please you means that you very well do have an opinion of him."

"I have no intention of talking about this."

Talia pulled up a stool and plunked herself down in front of him. "All right then, what indefensible thing has he done to you?"

The man mulled that for a long while, watching her mouth, then studying her eyes while some kind of confession perched on his tongue. He shifted finally in his chair. "He's done nothing."

"Then why is it that every time you see him, you act as though he carries the plague? You rarely use his name. Who is he to you?"

"Let it rest, Talia."

"Is Kyle your son?"

Alex burst out of the chair, went to stand above the brazier. "Christ, no! He's not my son—"

"But Kyle is blood to you."

"Damn it, woman, leave it alone."

"He is, isn't he? Related to you in some estranged way. A cousin? A brother?"

He went still, even stopped breathing, then whispered, "It doesn't matter."

"But it does, Alex. It matters very much if it's true. Is Kyle your brother?"

He let out a long sigh. "Half."

Which still didn't explain a single thing. "Kyle is your half brother?"

"We share a father," he said, as though the words left a vileness in his mouth. "Such as he was."

"Then your father didn't marry Kyle's mother?"

He stalked to the table, poured a cup of wine, looking suddenly reckless, his hair falling against his brow. "Or mine. My noble father made a practice of not marrying any of the women he bedded."

"I am sorry for that, Alex. But none of it is Kyle's fault. You can't blame him for your father's sins. That isn't fair."

"I don't blame him, Talia." He looked down into the wine cup. "I just don't need—"

—*anyone*. The man may have stopped midconfession, but she could have finished for him. Because she was beginning to understand.

"Never mind, Talia."

And she wanted to smooth the fretting from his forehead, to curl her fingers through his hair. "But that's the trouble, Alex; I do mind. Because you are such a puzzle to me, and we have so little time left together."

"The entire night, if need be." He thunked the chair into place. "I want to lay out the work schedule before morning. We're days behind."

So far behind, they would never catch up.

But she couldn't very well leave the man like this, to blindly stumble his way through the world. He needed to be cracked open, whether he wanted to be or not.

Chapter 14

❝**I**s he still alive, Alex? Your father?❞

"My father?" He glanced at her sideways, shook his head, his eyes looking weary and far away. "From what I understand, he was mortally wounded ten years ago, dying in the same way he lived."

"Was he a soldier?"

The long breath he took seemed to come from some very dark and desolate place. "Oh, no, my dear Talia. My father was a monster. Murderous, mercenary, a thug, loyal to no one but himself. A violent and venal and cowardly man. Monstrous to his black heart."

"I'm sorry for that."

"Don't be. I saw him but a half dozen times

in my entire life. He occupied himself defying King Henry and ravaging the countryside."

"What about your mother? Is she still alive?"

"No. I last saw her when I was ten—the day my father came to steal my brother and me by the scruff of our tunics."

"For what purpose?"

He laughed with a terrible coldness, shrugged as though it was obvious to her. "Because Gilbert and I had finally become useful to him."

"Gilbert?" He'd never mentioned the name before. There was a lightness about the sound. "Your brother?"

"Born of the same mother, older than me by two years."

"Where is Gilbert now?"

He touched the edge of the table, then ran his palm along the coarse grain. "Gil was hanged as a hostage when he was twelve."

Talia felt her heart flip. "Alex, no. How horrible. Who would have done that? Hanged an innocent boy?"

Alex shrugged as if this offense against God was an everyday thing. He sat on the edge of the table. "Henry, did. The late king."

"Dear God!" No wonder Alex had chosen Stephen above Maud's abominable father. "But why, Alex? Why was Gilbert being held?"

"Against my father's treacherous behavior.

Henry ought to have known not to trust a man with my father's reputation for falsehoods."

"But to hang a boy for his father's outrages!" She stood between the spread of his knees, wanting to see into his eyes. "You must have been overwhelmed with grief when you found out."

"Nearly paralyzed with it." He looked past her. "And terrified for my own life."

"Oh, the bloody bastard. Threatening you as well. Outlawing your entire family, I suppose. Sending out the hue and cry."

"No, my dear. I was there."

"What do you mean?"

"I was there with my brother."

Then she realized with a terrible dawning, the unforgivable thing his father had done. "Oh. Oh, no, Alex. Your father gave Henry two hostages, didn't he? Gilbert . . . and you." Her throat closed over.

"Aye. And me. You see, my father had lots of insurance against his own treachery. He had many sons to give."

"He wouldn't."

"Oh, but he did. Henry was raging when he learned that my father had continued his raiding, that he'd had no intention of retrieving a living son when he had so many to spare."

"Alex, no," she slipped his hand between hers, then held it tightly against her chest.

"We were bastards, all of us. Worthless to him. To anyone. A farthing to the dozen."

"But you said you were there when Henry . . . when Gilbert died. How did you not . . ."

"How did I escape the hanging, my dear?" He laughed again, a dry, tearless sound. "Timing. Chance. The outrage of my guard."

"He let you escape?"

"The king was breaking camp at the time and things were chaotic. But my guard had heard the king would be coming for me next. So he let me go."

"What happened to him?"

Alex looked into her eyes, brought her fingers to his lips. "Why did I know you would ask that, Talia?"

"Well, I . . ."

"Because you were worried about him."

"Why, yes, I—"

"This very courageous man who had risked his life to save mine, when my own father was perfectly willing to sacrifice me." He pulled her softly, slowly against him. His lips in her hair, and then his fingers at her nape, pulling her closer. "I've wondered that too, Talia. Through all of my life."

Oh, the delicious rumble of his voice inside her, seeking the deeper places she kept from everyone. "Did you never find out who he was, Alex?"

"Never. I was too terrified to come within leagues of Henry for years. And when I was finally old enough, Henry was gone, and I unwaveringly pledged myself to Stephen."

"The king had better damn well know what a fortunate man he is to have you on his side."

"That's high praise coming from you, madam."

Alex loved the feel of her, the scent of her wrapped in his arms. The warmth of her snuggled against him, her cheek now a print of heat against his shoulder.

Not to mention her belly pressed against his groin.

"Well-deserved praise, Alex." She pushed away slightly from him, studying him. "Stephen would be a feebleminded fool not to recognize your value to him. I'll tell him so the moment he arrives."

"I'd prefer you didn't." Preferred lifting her into his arms and carrying her the last few dangerous steps to his bed. "In fact, Talia," he said, setting her well out of the reach of his unquenchable desire for her, "I preferred your low opinion of me to this elevated one."

"I doubt that very much, Alex." She furrowed her brow, frowning as though she'd just caught him in a lie. "You're a practical man, and we didn't get anything done back then, did we? Before we settled things between us."

Alex felt anything but settled. Aroused and aching and ready to burst. "We're not getting much done now, madam." He sat down on the bench, then flattened and weighted the corners of the household roll, hoping finally to draw her to the table, to the rest of the evening's work.

But she disappeared into the darkness across the room, only to return with an armload of wood for the brazier. "It's just easier for me now, Alex, knowing for certain that we're not going to be married. Unburdens me."

It was easier to watch those perfectly shaped hips as she bent to the brazier, the gentle curves that beckoned to him. Though it irked him that she could just toss him off that way. "Aye, Talia, so you've told me."

"It's much easier for me to imagine a peaceful future for my people, knowing that you mean to try to do well by me when you go looking for a husband."

"As I've promised."

"Most important of all is that you won't ever try to kiss me."

He knew he was every kind of fool even to look at her, at the smoothness of her cheek, the ends of her hair rising and curling in the fire wind.

Every kind of fool for answering from his heart. For rising off the bench when he ought to stay rooted in sanity. "I've promised nothing of the sort."

She thought for a moment, wearing a danger-ously enigmatic smile. "But I know now that you would never press your attentions on me. Un-less . . ." She dangled the word in front of him, and he had to ask.

"Unless . . . ?" Foolish, foolish man.

She raised a carefree brow at him. "Unless I offered no objections." Hazardous banter—invitations and offers.

"Or *I* did." A last chance. A plea to himself to stop, not to gather her hair in his fists. Though she had hold of the lacing at the front of his tunic, worrying her lower lip.

"But I am right, Alex, that you have no wish to kiss me?"

He shook his head, knowing he was traveling toward a treacherous brink that he might not be able to pull away from. "No, Talia, that wouldn't be true at all."

She quirked an eyebrow, sly and hinting. "Then you do wish to kiss me?"

Quicksand. Softly scented, invitingly warm quicksand. And he was slogging through it gladly. "I do, madam. Through most of my waking hours, I do."

She seemed genuinely surprised. "Really?"

"Oh, yes."

"You mean . . . right now, Alex? Here?"

"Christ, yes, Talia. Right now. And yesterday eve. And today in the lists. And tomorrow when you take the bread cart down to the village." He'd pinned her against the table, wanting her, but not quite touching her, for that would be his final folly.

"But you wouldn't. Would you?"

A man could only talk about kissing a magnificently kissable woman for so long.

"The hell I wouldn't."

Talia knew she shouldn't have been testing him, teasing, or wanting him to touch her. Or so delighting in his breath against her mouth. Surely there were demons inside her, tickling, mischievous ones.

He was very close, and irresistibly tall. He was huge, with shoulders like a mountain—a warrior out of legend, so broadly muscled that she could feel them flexing through the thickness of his tunic.

Her backside was pressed against the table, and he was gently, insistently, spreading her thighs with his knee, leaving her to stare up into his breathlessly devilish grin.

"Well, are you going to, Alex?"

"Most probably." He stepped even closer, leaving her to indelicately straddle his thigh. "Though, God knows, I shouldn't."

"Why, Alex?" The man was a marvel of honor and respect, difficult to analyze. The light from the brazier planed his features in orange; the dimness of the chamber stole the lighter shadows and deepened them. His eyes sparkled like midnight and diamonds, made her blood heat. "You know your mind most times."

"Aye, Talia, and I know it right now. Clearly. As you must know it."

She did know. And felt his thoughts through his fingertips as he threaded them into the hair at the edge of her temples, taking his own exquisite time. He watched her intently when he caught her jaw and drew his thumb slowly across her lips.

"Oh, my!" And here she was, leaning against him, her eyes wide-open. "I think I've been a bit forward with you, Alex. Improper."

The corners of his eyes crinkled slightly, wickedly. "Oh, yes, Talia. Perfectly improper."

"Good." Because she wanted to be. Just this once. To wantonly shape the hugeness of his erection against her belly. To fancy a sanctuary with him that could never be, to imagine children who would never be born.

"Ah, Talia." He took close to forever making his way toward her mouth, touching his wonderful lips to her forehead, to her temple, breathing against her ear.

Tilting her chin as he brushed his kiss along her jaw, and then he touched his fingers to the center of her lips.

"You're soft here, Talia." He furrowed his brow as though his discovery troubled him, then drew another of the deep breaths that seemed to surround her.

"You're not soft anywhere, Alex." She couldn't help squirming against him just a bit.

"Holy Christ, Talia." He gave a worriedly surprised smile and, like the impatient, ungoverned woman she was, Talia shifted her head for a better aim, clutched his elbows to pull him closer.

"Perfectly improper, madam," he said, so close that every word touched her lips, blended with her own breath.

"Alex, I—" *Oh, my. Oh, unbelievable bliss!* He finally, deliciously covered her mouth with his, softer than she could ever have imagined, almost sweetly.

"God save me, Talia." With a driving, soul-hungry groan, he possessed her utterly, a searing jolt that shot sparks to the ends of her fingers, that seemed to plunge to the center of her.

"Just for tonight, Alex." Just between them. No one else in the world mattered.

He rose up from his kiss and stared at her, and the table rocked and the candle danced as he caught her up in his arms and gathered her hard against him.

"It'll be all right, Alex." But it wouldn't. Not ever, after tonight. Her heart thudding with stolen wonder, Talia climbed more deeply into his embrace, throwing guilt over the battlements, moving her hips against the length of his wonderful hardness, wishing for a lifetime of him, willing to steal just the moment.

And so she kissed him with a full measure of passion, traced the planes of his midnight-bristled jaw, brushed her lips across the soft play of his eyelashes. He tasted of sweet wine and leather and ink.

He groaned and slanted another hot, slippery kiss across her mouth, then slid it down the front of her chemise, blowing hot through the linen. His breathing ragged and pleasuring as he shaped his hands beneath her breasts and lifted them, as though he might kiss them as well.

A heady, wholly impossible thought.

He watched her face as he grazed his thumbs across her nipples, sending a deliciously feverish clenching to the joining of her thighs.

"Oh, Alex. Oh, yes!"

She didn't know what else to say to this unexpected intimacy, because she could imagine so very much and had lost her will. He was such a large and powerful man, crowded with courage, too big for her castle, yet he was trembling as he enfolded her tightly in his arms, as if to rescue her from the tangle that she'd caused on her own.

"You're very good at this," he said against her temple.

"At kissing, you mean?"

"Aye."

"Inspired completely by you, Alex. I've never been kissed before. Not like this." Not by a man of honor, who seemed to care. Who didn't smash his bristly, ale-reeking mouth against hers.

He frowned at her with half a brow, steadied his breathing. "Betrothed a half dozen times . . ."

"Nothing ever like your kiss, Alex."

This seemed to please him only for a moment, then sent him frowning more fiercely. "If only I could . . ."

"Stay, Alex?" Oh, this suddenly riled her, set her cheeks ablaze and her heart racing with a kind of helpless anger that she'd been stifling for days. Alex and his bloody heiress. She twisted out of his embrace and went to a safer place across the table. "And collect all of my embraces for yourself?"

"Talia, if only . . ."

If only she were wealthy and pregnant with titles and ensconced in a tower of gold. Not that it mattered anymore. Carrisford would be gone, and so would he.

And she was beginning to feel reckless and ill-mannered. "Then you think Conrad will be pleased?"

He settled his gaze on her like a weight. "Pleased?"

"With me, Alex? With the way I will kiss him? Though my way is far from proper, as you said. Do you think Conrad will understand?"

He cleared his throat. "I think that's quite enough, Talia."

"You're right. Any more of this, and we might have ended the night tangled in your bed linens. And then I would no longer be a virgin. And then *whoomp!* there goes the price of my marriage bed. Right into the ground."

He eyed her soundlessly, his wondrous mouth now a coldly firm line.

"Then let's get to work," he said finally, flatly.

Aye, it was much better that way. Talking of board feet of lumber and buckets of lime.

It seemed easiest to go along with him, to pretend to reinforce the very thing she intended to destroy.

Feeling utterly joyless about the whole mess, her heart still aching for more of him than she should want, or could ever have, Talia knew better than to glance his way as she sat down at the table and took up the quill.

"Where do you wish to begin, Alex?"

Begin? Alex thought. Bloody hell! He didn't want to begin anything. He wanted to return to the safety of a half hour ago.

Before he'd tasted her. Before he had turned his unbearable curiosity into this blood-thickening craving. Into this sizzling need.

He would suspect her of toying him, but she wasn't that kind of woman. She was direct, even brutally honest.

Then you think Conrad will be pleased?

Damnation!

"I've sent for three cartloads of reeds to repair the roof of the stable."

To hell with the stable. He watched her bend over the neat lines of her script, still reeling from her immodest, inventive touch, still dizzy from her scent.

Conrad would be more than pleased; he'd be bloody knocked bloody out.

Which ought to delight Alex. Instead, the closer the day came to the king's arrival, the more certain he became that Conrad would be eager to marry Talia. Quite eager.

Which sat hard on him. Bruised his ego. Weighted him down and unfocused his strategies so that he could barely see the details.

"How much slate do you think you'll need?"

"Slate?" He knew he'd barked the word by the way she huffed and shifted positions.

"The kitchen roof, Alex. You said you had calculated how many tiles—"

"Three dozen." So businesslike. Her father had taught her well. Hell, the man had probably learned from her.

"Good, then I'll get you slate from the scree. Will late tomorrow be soon enough?"

"Yes." *Yes. Yes.*

"Then I'll have Quigley see to it."

Damned efficient woman. "Have him come find me early in the morning."

She idly wound a lock of hair around her finger as she studied the rolls and wrote something that ended with a quick flourish. "I suppose the king will be interested in the state of your siege stores."

He sat down on the edge of the table, a safe enough distance, if he kept his mind on the king's visit and not on the tendrils of vanilla curling around him.

"As you've told me yourself, since castles are mostly taken after a lengthy siege, where supplies and water are really all that matters, yes, he'll be very interested."

"Ah, then, I'll see to the stores myself."

"*You* will?"

She turned her face up to him, brightened and softened by the candle flame. "It makes good sense, Alex. I'm far more familiar with the cellars of Carrisford and the storage space than you are, don't you think?"

I think I don't trust you, madam. Though he couldn't put his finger on the immediate reason.

"Oh!" she said—a completely unbelievable exclamation lighting her eyes, deepening his suspicion. "I'm sure, Conrad would find a tour as interesting as the king. Because a siege-ready castle will add a great deal of value to my wardship, and therefore to his desire to marry me."

He swallowed back an irrational clot of jealousy. "Exactly, Talia."

"So you will concentrate on the battlements and the courtyard, and I'll take on the cellars stores and the village."

"And you will clear everything through me first."

"Of course, Alex. And to accomplish as much as possible, I give you full permission to employ my villeins as you see fit. As long as you don't endanger anyone."

He pitied Conrad the woman's wheeling, seductive logic, the dampness on her lips as she sipped from the cider cup and went back to her notes, because he damned well needed her cooperation and all of her people.

"Have you lost anyone yet, madam?"

"Not that I know of. No complaints either." She chewed on a half smile, then threw him off guard with her next question. "What do you plan to do with Kyle now?"

"*Do* with him?"

She tilted her head and sighed. "It must hurt him deeply to know that you go so far out of your way to avoid your own brother. I pray that you'll be kinder to him, include him in your life."

He left the table to add a log to the brazier, to put more distance between them. "The boy doesn't know, Talia." Sparks rose and sputtered as he laid an oak log on top of the blaze. "He doesn't know of our . . . connection."

"Doesn't know?" He heard the cracking of the

chair as she sat up sharply. "You don't mean it, Alex."

Alex sighed and turned, facing her as her gaze burned through him. "The boy has no idea, and I plan to keep it that way."

She clunked her cup onto the table. "How the devil could Kyle not know?"

"Though it is none of your business, Talia, I've made it my policy not to seek out any of my father's bastards."

"You mean your *brothers*."

"I mean that my personal life is none of your business, madam."

"So you have no plans to tell him?" She stood up with a stomp, meeting him at the brazier. "That innocent young boy hasn't a scrap of family in the world except you."

"It wouldn't serve either of us, Talia."

"It would serve Kyle. He needs you, Alex, and you know it."

A surge of guilt shoved at him, but he shifted his weight and stood his ground. "I insist on your silence in the matter, Talia."

Her face became a flickering show of raw emotions: disbelief and anger and confusion. It was the disdain that injured him, because he doubtless deserved every ounce of it.

"I take all my compliments back, Alex. And my kiss. And every other exemplary thought I've ever had about you. You're a despicable, stone-headed, self-centered blackguard, and I pity the poor heiress who finds herself saddled with you for a husband."

Directly to the point in all things, my dear. He *was* a brute and a bastard and certainly didn't deserve a woman as decent as Talia.

"My orders to you remain unchanged. You will say nothing to the boy."

"I would never tell him, Alex." She huffed and flung herself back into the chair, then started writing furiously. "You'll have to confess that sin yourself. The last thing I want to do is to hurt Kyle's feelings."

"Good."

"Because nothing could hurt him more than to learn that you are his brother and that you want nothing to do with him." She plopped the quill into the holder and stood, pointing to the curling strip of parchment. "Our schedule, my lord. I'll keep my part of the bargain, if you keep yours. Sleep well."

Bloody hell, he hadn't had a good night's sleep since he first met the woman, and he doubted he'd find any tonight.

Chapter 15

❦◦◦◦◦∽◦◦◦◦∽◦◦◦◦❦

"How thick is the base of this tower wall, Jasper?"

"Eight or ten feet, my lady."

"Then we can safely pull out another two feet do you think?" Talia grunted as she shouldered another shoring timber up against the ceiling beam, barely able to straighten from her knees in the cubbyhole they had made directly under the east tower wall.

"No more than that, my lady."

"Please God, we don't need an early cave-in." Aching to the bone, Talia knelt and tied a rope around another timber, knocking the opposite end on a side of salted ham that hung from the cellar rafters in a forest of other meats. "And I don't want to progress too far before the king arrives and His Lordship leads him on a tour of every inch of the place."

She couldn't bring herself to mention Conrad, even to Jasper. Wedded and bedded to a stranger.

If this marriage actually came about before she was able to bring down her dear castle.

"So, I'm thinking that we'll be lifting some of the king's wagons when he arrives, my lady. Quite a plush treasure that'll be."

And an inescapable fate, if they were caught.

"No choice, Jasper," Talia said, tugging the timber into place. "One day soon we'll all be living in our ramshackle little village, relying on whatever grain and seed and salted meats we can hide in the caves from Stephen and Maud and their marauding armies."

A sudden flight of footsteps startled her, bringing her out of the cubbyhole.

"Talia, oh! What's going on down here?" Brenna's face loomed out of the paleness of the single candle, her dress was streaked in broad white swaths. "Are you planning the king's supper?

"Brenna! Blazes, what are you doing? It's too dangerous down here! Now go!" The girl knew too many of her secrets already.

"Lord Alex sent me to find you." Brenna shouldered her way to where Talia and Jasper had been working. "But what is this, Talia? Is the tower broken?"

"Yes, Brenna. Jasper and I are fixing it. Now please leave before it falls—"

"Falls? Oh, dear!" Brenna started plowing back through the still-swinging hams. "I'll go get Lord Alex. He'll know what to do."

Mother Mary! "No, Brenna. Stop!" Talia nearly had to tackle the girl. "Alex can't help us. And you can't ever tell him what you found here!"

Brenna stared at the huge hole and Jasper's owlish, stone-dusted face peering out at them. "But, Talia, His Lordship will know exactly what's happened and how to fix it."

"Aye, Brenna, and that would be the end of it." She had no choice but to tell her everything. Brenna was honest to a fault and said whatever came into her head, unless she was charged with keeping a deep secret. "It doesn't need fixing."

Brenna stepped closer to the hole and peered inside. "But look how much of the tower is gone. What's done it?"

"I did."

"You?" Brenna wrinkled up her nose in disbelief. "Why would you undermine the tower, Talia? It'll fall down, and the castle will, too, and then anyone can get in."

"Yes, I know." Brenna had to believe in a secret before it was completely safe with her.

"But why would you want that? Lord Alex

can't very well defend a castle that's missing part of its wall."

"No one can. And that's the idea. Carrisford Castle has to come down, sweet. It has to be destroyed so it can never again be used in a war."

"Not even to protect us? And all the people in the village?"

"The castle hasn't been able to protect us since the war started, has it? We've been seized seven times so far, and the war is far from over."

"But what about the village?"

"Without the castle as a beacon to draw the armies, no one will be interested in the village, and we can finally live there in peace."

Brenna sat down hard on a salt barrel. "What a horrible thing, Talia."

"It is."

"Are you and Jasper going to take down the whole castle? All the towers? And the walls?"

"Not just me and Jasper, Brenna." Talia knelt in front of her and tucked a stray strand of hair back under her cap. "There are a lot of us. And in the end fire will finish it off. When everything is ready."

The girl's sorrow dipped the corners of her mouth. "How long from now?"

"A few weeks, maybe less."

The girl twisted up her face in heartbreak, chewed on her lip. "Lord Alex doesn't know you're tearing down the castle, does he?"

"He mustn't, Brenna. He would stop us."

"Are you going to marry him?"

"I can't."

Brenna took Talia's hand, held it against her cheek. "You should, Talia. He's the best."

No time for regrets. "It isn't going to work out, sweet. He's not even planning to stay here as lord. Even if there were a castle left for him to garrison."

"I'm awfully sorry for that." Brenna took in a long raspy breath.

"So am I." Talia had to swallow back her tears. "Do you understand what it all means? I need you to."

Brenna heaved a large sorrowful sigh that left her shoulders hanging. "Unfortunately, I do."

Talia kissed her cheek, relieved and wondering when Brenna had gained all this maturity. "Thank you."

"Well, then, what can I do to help?" She canted her head at the timbered struts.

"Keep an eye on the girls—they are little ferrets when it comes to digging up trouble. And do as Alex tells you. Be my spy—"

Brenna clapped her hands together, her face lighting with joy. "A spy, Talia? Oh, yes!"

Mother Mary, save us all! "Act as you would normally, Brenna. Don't do anything to bring suspicion down on us, or that will be the end of us."

"I know just what to do. Lord Alex won't learn

a thing from me. Oh! Remember he wants to see you, Talia. Right away."

"So you said." Talia lifted a corner of Brenna's kirtle. "What happened to your clothes?"

"Limewash. I was helping His Lordship with the barbican walls."

"And he wants to see me?"

"Something about needing more lime."

At least it would keep Alex from poking around in the storage cellars.

"Show me."

"What are you doing, Lord Alex?"

Alex had to spin on his heels to find Lissa and Gemma standing directly behind him, grinning up at him in the bright sunlight. No sign of Talia or Brenna with his message. "Well, good morning, ladies."

"Good morning, Lord Alex." Lissa curtsied deeply, and Gemma hugged his knees fiercely, a gesture that he'd come to look forward to because it always came pouring from her heart, right into his.

"What are you doing, sir?"

The girls stared up at the web of ladders and scaffolding leaning against the barbican walls, gaping at the men scrambling up and down. There was so much activity, it looked like an anthill torn away from its side.

"We're limewashing the barbican walls. After

that, we'll move into the bailey." Alex poured a bucket of water into a pail of powdered lime, narrowly missing Gemma's head as she peered into the mixture.

"What's limewash?"

"Careful, Gemma!" Alex grabbed Gemma's wrist before she could dunk her finger into the mess. "Lime and water and other things."

"Why, Lord Alex?" Lissa stood over the bucket, securing Gemma's hand, enabling Alex to stick in the paddle and begin stirring the thickening liquid.

"The wash will make Carrisford look bright and shiny for the king."

"Yummm! It looks like milk."

"It's not milk." Alex missed the darting hand this time, grabbing back Gemma's little fingers, now dripping with limewash.

"Ooops!" The impish face was the picture of strawberry-haloed innocence, melting away any scolding he could have mustered.

"Can we help, Lord Alex?"

"I'm afraid the lady Talia wouldn't be very pleased with me if you got your clothes full of limewash." He could just imagine Talia's reaction, augmented by their unwise intimacy a few days past, that had only sharpened her dealings with him.

But she had kept her promise, hadn't said a word to the boy about the connection between them. A connection that seemed to have tightened in the days since. That made Alex watch for the boy, to ask after him in the lists.

To worry. To know that right now he was with the crew repairing one of the pier posts on the quay.

A sharp tugging at his elbow made him look down at Lissa. "But Talia told us this morning that we should help you in any way we could. Besides, Gemma is already all limewashed. And I'm very careful."

Fearing the worst, Alex turned to follow Lissa's point only to find Gemma working the paddle herself, splashing thick waves of gloppy white out of the bucket and all over the front of her kirtle.

"Ah, Gemma, no." He grabbed the paddle, but she kept on stirring.

"I'm helping, Lord Alex. See!"

"Me too!" Lissa had found a brush and was halfway up the nearest ladder.

And I'm in deep, deep trouble. Deeper than ever, by the looks of the two girls.

"I'll tell you what, ladies," he said, resigned to his fate. He hooked his arm around Lissa's waist and lowered her safely to the ground. "I'll welcome your help with the limewash, but only with a few conditions."

"What, what, what, Lord Alex?" They jumped

up and down, making him wonder if he wasn't about to make a grandly foolish mistake.

"All right, ladies." He took a stern, lord-to-villein stance and glared down at the messy young girls. "You're to keep the wash only on the wall—not on the ground or on yourselves or me or anyone else. You're to stay off the ladders and the scaffolding, and you will mind Wallace here."

He pointed to his horrified sergeant, who had balked earlier at letting the much older Brenna help with the limewashing. "He's in charge."

"We will!" The girls would have dived into the buckets with both hands if he hadn't caught them and carried them to the supply table.

"Some instruction before you start, ladies." Though certain that his advice wouldn't stick nearly as well as the soupy white stuff, he handed each a thick brush and showed them the proper way to apply limewash. "Small strokes, applied lightly, neatly. Do you see?"

"Yes! Yes! Lemme try!"

"Easy, Gemma. Don't miss a spot, else the stone beneath will show in blotches."

"Like this, Lord Alex?" Lissa frowned as she concentrated on an area, doing a fine job, actually.

"Excellent, Lissa."

Gemma hadn't a chance at any kind of accuracy, but she was squealing in delight, running along beneath the scaffolding, barely able to lift the brush as she trailed it along the wall, and then running back to the bucket beside him, a streak of white now adorning her cheeks.

"That's one way to do it, Gemma." Lord, Talia was going to kill him.

"Thank you, Lord Alex." Gemma's aim was impeccable, clipping him across the knees with a spray of white as she drew the brush out of the bucket and ran to a new part of the wall.

"Watch out for them, please, Wallace. I don't want them falling off the ladders."

Wallace flinched. "But my lord—"

"They'll soon tire of the game."

"Are you sure? They look wound enough for days, my lord."

"I'm sure, Wallace." Though Lissa had already covered quite a bit of wall and Gemma was concentrating on her third thick line of limewash.

"But what about till then, my lord—"

Alex glanced again through the gate into the bailey and saw Talia striding toward him, Brenna on her heels.

"Bloody hell." Though he felt a wild relief at the sight of her.

"Looks like trouble, my lord."

And all he wanted was to carry her off into a deserted tower, to run his fingers through her hair, and—

"Talia! Look! We're helping!"

"So I see, Gemma."

Talia shifted her gaze along the length of the wall, then blinked up at Alex with those clear blue eyes. He'd been holding his breath, expecting a ringing harangue. Finally, she sighed.

"You're far braver than I, Alex."

The smile she'd been so poorly hiding broke across her face, followed by the sort of laugh that he wanted to tuck away deeply into his heart. Broad and homey, including him this time, with a shake of her head that made the red in her plait glint in the sunlight.

"Oh, Alex, you're as full of limewash as they are." To his amazement, his great pleasure, she reached up and drew her palm across his cheek and just under his jaw, then showed him the streak of white.

"See what I did, Talia?" Lissa slapped the wall with her brush, spattering limewash in a fan above her head.

"Lord Alex showed us how!" Gemma ran toward them and threw her arms around his legs again, clobbering the back of his thigh with the brush.

"Careful, Gemma!" Talia said, as she loosed the girl from his legs. "I think His Lordship's got just about enough limewash on him."

"Near as much as me!"

He could plainly see the woman hiding her smile again as she sent Gemma off to the bucket. "You needn't put up with them, Alex."

Alex followed her gaze, lighting with hers on the three girls, diligently at work on the wall.

"I don't mind." And damned if he didn't. In point of fact he wanted to laugh. To throw back his head and revel in the pure, reeling pleasure of the moment.

But he held it inside, restraining his smile, even when he felt her eyes on him, felt the softly probing questions she asked.

"You've been so very good to them, Alex. They'll miss you terribly when you leave us."

She might as well have stuck her dagger in his heart. He swallowed hard and looked away, pretending an interest in the stone finials that lined the barbican wall. "Your family is distracting, to say the least."

"They are everything to me, Alex." Her eyes shone as she watched them, love and loyalty sparkling brightly.

Oh, to be loved like that.

And to love as freely.

"By the way, Alex, Kyle is helping Rolf at the quay."

"I know."

She stood in profile, a half smile perched on her lips. "I thought you might."

"It means nothing, madam. I also know that William and Garin are making arrowheads. That Gordon is fitting out the lists for a demonstration—"

"Fine, then. What's this about needing more lime?" She fluttered her gaze down the length of his hauberk, then raised it to his face, the picture of innocence. "You seem to have plenty."

Ignoring the jibe, he nodded at the girls' messy industry. "Not at this rate. Have you more anywhere?"

"Tending to the state of the walls has never been very high in my recent guardians' priorities. Father always kept a plentiful store of it at the lime kilns, just beyond the orchards. I'm sure it's still there. Shall I have Quigley show you?"

"We've three days left, Talia. You'll show me this afternoon. The carts can come later."

"You don't need me, Alex."

Oh, madam, I do indeed. "We'll conference as we walk. Bring a sack of dinner."

"Alone, Alex?"

He wondered at her coyness, delighted in it. "We've been quite alone before, madam."

"If I didn't know your plans better, Alex, I would think you were courting me."

Talia didn't know what to make of his crooked smile—to be wary of it or flattered or just plain faint away. But he wound her plait in his fist and pulled her close.

"Believe me, Talia, if I were courting you, you'd have no doubt of it. None at all."

Chapter 16

❧◦❧

"This a lime kiln, madam?" Alex stalked imperiously around the deserted site, frowning at everything, obviously thoroughly disgusted with the state of it.

"It was, back when my father was alive, and Carrisford was kept at its best. Now, I'm afraid—"

"What's all this?" He picked up a small chunk of limestone off a tumbled pile.

"Where it all begins. The bare rock is crushed nearly to a powder, then heated in one of the ovens, using peat or charcoal. Eventually all that's left of the original stone is the lime. The same kind that is used in mortar."

"Do you mean to tell me we have to go through all that in order to finish the limewash?"

"No, we have some stored." Though she

couldn't take him too far afield; the limestone caves nearby were filled with contraband that would save so many lives.

The powdered lime was kept in two long buildings, lead-roofed and constructed of limestone blocks. "See, Alex," she said, leading him into the dimness, "all the cribs are full of lime and ready to be carted away."

He grabbed a handful of the powder and let it sift through his fingers, then raised his eyes to hers. "Is there anything you don't know, Talia?"

It was a difficult question, made almost morose here in the near dark. She started out the door, needing fresher air. "I don't know how it'll end."

"How what will end?" She heard him brush off his hands, felt him behind her as they came out into the fading afternoon light.

"All of this. I wish I did. Waiting is the worst thing. Waiting for the king. For a husband. For this war to end. Does he snore, do you think?"

"Does who snore? The king?"

"Conrad, of course. I don't know that I could take much of that, unless we had separate bedchambers. Will he insist that we share one, Alex?"

"Good God, madam, I have no idea what Conrad prefers regarding his bedchamber."

"What if I don't like him?"

"We'll see."

"How old is he?"

She felt a purely devilish delight in his reddening face, in pulling that frown out of him and making him nearly growl. "Conrad is my age."

"Ah. Which is what . . . ?"

"Nearly thirty."

"Is he as good with children as you are?" She stopped beside the stack of limestone and made a point of staring up at him. "Patient, encouraging? With Lissa and Gemma underfoot, and our own children who will come along quickly, I must insist on a patient man."

"Great Heavens!" There. He actually growled and gnashed his teeth. "I know the man on the battlefield, not as a nursemaid."

"Then please find out for me before you actually offer me to him." She started away, heading back into the woods before it got too much darker.

"Talia—"

"Do women flock to him? Is he that handsome, do you think?" She threw her questions at him over her shoulder, satisfied that his long stride followed, strong and steady, making her heart leap. "Does he play indiscriminately at court and when he's waiting out a siege?"

"I'm not going to answer any more of your bloody questions, Talia. I want to know about—"

"Because I want a faithful man to husband me and be a father to our children, Alex. Not a man who makes a hobby of spreading his seed. Will he be faithful, do you think?"

"Dammit all, Talia, I don't know."

"Will you be faithful to your heiress when you find her, Alex? I do hope so. But you're such a fine-looking man; you must have women falling all over—"

"Talia—"

"So very much to learn about him, Alex. Conrad will be here in three days, and I don't even know if he has a family. You said he has brothers, but does he have sisters, too? Older or younger? Does his mother still live?"

"Enough, woman!" She knew she was baiting the man, but she couldn't stop herself, even when he captured her shoulders and made her sit down on a stump.

"Now you'll sit, with your mouth miraculously closed, and you will listen to me."

"I always listen—"

He put a finger to her lips. "I won't have the king's visit disrupted by your distractions. I'll do all the talking to Conrad."

She grabbed his wrist and pulled his hand away from her mouth. "How could my simply interviewing a prospective husband possibly be a distraction to the king?"

"You're going to leave Conrad alone unless I'm there with you."

"That's not very private, Alex."

"You're not going to pin his ears back with your endless quizzing."

"How else can I learn enough about him to make a decision? You've been no help at all."

"You're not the one making the decision in the matter, Talia. I am."

She wagged a finger up at him. "But only if I approve of the man."

"Not necessarily."

"Yes, *absolutely* necessarily. You gave your solemn word that I will have a say in whom I marry. Do you now intend to break it?"

"Talia, you can't just seize the situation without a thought to the consequences."

"Believe me, Alex, I'm thinking only of the consequences. I've dealt with nothing *but* consequences for more than two years."

"Then think carefully on these, madam: you will attend the king and his court on time, and in your best; you will smile pleasantly; you will not accuse His Majesty of crimes against your people; you will speak only when spoken to and answer politely, without your baiting, biting wit; you will adopt a position of deference in front of Conrad; and you will obey me without comment."

Alex knew very well that the woman was dismissing each of his edicts as he pronounced them, already mounting her defense, blinking at him in that stubborn way of hers.

"Do you understand me, Talia?"

She harrumphed and reached into the woolen

sack she'd been carrying. "I understand more than you know. Here." She handed him an apple.

He took it from her but shook it under her nose. "This visit means a great deal to me and my future."

"So you've told me." She pulled another apple from the sack and polished it on her kirtle.

He knelt a knee beside her on the stump and leaned down closer. "And to you."

"Obviously, Alex." She bit into the apple, leaving an enticing drop of juice sparkling on her lower lip. "But you hardly need my recommendation to the king; you seem favored enough."

He didn't trust a word of the woman's wide-eyed flattery, but at least they were discussing the matter. "A man is only as favored as the memory of his most recent act of loyalty. I took Carrisford—"

"You stumbled on it."

"Damn it, Talia." He lifted her chin, gaining her clear-eyed attention, pools of crystal blue, long sable lashes, and beads of apple juice.

A foolish moment later he was touching his mouth to hers, the very end of his tongue to her lips, and that small, ripely surprised space between them.

"God, you taste good." And felt good, and smelled marvelous; of the rowdy, skin-tightening scent of apples and autumn and longing. He drew in another breath of her soft cheek, rousing him instantly, fully, filling him with a sultry yearning.

"Mmmmmmm . . ." God save his sorry soul, she was leaning into him, her head tilted, collecting his kiss a bit at a time.

Their last kiss had left a need for her roaring inside him like a fiery furnace, left traces of herself humming through his veins.

This kiss was even hotter, sweeter, needier. It made his fingers itch to tangle in the ends of her hair, to lose himself in the clear brightness of her eyes. To pull her hips against his erection, to carry her to the ground, to enfold her, weight her, to wrangle and writhe together, to fill her with himself, to hear his name come calling from her lips.

"I do like the way you taste, Alex. Right here." Her lips were hot against the bridge of his nose, then brushed like an angel's across his eyelids. "And here." She touched her fingers to his mouth and it took every ounce of restraint not to take her against him.

"A dangerous thing to say, madam." But he couldn't stop this succulently restrained exploration of her perfectly bowed mouth, the teasing tip of her apple-sweet tongue, the sharp glance of lightning that dizzied him.

"Should I refrain from this, too, Alex?"

"Refrain?" No. Never. Christ. His heart stuttered and reeled around inside his chest, his pulse raged in his ears, deafening him, filling his groin with a need far deeper than release, a need that could be satisfied only one way. That ought to last forever.

"Should I kiss him, Alex?"

"What?" He was breathing unsteadily, taking in her scent and savoring the soft brush of her words across his mouth, having the devil of a time keeping his hands off her.

"Or should I wait for Conrad to kiss me?"

Conrad? His head was spinning wildly, from the tracing of her tongue, this intimate dance between them.

"Which, Alex?"

Which? And then he realized and pulled away, fighting for balance.

Conrad! The bastard. He ought to punch the man the moment he crossed through the gatehouse.

This was jealousy. Hot and seething, and impossible.

Conrad was an utterly innocent man, who'd become his greatest rival for a woman he couldn't allow himself to have.

"Or do I just play it as I feel it, Alex? Like this. Like us?"

As she felt it? Christ. "You wait for the man, Talia."

For me.

No.

Bloody hell, where was the rightness of all this, the reason? Where was the fully formed sense of himself that he'd tempered in the fires of hell? Unrecognizable now, ill fitting, and he hadn't a clue what to do about it.

"What if he doesn't, Alex?"

"Doesn't what?"

She stomped her foot and huffed. "You're not paying attention, Alex. What if Conrad doesn't kiss me? How will I know if he fits?"

Fits? Holy Christ, the woman was killing him, one question at a time, one staggering image after another.

"Then I will be the most astounded man in the entire kingdom."

"Why do you say that?"

She had the nerve to ask that while the last of the sun gilded her hair, and her cheeks still glowed with the remains of their kiss. He could have offered a dozen reasons, cagey and confusing. But there was only one true answer.

"Because he won't be able to resist, Talia. Because you are the most magnificent woman I've ever met. And I can only assume that Conrad will feel the same way."

That widened her eyes. "Oh."

"Come, madam. I want this lime in the bailey

by the morning. And the walls finished by tomorrow evening, ready when the first of the king's caravan begins to arrive the next afternoon."

She stood sharply and brushed off her skirts. "I thought he wouldn't be here for three days?"

"He won't be. But his caravan is leagues long, and precedes him by a half-day so that all is in place when he arrives."

"Too soon, Alex." She touched her fingers to her lips and shook her head. "Much too soon."

Unable to disagree, to risk imagining what his life would be without her, Alex followed the woman's determined stride through the oakwoods. The quickening fall of leaves was lit by the deeply setting sun, gilded ones and fiery orange, a path of gold beneath her feet.

He could taste her still as he marked the taunting sway of her hips. His hands would fit right nicely against them.

Hell, they had fit too nicely already. Was that but a few weeks ago when she'd thrown herself onto his back and pounded on his helm.

A lifetime ago. Forever.

She paused at the rise of the orchards, as though assessing the two rolling hills and the deep valley between, the branches heavy with apples and dark plums and walnuts.

An unsparing sight, sweeping in its beauty, the sort that seeps into the marrow and stays. So like the woman who fought so audaciously to keep it all in place.

He stepped in behind her, fully mindful that he was crossing his own boundaries as he slipped his arm around the slender slope of her waist and rested his hand on her hip.

He felt her breathing catch and slow, and her weight shift slightly, familiarly against him. Aye, a flawless fit, her bottom tucked against the length of his arousal, the top of her head inches below his chin, her shoulder pressed against his chest.

"A good crop this year?" he asked, the question slipping from a surprising part of him, because he hadn't the slightest idea what a good crop looked like, let alone a bad. And it seemed that he ought to know, for her sake.

She tilted her head back, her ear against his chest as she glanced up at him. "Modest, Alex, but it will have to do for the long winter. The picking will begin after the king leaves. No time before then."

He waited for a sharp-edged comment about his using the value of the crops to flog her wardship. But she merely sighed and continued down the hill, through the rows of trees.

Feeling the loss of her warmth, and somehow changed, Alex followed her through the orchards and the village, bantering lightly with her, until they finally joined the parade of supply wagons lumbering up the incline toward the castle gates in the last light of the sun.

And once again, he found himself looking for the boy among the figures he could see on the darkening quay.

The tide was in and lapping at the piers, bobbing the small boats. He hadn't realized that he'd stopped to look until he felt Talia beside him.

"Do you see Kyle?" she asked.

He didn't like the growing panic in his gut, focusing on one figure with a rope and then another hammering at a plank.

Too tall. Too bulky. Too old.

"There he is, Alex, just popping up out of the water. He'll be cold when he comes home."

"Where?" His heart raced ahead, as his search led from this pier to the next because she might be wrong.

She quietly slipped her hand around his, enfolding his fears, dissipating them. "There at the far end, Alex, the last pier."

"Yes." Alex let go a breath, laughed actually, startled at the relief as he recognized those lanky shoulders straining to pull all that gangling eagerness onto the dock, until the boy landed spread-eagled.

"There, he's safe," she said.

For now. An odd thought. Made more odd because she held his hand firmly and he held hers right back.

* * *

A quick rap on Talia's chamber door brought her out of the chair. She opened it to Quigley, shivering, his eyes huge and his face moon pale in the darkness.

"They're coming, my lady, the first of the king's wagons."

She pulled him to the brazier, tossed a blanket over his shoulders. "Where?"

"A half dozen leagues. It'll be midnight before the first arrives at the cut."

"Then you know what to do." Supplies to last this winter and next, when Carrisford was no more.

Quigley clasped his hands together and sank onto the bench. "Please, no, my lady. Reconsider. This is the king."

"It's an ordinary train of wagons, full of grain and cheese and dried peas. We need it all, Quig. We've never failed and never been caught, and time is wasting."

" 'Tis luck, my lady."

"Good planning," she said lightly, turning away to the fire in the brazier.

"Good planning for what, madam?" The voice didn't belong to Quigley.

She turned and found Quigley as rigid as a statue, as though hoping that Alex wouldn't notice him standing in the middle of the room.

"For the king's visit, my lord," Talia said. "The

sins and neglect of more than two years eradicated in two weeks. Possible only through good planning."

He lifted that skeptical brow. "Indeed, madam. And just in time, it seems. I've just gotten word that Stephen will arrive tomorrow afternoon."

A stone dropped into Talia's stomach, heavy and hot with regrets and fear and wishes that would never come true.

"Good. Then thank you, Quigley," she said to the beleaguered man, "for everything."

"My pleasure, my lady." Quigley left her with a deep, pointed frown as he bowed out into the tower stairs and disappeared, hopefully on his way to gather his team to relieve the king of a few extraneous supplies.

Alex must have already been to his chamber; he looked finished for the night, homey in his soft woolen tunic and leather slippers, thoroughly satisfied with himself, as he moved to the worktable where she'd been making another list.

"We're in fine shape for the king's visit, Alex."

"I'll be riding out of here at noon to meet the king and his escort."

Mother of Jesu, don't ask me to go with you, Alex.

"Then I'll stay behind and show the king's chamberlain to the royal chambers above the chapel, and make sure the sumptuary wagons are safely stored, and tour the kitchen with his cook, and see that his horses are stabled well."

Alex took a long time to nod, lighting a second candle with the first. "A good plan, indeed."

"And just to ease your mind about my participation, Alex, I've drawn up the full set of your rules—as I understand them—which I intend to follow."

He laughed and dropped himself into a chair, thrusting his long, powerful legs toward her. "This I must hear."

Not that she planned to abide by any of his edicts that might affect her own operations.

"I want to make sure that I understand exactly what you expect of me. It's not a long list, but inclusive."

He looked smugly pleased with himself, large and lordly as he gestured for her to continue. "Please proceed."

Though she'd memorized the list, Talia picked it up off the table. It was better to ignore his smirk than to resort to physical combat.

"First, I will greet the king and the members of his entourage with all due respect."

"Admirable. Go on."

"I have instructed my villeins and my staff to cooperate fully with every request made by the king's guests as well as the royal household."

"Good of you."

"Thirdly, I will represent your interests honestly and with a mind to your goals. The big castle and the wealthy heiress and everything."

He said nothing, hardly needed to, with that arching brow and the skeptical frown.

"And lastly, I'll do my level best not to send Conrad running from me in fear and loathing." She dropped the list on the table, wishing for it all to be over. For Carrisford to be in ruins and to have all thoughts of a marriage—to anyone—be in ruins as well.

For this increasingly distracting man and his fathomless dark eyes to be gone from her life and her dreams. "Any comments, my lord?"

He leaned over to the table and snagged the parchment, then idly studied it. "Interesting, Talia, but I don't believe a word you've written here."

"My promise is every bit as binding as yours. And the sooner this royal visit is over, the better off we'll all be."

"I'll agree with you there, my dear. But I don't trust you not to speak your mind in the face of . . . say, a royal temper tantrum."

Now the blackguard was sparring with her, a sport she'd come to adore. She thunked a stool in front of him and sat down to stare. "Meaning that you think I'm so wild-minded that I haven't the sense to hold my tongue, should good king Stephen decry my frumenty and throw it against the wall."

He discarded the list and leaned forward on his

elbows, hovering, matching her stare with those darkly lashed eyes. "Frankly, madam, I doubt that you'd be capable of holding your tongue even in the presence of God Almighty Himself. And that goes doubly for your householders. Not to mention your opinionated little family. Every one of them cut from the same cloth as you."

"Just because I respect the sensible opinions of those people who—"

"And as for defending my interests, Talia, please don't." He took hold of her plait, mock horror etched on his brow.

"But who knows better than I what Carrisford is worth? As well as what you're looking for."

"You'll keep it all to yourself, madam. And I will hold you to your promise not to bait Conrad."

"Bait him?"

"He's not used to women like you."

"Like me? You mean with brains and the ballocks to use them?"

He smiled. He was very close again, very large, spicy, dazzling. "Exactly."

"Why did you come here tonight?"

He studied her for a long moment. "Because I'm a selfish man."

"And to provoke me."

"No, not that." He gazed at her mouth as though he'd been lost in a desert and she was a cool oasis.

"Then what?"

"Proof that I am the devil you think I am. To beg one last kiss from you."

"Oh." A kiss wouldn't be very wise, even a last one. Not with the way her hands were trembling, the way her heart was pounding, and the stone wall she ought to be building between them.

"Oh, Alex, I wish—"

"I know what you wish."

No, he didn't. He couldn't possibly. Because she was only just beginning to realize that she wanted him completely, wanted him to stay and stay, wanted children with him and to be his lady wife.

To be heiress enough for him.

But his life was warring, and hers was to keep her family safe.

And if she kissed him first, he wouldn't go tying himself up in guilty knots. And she'd have this last moment to remember him by.

And so she kissed him, took his mouth as he'd done hers, teased and toyed with her teeth and tongue, until he made a sound like her name, and was growling low in his chest, his breath shuddering out of him, brushing past her lips, until he plowed his fingers through her hair, tilted her face to him, and plundered her mouth.

Hot tears gathered in her throat, unshed and aching. His lips were softly searing, his kiss leaving smoldering trails of steam and longing.

Leaving a new emptiness where her heart had been, when he left her a moment later.

The first wagons began arriving in the bailey just after midmorning, wagon after wagon, most of them lighter now. Talia had managed to slip away in the middle of the night to help with the royal looting. Despite a wild storm that dropped buckets of rain through most of the night, Quigley and the rest of her band worked with their usual efficiency, moving the purloined goods from the caravan into the byways of the forest, and finally to the dozens of caves and sheep cotes and tumbleddown, inconspicuous-looking barns tucked away throughout the countryside.

The sumptuary wagons made their way into the bailey as Talia watched Alex ride out through the castle gate, feeling in control for the first time in weeks.

Despite the imminent husband.

And the king.

And Alex's kiss.

In control, indeed.

"The king should be quite comfortable in his chamber, my lady."

She turned from her mooning malaise to be the image of cooperation for his chamberlain. "Then I'm so pleased, Sir Tobin."

"And now I do need you to show me where to put the king's stores."

Quigley hobbled into view in the great hall, motioning for her attention, his eyes in a panic.

"Sir Tobin, it seems my steward needs me for a moment. If you'll pardon me." The man nodded, and turned away to his own staff.

Talia pulled Quigley aside, fearing to ask "What is it, Quig?"

"Trouble, my lady," he whispered behind his hand. "Crossing the broad creek."

"What kind of trouble?"

"The wagon bridge, my lady. 'Tis gone, in a heap downstream. Taken in the storm last night."

"Wonderful."

"I do hate to ask you to come see what we need, with the king coming and all."

And Conrad.

And the end of Carrisford.

And Alex.

"Of course, I'll go, Quig. Just as soon as I can rid myself of the king's chamberlain."

"Too soon to set the place ablaze?"

She gave him a kiss on his hoary old cheek. "Just a bit too soon, Quig. Just a bit."

Chapter 17

❦❧

"**A**lex, old man, you're looking in high spirits!" Stephen shouted as he rode free of his escort, an arm extended in a hearty greeting.

"And you as well, my liege, I'm glad to say." Alex maneuvered his horse head-on beside the king and shook his hand, truly pleased to see him in excellent health. "Welcome to Carrisford."

Stephen squinted ahead at the neatly timbered pickets of the castle, just visible on the hill above the bay. " 'Tis looking well from this distance."

"Aye. In spite of Rufus and the rest of his illgotten brethren. You didn't warn me of its sorry condition, my liege."

Steven eyed him with a wise smile on his weathered face. "Would that have mattered to you, Alex?"

"Not in the least." Alex smiled back, never surprised at Stephen's insight. "Come, I'll show you."

"Besides, Alex, I knew very little myself." The king followed Alex along the narrow foot track.

"Utterly undefended, nearly indefensible when I arrived. Bloody hell, as I wrote in my report to you, I merely rode through the front gate. Little bloodshed—"

"And no hostages, as usual. Hostages are a lucrative bounty, Alex." But Stephen knew the reason that the practice repelled him.

Alex held aside a branch as Stephen led his horse through the track, formed a sober reply. "Hardly a crowd worthy of a ransom anyway."

"Ah, but what about the Carrisford wardship itself, Alex? I hope it's been worth your efforts, and not a dark hole in the ground."

Talia's remarkable smile came to him, her kiss the night before. "Most definitely worth the effort."

"Then you ease my mind, boy." Stephen turned back in his saddle as Alex came forward, with a question that Alex had fully anticipated. "So I suppose you plan to marry the woman yourself."

However certain he'd been of the question, Alex hadn't been prepared for the dryness of his mouth as he answered with a shake of his head, "No, my liege."

Stephen gave an unkingly snort. "Rumors are

that she's a raging beauty, Alex. Are you sure you won't take her for yourself?"

"Quite certain." He couldn't—not when everything had fallen so perfectly into place. "It was never in my plans to marry my ward."

Stephen gave him a long, practiced eye. "Is she a shrew then, Alex?"

Alex smiled broadly, aware of a sudden warmth in his chest, the memory of the woman's power to topple his composure with her maddeningly impeccable logic. With the sweetly heated scent of her as they wrestled with the accounts and the war, over buckets of nails and the weather.

"Lady Talia is independent-minded, Your Grace. Stubborn and spirited and too quick for her own good, but she's far, *far* from a shrew."

"Ah, then the rumors are false and the woman is too hard on the eye?"

Soft and sultry and golden-skinned. "On the contrary, my liege. As easy as the dawn."

"All these sterling attributes and you've no plans to marry the girl?"

Alex had been staring up at the castle, at his banner floating freely above the gatehouse tower. "Carrisford is not for me, Stephen."

Stephen stopped his horse and took a long, assessing look at Alex. "Meaning?"

"You know very well that I'm looking for a

larger holding, Stephen. Carrisford is insignificant. It carries no title. Little power."

"True." Stephen rode ahead through a narrow muddy patch of ground. "So you still plan to sell the wardship, as was your original intent?"

"To marry it off to a suitable knight." Alex caught up with the king. "One loyal to you, of course."

Fierce and determined and strong and capable of protecting everyone and everything that Talia held dear.

"Have you a particular candidate in mind?"

The thought brought on unwanted images: rushlight and a tousled counterpane and Talia's sighing laughter. "I assume Conrad is with you."

"Conrad FitzWarren?" Stephen sent a glance toward the trailing retinue, then nodded. "A good man, if you mean him, Alex. An excellent choice."

A chill settled across his shoulders, a foreboding that usually signaled a blindside attack. He whirled in his saddle, before he realized that he was nowhere near a battlefield, that the clanging sound was his heart battering at his ribs.

"So he's here with you?" Alex finally asked, feeling skittish and a bit dazed.

"Aye, Conrad is here. And doubtless in the market for a worthy bride such as the one you've described."

Alex searched for a measure of relief and found

only a sinking sense of loss, of wrongness that he couldn't afford to explore.

"I'm glad you approve, my liege, and I think you'll be pleased with the progress I've made restoring Carrisford's defenses."

Alex tried to make little of this peculiarly possessive feeling of pride at the neatness of the village, the glitter of helms on the ramparts, at Stephen's own banner now flying beside his own, but higher.

He searched the incline and the gatehouse and the towers for Talia, certain he would see her watching for the entourage.

She'd promised a welcome befitting a king, and though he knew it galled her to invite the war into her home, he trusted her to keep her word.

Stephen seemed pleased at the turnout of villagers, amused at the proud young man who offered up a leather pouch.

"Lavender, Your Grace. With the compliments of my mother, the herbalist."

Ever the king, Stephen stopped in front of the young man, opened the pouch and sniffed. "Excellent, young man. My compliments to your dear mother."

Others crowded around, offering small tokens from the village.

A finely tooled tin cup, a thick beeswax candle, sugared plums.

A fine show of pomp and devotion on Talia's part, obviously pleasing to the unsuspecting king, but deepening Alex's own suspicion because he knew the woman would try most anything if she thought she had a chance to succeed, to make all the hurt and horror disappear.

The sky rumbled and quickly clouded over as Alex followed the king as they continued through the parade of celebrating onlookers, finally crossing the drawbridge and riding into the bailey.

Stephen dismounted and looked around him in admiration. "Blazes, Alex! You've done a right fine job with this castle, and in damn little time. Takes a bloody good commander to manage it. What is your secret?"

"Loyal and skilled men-at-arms, my liege." Alex caught the king's saddlepack as his squire untied it, then hoisted it over his shoulder. "Cooperative tenants."

"And a devilish mind for politics and negotiation, Alex!" The king clapped him on the back and started through the barbican. "Come show me the rest of your marvel, then we'll talk about the spring campaign and a certain father who might be persuaded to part with a particular heiress for the right price and a request from a grateful king."

"Bloody good to see you, Alex!"

Damnation. He'd been avoiding Conrad since

the crowd of Stephen's knights and his own had begun collecting in the courtyard.

Alex turned sharply, grabbing Conrad's outstretched hand and shaking it hard. A soldier's greeting, with a lot of backslapping.

"Conrad, you're a sight for sore eyes." Nearly as tall as Alex, battle-hardened, slow to anger, God-fearing, gifted with good sense and good humor, wisdom and the bare-assed confidence to use them.

Does he snore?

The question had clung to him like a storm cloud.

Conrad glanced around the courtyard, grinning. "Seems this life of sleeping dry and eating regularly suits you very well, Alex."

It all suited him far too well. He tried to sound matter-of-fact. "It does, though there are endless details and responsibilities that I'd never realized."

"But in all, you do recommend it?" It galled Alex to see Conrad studying the pickets and the stables, making an uninvited assessment.

"Aye, Conrad, I recommend it." Bloody hell, this was to be his interview of Conrad, not the reverse. "Have you ever thought to take up a holding yourself?"

"In keeping a garrison and accounting for swine, Alex? Commanding a castle of my own? Are you mad?"

A flood of relief swept against Alex's chest. "If you're not interested in such a life . . ."

"Oh, but I bloody well am. You look fat and well contented, man. Happier than I've seen you for years. I'd gladly take such a chance as you have done."

Bloody hell. "Would you, then?"

Alex was about to turn the conversation back toward the subject when Stephen came up between them, his eyes full of mischief. "Well, Alex, have you told Conrad of your plans for his purse?"

"What plans?" Conrad waved off the suggestion. "If it's a horse you're trying to pawn off on me, Alex, I've no need for a new one. I'm quite happy with the destrier I stole out of the earl of Gloucester's own stables."

"Great God, Alex. Does the woman truly resemble a horse? Is that why you've kept her hidden?"

"What woman?" Conrad asked, glancing between them.

Alex frowned at his nosy king. "I hadn't had the chance to present Conrad the offer, my liege."

"Why the hell not? You're so ready to rid yourself of the woman."

Both men were staring at him; Stephen with an unrepentant smile of triumph, Conrad with too much interest.

"What His Grace is talking about, Conrad, is *this*"—Alex raised his hands, indicating the courtyard and the battlements and so much more than that—"Carrisford itself, the castle, the village, and its entailing wardship."

"Ah, yes! I recall now, Alex. You've become guardian to . . . whom?"

A handful of sunlight. "To the lady Talia, heiress to Carrisford."

"A lady?"

"And not a horse at all," Stephen said, patting Conrad on the back, "according to Alex."

"Oh?" Conrad's gaze sharpened. "And what has my particular purse to do with this lady, Alex?"

Yes, this *was* the right move, despite the bank of coals lodged in his gut, and the lagging of his pulse. It was going well.

"You haven't married or gotten yourself betrothed since last we saw each other, have you, Conrad?

"Why? Have you taken to matchmaking, Alex? Have you found me a wife?"

The words lodged in his throat; he forced them out. "And a castle, if you're interested. Carrisford—it has served me well, but I've no plans to keep it—"

"—Or the lady Talia," Stephen said, fixing Alex with a hard gaze.

"However, His Grace has given me leave to arrange a marriage between my ward and a suitable bridegroom."

Conrad preened. "And you mean to say, Alex, you believe that I am suitable to marry your ward?"

Alex forced himself to ignore the prickling anger at Conrad's easy reaction, the rocky feeling of the ground falling away. "Indeed, Conrad. For the right price, of course."

"And that is?"

"I'm a reasonable man, Conrad. Tour the castle while you're here; the grounds, the defenses, the stores. Examine the accounts—"

"And meet with Lady Talia, of course," Conrad said with a lift of a brow.

"Of course." Alex's heart thunked against his throat. "Then you can make an offer. Or not."

Conrad eyed him for a long moment. "So where is this marriageable ward of yours?"

Yes, where? "She'll be here for tonight's feast."

"Is she that shy?"

"That busy, Conrad. Probably releading the chapel roof." At least she'd bloody well better be, after promising him promptness and grace. With a feast being prepared in the kitchen and a king who'll be peckish in no time at all.

"Your pardon, my liege," Alex said, filling Stephen's wine cup. "Do make yourselves comfortable in your rooms. I'll go check on the lady's progress."

And she damned well better have a spotless excuse for not greeting the king as befitting his ward.

As she'd promised him.

Alex is going to have me drawn and quartered. Right there in front of the king and my maybe-bridegroom.

Talia fought her sopping skirts as she climbed the stairs into her chamber.

Her bath was cold but thankfully waiting for her so she could make quick work of the mud caked into her hair. She threw off her drenched cloak and hung a water kettle over the brazier and raised a larger fire, hoping that Quigley was taking care of Brenna.

And the barley and the cheese and all her hopes to get her family through the coming winter.

"Bloody, bloody hell!" The harder she worked at loosening the knotted leather ties at the bodice of her kirtle, the more her fingers stiffened. Bending as close to the brazier as she dared, Talia cursed the sudden chilling breeze at her back that made her shiver, then heard the door shut quietly.

Alex! She could hear him breathing far too steadily, his temper under tight control.

Better to face the beast full on. She turned, never ready for the dizzying power of his gaze, its staggering darkness when he was angry. Or disappointed.

"Ah, Alex! I assume the king has arrived and is

comfortable. I was just—" She stopped because his anger seemed ready to overtake her, his eyes darkly glittering shards of ice.

"Is this the way you keep your promises, madam?"

She wished he had bellowed instead of leveling his voice as he scanned the length of her, his eyes catching every leaf and clot of mud.

"Well, Alex, I . . . uhm . . ." Her brain had emptied, and he was on her in the next instant, his wall of heat overwhelming the fire in the brazier behind her, making it impossible not to look up into his blazing eyes.

His breath puffed at her lashes and he whispered through his teeth, "You promised that you would greet the king with all due respect. For *me*, Talia."

"Yes, I'm sorry, Alex. I was taking—"

"You promised that you would honestly represent my interests—"

"I will."

"And that you would not send Conrad running in fear and loathing." His teeth were shiny white as he glared down at her. "Your very words, spoken right here only last evening, if you recall."

"I do recall, Alex." She couldn't look directly into his dark eyes, for fear of losing her will and her reason. "Believe me, I'm doing my best to—"

"Enough, Talia. I've seen you at your best, and this isn't it. Bloody hell, madam, you are late for a royal visit, and now you think to make an entrance dressed like . . ."—he sputtered, as though he hadn't words enough—"like something coughed up onto the sand by a storm tide."

"You can't possibly believe that I've made a mess of myself on purpose. To what end? Just to embarrass you in front of the king?"

"Then why, madam? And this?" He lifted a handful of her hair in his huge fist, and then pulled out a leafy twig. "Is this your unsubtle attempt to convince Conrad that you're a lunatic?"

"Don't be ridiculous." Her heart skidded to a stop when she realized. "Dear God, he's here, isn't he? Conrad. And he's interested in me?"

Which only made Alex growl, wolf-wild and low. "Enough, madam. You're going to clean up and dress in your bloody best gown, then you will greet the king and Conrad with your bloody best smile."

"Aye, my lord, that's exactly what I had planned to do before you came barreling in here." Heated to her bones by her outrage, Talia pointed toward the very tightly shut door. "If you'll please take yourself out of here."

He stood like a wall, his arms crossed over his chest. "Not without you, madam. Now, out of those filthy clothes and into this bath."

All she could do was stare as he stalked to the brazier, pulled the kettle off the hook, then poured the hot water into the bath, raising up a cloud of steam.

"What did you say?"

"Into the bath."

The man was mad. "With you here? I will not."

His long, exhaled breath made her skin sing along her arms, made her imagine it playing itself against her ear as he said again, each word a diabolically, deliberate suspension, "Take off your clothes."

Such indecent rudeness. Oh, then why the devil did she want to demand the same of him? To see him one more time, as she had that first evening.

"I absolutely will not." She grabbed the front of her sopping kirtle, then stepped back two paces until she bumped into the blanket chest.

"You'll do just as I say, Talia. And you'll waste no more of my time at it." He seemed to grow larger, hotter, more deliberate as he came toward her in his slow, inexorable stride until he was standing over her. "This night means the world to me. I plan to keep you from ruining it."

"By forcing me out of my clothes like a brute and into that tub?"

"By making you presentable any way I can. Now, undress, else I'll take your clothes from you myself."

It was a long, licking gaze he gave her, an un-yielding promise that he had every intention of going through with his threat.

A threat that seemed too much like an invita-tion, that lifted and embraced her in his smoky en-chantment, that fanned an already disorienting blaze and burned right through the damp thick-ness of her kirtle and her chemise and gathered and spread like sunlight, low in her belly.

A falling toward him feeling, a tantalizing taut-ness, a threading through her, through him, bind-ing them together, as though he could give the slightest tug and she'd do his bidding gladly.

Damn the man, but she wanted to! She also wanted to kick him in the shins. She put her hand in the middle of his chest and gave a shove.

"Then you will at least turn away, my lord."

Her shove hadn't moved him in the least, but he did finally, slowly, step backward, then left her to add more wood to the brazier.

"Hurry yourself, madam," he said, as the sparks sputtered into the air.

Hurrying didn't help at all as she tried again to untie the leather lashing that crisscrossed its way upward toward an implacable knot between her breasts.

"Have you told him anything?" Talia asked, feeling the unremitting heat of Alex's gaze sliding along her fingers as she worked. She tried to focus on the irritating task, only making it worse, and moved nearer to the light of the candle on her dressing table.

"Him?" A grumbling, distant sound.

She gave a tug on one end of the lacing, frustrated to her bones. "Conrad."

"Damnation!" Suddenly Alex was standing in front of her, encompassing her, his warm fingers dancing with hers and the leather lacing, his rumbling words at her temple. "Did I tell him what, madam?"

He made her breathless and clumsy with his enthralling efforts, his fingers a stunning pressure and release against her bodice, skiffing along the margins of her modesty. "Did you tell him about me? About . . . things."

"Hold still," he said sharply. He brushed her fingers away and leaned closer to the tangle, inspecting it, the lush course of his breath gamboling hot against her chilled skin, steaming down the cleft between her breasts.

She swallowed hard, trying not to sigh into the softness of his hair, not to make too much of her heart banging around beneath his hands.

"Did you tell him, Alex?" Her mouth was so near his temple she could easily kiss him there.

So easily lose herself, and everything that was dear to her.

"Yes, I told him, Talia. Some." He tugged on the knot, hopefully unable to read her thoughts, or the invitations lurking there, the regrets that perched upon her tongue.

"You told him *some*, Alex? What exactly, beyond that I was for sale?" She'd meant that as a jest between them, a jab, but it only deepened his features.

"I told him, that my ward was insolent and troublesome and inconvenient. Now hold still." He bent his head to that tangled place above her heart and his breath exploded across her chest like a searing storm, traveled everywhere, carrying her imagination along with it. His forehead against her collarbone, his hair dancing along her shoulder.

Steamy, close. So intoxicating! Damned forever as a strumpet, grieving for these moments with Alex that would be lost to her after tonight, Talia simply threw back her head to give him leave for more.

"Alex, what are you doing?" And don't stop, please. Not ever.

He looked up sideways at her, his nostrils flaring. "The knot, dammit!"

"Ah!" She caught her laugh between her lips, aware that she was clinging to him, her palm against his hips. He was using his teeth on the tie, and then his fingers and his growl. She ought to tell him that the dagger at his belt would do just as well. It was only a thong; a quick cut and her kirtle would come right off.

But this was too marvelous, his growling between her breasts, his fingers softly ravishing, his muttered cursing, until he finally broke away.

"There!" he bellowed, backing away in triumph. The knot was gone, the two ends dangling. And he was breathing like a hunt-driven stag. "Now undress and get into the bath, this minute." He pointed to the steaming tub.

The air crackled between them. This wasn't wise, not with all that had passed between them.

But when he only stood there, watching, his face a mask, Talia began unlacing her kirtle, her heart aching for all that might have been.

Chapter 18

Alex knew bloody well that if he moved at all, it would be toward Talia and right on to the end of all his carefully constructed plans. So he planted his heels firmly into the planking and watched and burned as her heavy kirtle fell into a heap around her ankles.

He forced himself to focus on the depth of her deceit instead of the clinging, linen-draped silhouette of her calves and thighs and hips, the shadowy, shifting shape of her breasts. He tried not to think of the softness beyond the ties and her wet chemise. Or her cool skin, the clouds of that woodland scent of hers.

Sweet pine and moss and yew.

And the soft light in her eyes.

He could control the rigid heat collected in his

groin, his palpable need for her, as she grabbed the chunk of soap and walked to the bath. Hell, he'd been managing that since the moment he'd first laid eyes on her. But his restraint was brought to the brink when she bent and picked up the hem of her gown.

Christ.

He turned away from all that loveliness, paced to the door, then to the window.

"Where were you tonight, Talia?"

A sloshing splash, the stunning sound of her chemise hitting the floor. He closed his eyes. "When do you mean, Alex?"

"When you should have been entertaining the king in the courtyard."

"I was in the orchard," she said, too easily.

"Doing what? And keep scrubbing." He could only hear as she stepped into the tub, didn't dare look in her direction.

"Because Derwent's hogs got loose in the afternoon and went straight for the windfall apples. And then Margaret, the baker's wife, finally had her baby."

"A son, I know. That was much earlier. Where were you tonight?" When she didn't answer, his anger turned him, but she was gone. "Damn it, Talia!"

He came around the table, certain that she'd escaped through some hidden trap in the floor, only to discover her in the tub, on her knees, her head completely under the water, her hair drifting on the surface like seaweed.

He should have turned away from all that golden splendor, her naked back, the curving moons of her bottom. Before he could fully form the thought in his head, she sat up fast, in a shower of water that fanned across his chest, dousing him completely from head to toe, talking overloud.

"Margaret was having trouble afterward, so I took her some feverfew."

Alex swabbed the water off his face and opened his eyes to a golden selkie, still kneeling in the tub, her hair now swift runnels of red-gold silk coursing over her breasts like a curtain, shielding the joining of her legs.

Her eyes tightly closed, the bewitching woman stood up and stuck out her hand and felt around for the towel that had fallen from the bench.

He took a silent breath of pure strength and put the towel into her hand. "Here."

"Alex!" She gasped and her eyes flew open, her lashes starred as she gaped at him. "I hardly expected such service, considering."

Considering that she dizzied him, drenched him in need; she was the course of the seasons, the breath of him. It was all he could do not to cross the short distance between them, lift her into his arms, and take her to the bed, to enter her sweetness and claim her for himself.

To plunge and thrust and possess her, to make

her feel the pounding in his veins, the throbbing in his lungs; to prove to her that he would stay with her if he could.

And God save him from his sins, she just stood there to her knees in the water, buffing her bewitching hair with the towel, uncovered and proud and tempting him, so breathtakingly familiar with him.

So like a wife.

"Talia." Her name had escaped him too easily, filled in the empty places in his heart.

"I'm hurrying, Alex."

"You're beautiful."

She paused inside her cloud of damp hair, then frowned. "Another point to be sure to make with Conrad tonight."

"Damn it."

"I agree. It's a damnable thing we're both doing." She looked determined, as though she'd suddenly joined his side. "It's like an endless abyss, Alex—filled with nothing and everything. In the beginning, you gave me hope, when I was sure there was none left in the world."

"Christ, Talia." She was candlelight and confidence, sleek and curved, dazzle-eyed and fearless. He willed his heart to keep a steady pace, but she was a quickening inside him, and his hands ached to hold her.

To keep her.

And he probably would have been able to walk

away right then, if she hadn't stepped to the edge of the tub, if she hadn't put her lips to her fingertips, and then her fingertips to his mouth.

A fleeting, feathery touch that lifted the hair on his arms and drew the air from his lungs.

"I'll do my best for you, Alex."

His will tattered beyond use, Alex cupped her hand against his cheek, losing himself in her eyes, his need for her, for more of her, all of her, coursing through him like quicksilver.

"Please don't, Talia." But her mouth was moist and rosy full and she was too willing, too bright-eyed.

"Don't what?"

"Please don't help me."

He could find his way to hell on his own. By combing his fingers through her hair, touching his lips against her ear.

By cupping her chin and tilting her mouth to him.

Whispering words she shouldn't hear, that he shouldn't ever say.

And finally, dangerously, tasting her mouth, covering it fully as though she belonged to him.

"Alex . . ."

These were his as well, her naked, soapy-slick, lithely rounded curves that so perfectly fit his hands, and the lightning that ripped through him, blinding white and deeply hot.

His.

Her soft belly and the rock-rigid erection she'd raised and now cradled against herself.

Her heady sighs and her whimpering.

Her damp arms around his neck.

Her dreams.

His.

The sultry way she was climbing into his embrace, her fathomless kiss.

His. Every inch of her. "Talia!"

She pulled away slightly, breathless, blinking blindly. Her mouth was as darkly rose as the tips of her breasts. Then she shook her head sadly, her curling cascade of hair becoming a curtain against him.

"Oh, what we could have been together, Alex."

Children and family and this needy old castle, her belly growing large with his sons and his daughters. So much to regret.

He managed to turn away from her, from the burning at the backs of his eyes. He stopped at the door, his hand on the latch.

"You'll come to the great hall when you're finished here."

He heard her step out of the water, but didn't dare another glance at her.

"I really didn't mean to disrupt your meeting with the king, Alex. My deepest apologies to him. And to you."

There was no way she could not have disrupted it. Talia being Talia. "I know."

He left while he was still able.

Alex stomped away from Talia's chamber, stumbling over his guilt, this relentless yearning, the inescapable images of the future.

He dressed in his best, then slipped into the great hall through the kitchen and discovered Stephen there, poking at a plate of meat.

"Alex, old man! I'm stealing away your cook for my own!" Stephen tucked a morsel of venison into his mouth and garbled something about "stale oat cakes" and "boot leather" which reddened the cook's usual damp blush.

He'd missed Stephen's sense of humor; falling back into the familiar banter was easy, because he truly liked the man. Alex crossed his arms over his chest and leaned back against the chimney wall. "Sorry, my liege, but my loyalty to you does have its limits."

Stephen laughed. "See, Conrad, how the man chooses his battles carefully?"

Christ, he hadn't noticed Conrad, sampling his way along the serving table.

"Aye, Alex, I had just been wondering if your cook comes with the woman and the castle."

Unable to conjure a response beyond punching the man in the gut, Alex ignored Conrad and nodded to the king. "Lady Talia sends her deepest apologies to you, my liege. She'll join us in the great hall momentarily."

"Leading the chapel roof, was she?"

"Aye, Your Grace, she was."

The great hall thrummed with knights and soldiers, a royal court of good-natured mayhem, a sound that quieted when Stephen stepped into his place at the table, and roared back into full voice when he gestured broadly for them to continue.

Stephen dropped into a chair, one long leg hung over the arm. "You're out here in the wastes, Alex. You did hear about the end of De Mandeville, didn't you?"

"Aye, Your Grace. A suitably ignoble end to the bastard's barbaric career," Alex said, keeping a watch out for Talia, for his heart, because he didn't trust her with it.

Conrad laughed in that confident way of his and poured himself a cup of wine. "Imagine De Mandeville taking an unlucky arrow in the head because he'd removed his helm in the midst of directing a siege that he was winning."

Stephen smiled wryly. "Arrogance. I never trusted Geoffrey de Mandeville completely, and he burned me at the last, didn't he? If ever I arrest another man like him, I bloody well won't release him. No matter what pledges he makes."

"Alliances rarely last, my liege," Alex said, thinking of his dead brother, riding out the grief,

Talia's compassion, her outrage. "Press a man and he will bend; make him feel betrayed and anything can happen."

He never learned what Stephen was going to reply, for a pair of squealing, laughing voices and running footsteps came dodging toward them through the hall, around the labyrinth of men and tables.

Dear, familiar voices.

"Lord Alex! Did you hear? The king is here!"

Alex braced himself just as Gemma threw herself around his knees in her usual enthusiasm, nearly knocking him off-balance. He lifted her into his arms. "I know, Gemma, but you're supposed to be in bed."

"Did you see him yet, Lord Alex?" Lissa tugged at Alex's sleeve.

Gemma leaned out from Alex's arms toward Stephen. "Who are you, sir? Do you know the king?"

"He does, Gemma," Alex said, oddly proud and protective of this little band of noise. "This *is* King Stephen."

Gemma peered closer, studying the man. Fortunately His Grace was the doting father of a son and two daughters and seemed genuinely at home with Gemma's questions. "Are you really a king?"

Lissa gasped and sank into an ungainly curtsy. "Oh, my, Gemma! He is! Your Grace."

Stephen took Lissa's hand and lifted her to her feet. "And who are these lovely subjects, Alex?"

"Lissa and Gemma." Alex glanced at Conrad, watching for coldness, but finding only amusement and the memory that the man had five younger sisters, each of whom had wrapped him around their little fingers.

"Talia, look, the king is here!" Gemma waved toward the end of the dais and everyone turned.

And Alex stopped breathing.

It wasn't the shimmering, wine-dark silk of her gown, or the gold threads entwined along the sleeves that had staggered him, nor her cascades of unbound hair captured by a simple circlet of garnets at her temple.

Or her elegant grace, or the deep rose her mouth set into an enigmatic smile.

It was her eyes and the challenge there. The hotly arousing effects swirling around in his chest, lighting deep fires in his heart with the softness of her smile.

"Come meet him, Talia! The king is very nice." Gemma wriggled out of Alex's arms and flung herself into Talia's.

"Your Grace, my humblest apologies for causing you to wait for me. Welcome to Carrisford." She managed a sweeping curtsy even with her arms full of Gemma.

Stephen rushed to her side and raised her, obviously charmed to his ears. "My dear Lady Talia, would that all things were as worthy the wait as you."

"Your Grace is very kind." She leaned in to the king and said softly, "Supper is on its way, and I pray that you feel the same after our humble feast in your honor."

She glanced at Alex, gracious, welcoming, as though they had often stood together here in the hall, welcoming guests.

Domestic.

Pleasing.

Distracting.

As though they were lord and lady of Carrisford.

Christ, his bones ached. And his heart.

Conrad had wedged himself into the mix and stood preening like a barnyard cock. "Fear not, my lady, our king already has plans to steal your cook."

She flicked a startled, quizzical glance at Alex, then looked back at the smiling Conrad. "And you must be . . ."

"Conrad FitzWarren." The blackguard took her hand, bent over it for far too long, before he raised his cocky smile to her. "Delighted to meet you, my lady."

Nay, she's mine, Alex thought. But she wasn't his. Not in the way he would like.

The way he needed her to be.

"Welcome to Carrisford, my lord. Alex has spoken very well of you."

"And not nearly well enough of you, my lady, I'm sorry to say."

Now the woman was actually blushing! *Beaming*, to put a bloody fine point on it. And Gemma was fiddling with the shiny fox-headed clasp on Conrad's jerkin.

Bloody hell!

"Aye, FitzWarren," Alex said, elbowing past Conrad to stand beside Talia, slipping one hand around the trim of her waist, "because I neglected to tell Her Ladyship the full truth about you."

"Will you save us some sugared plums, Lord Alex?" Gemma reached out to him, yawning as she crawled from Talia's arms into his and tucked her head against his shoulder.

He planted his usual good night kiss on the spray of curls on the girl's forehead, wondering how the smile that Talia gave him over the top of Gemma's head could reach so damn far into his chest that it had gotten hold of his heart, warmed it, and gave it a good, aching twist.

An instant of time, a tiny measure of his life, but with unimaginable implications.

He cleared his throat and stood Gemma on her feet. "I'll save two for each of you, Gemma, if you and Lissa go to bed now. And stay there."

"Hooray!"

"Ooo! Thank you, Lord Alex!" Gemma gave him a wet kiss on his cheek. "And good night, Sir King." And then jumped from the dais and took off with Lissa.

Alex turned to take his place at the table beside Talia, but she was already well flanked: the king on her left and bloody, drooling Conrad settling himself on her right.

Hell. Astounded at a world going ever madder, Alex sat down on Stephen's left, feeling as pouty as a child, chafing at the blathering chatter between Talia and Conrad, trying to concentrate on Stephen's questions about the terrain around Carrisford and the state of its armory and the best routes through the valley, when all he wanted was to separate Talia from Conrad, and Conrad's head from his shoulders—

Bloody hell.

Chapter 19

"**Y**ou were right, Alex," Stephen said, frowning down at the armory inventory. "You've not enough here to defend the castle for more than a week or two."

Alex's meeting with Stephen and his counselors in Alex's chamber was lasting deep into the night. A distracting, disorienting eternity, while Talia was somewhere with Conrad.

"My armorers are fine craftsmen, my liege, quick and skilled, and have been working long hours. But as you've seen, I've only got two of them."

"And I need Carrisford well equipped, Alex, if this campaign we've just planned against Gloucester is going to succeed. No matter who is here to lead the defense." Stephen set down his cup of wine and tapped on the parchment in front of his chamberlain. "Make a note to send a half dozen of my own armorers and enough iron to do the job."

Alex knew that the king's offer had all to do with his own royal interests, but he did appreciate Stephen's ability to make it seem like generosity.

"My thanks to you, Your Grace."

The remainder of the night was a mad turmoil of maps and charts, opinions and prognostications, all of which led unerringly to the near certainty that the king's war was coming here, to Carrisford, to Talia and everyone she loved.

Stephen was sending more men as well, more weapons, and horses.

And Alex couldn't do a damned thing about it.

When the crowd dispersed, Stephen finally propped his booted feet onto the table and leaned back in his chair. "They seemed to get on well, Alex. You must be pleased."

"I've no complaints against your advisors, Your Grace. Save for William, who's—"

"An ass, I know. But I wasn't speaking of them. Have you no curiosity about FitzWarren and your ward? How they got on this evening . . . without us?"

To counter his probing, Alex looked right at the king and said, "I'm sure they got on very well, my liege. At least I hope so."

What a damned liar he was.

Stephen rose, stretched and yawned, then made his way to the door. "If you truly believe that FitzWarren is the right and best man for Lady Talia, Alex, then I give you leave to make the match. If . . ."

Stephen said good night, leaving the rest of his statement hanging there. Leaving Alex to wrestle with it through his dreams and long into the morning as he finally sent the royal entourage on its peripatetic way.

Without ever setting eyes on Talia.

Or learning of Conrad's opinion. Only that the man had left sometime before the king.

Alex had loved only once in his life: his brother. He'd had no idea at the time that love could be so precarious, so rare. Or the lack of it so debilitating. And now here it was, terrifying him again, making him feel powerless and aching to ask for more. For a family, just like this one that Talia had offered him so plainly.

The family he'd so roundly refused.

Feeling like a ghost, terrified now of actually finding Talia and learning that she had fallen deeply for Conrad's charms, Alex wandered down to the lists, rounding the corner of the armory just in time to see Kyle on horseback, running full out for the quintain.

Aiming badly.

Bloody hell! The boy went down cracking hard, and Alex ran. He shoved the squires away. "Let me see him."

The boy was staring into the sky, his eyes fixed on nothing, his mouth open, his body still as death.

"Christ, boy, breathe!" Alex gave his chest a thump with his palm. The gasp that came braying out of him sounded more like a wheeze from an old sackbutt than from a pair of human lungs.

Then a whole lot of coughing rolled the boy and brought him up onto his hands and knees. And started Alex's heart beating again.

Knowing the shame of the first fall, and the second and the twelfth, Alex waved the others away, but stayed beside him, patting him on the shoulder. "You'll be fine, Kyle."

The boy finally sagged flat out on the ground again and whispered something unintelligible but universal.

"I know, lad. First time I landed on my back, I didn't wake up for a full quarter hour."

The boy turned his head, a watery eye showing over his crooked elbow, through his shock of de Monteneau hair. "You fell?" he asked, barely a sound at all.

Alex laughed hard. "So many times, Kyle, I stopped counting before I was seventeen."

The wheezing slowed and Alex stood, lifting

the boy by his shoulder. "Come, boy, I have something to tell you. But not here; we're liable to be run over by one of those young squires on horseback."

The boy gave him a look of horror but followed Alex up the stairs toward the wall walk and the view of the bay beyond, his head drooping, his stride heavy, like a man approaching the gallows. "I'm sorry, my lord."

"For what?"

Those eyes peered through that shock of hair again. "For falling."

"You'll fall a thousand times before you get it right. And then you'll only fall on the odd Sunday. Be sorry only if you never try again."

"Aye, my lord."

How did one go about telling a young man that one was his brother?

All the time he'd wasted. The loss.

So many of them.

"Kyle," he began, but then his mouth went pasty. "Well, uhm . . . 'tis past time that I tell you this . . . this particular thing."

"I know." Kyle groaned and sagged against the short wall. "You don't want me to squire any-more. I can't blame you, my lord."

"That's not what I mean, lad." Alex sagged too, feeling ancient and guilty and unfocused. "You're a fine squire. And you'll be an even finer knight."

"You really think so?"

Alex saw Gil again in the eager honesty of the boy's eyes. " 'Tis in your blood."

"How can you tell that?"

"I just know, Kyle. Because . . ." He truly wanted to tell him, but this was a profound truth that he himself was only just realizing, and the words seemed caught up on the lump in his throat. "Because you and I have a lot in common."

"Oh, I double-doubt that, my lord." Kyle laughed and brushed a piece of grass off his shoulder. "You an' me?"

"Yes, and I'm not sure how to tell you this . . ." Because it will change so many things.

"The news that bad, is it?"

He'd once thought so. Learning of these brothers his father had left him. Spare ones. But now it seemed the opposite—somehow more than good.

Alex looked the boy in the eye, praying that Kyle wouldn't hate him too much for having held back. "I should have said before this, when you were first sent to me. I didn't because . . . hell, it doesn't matter why . . . just that I'm saying it now. That you're . . . Kyle, you're my brother."

Kyle raised his chin, cocked his head. "I know that, my lord."

The wind caught his banner nearby and gave it a good snap. "What did you say?"

Kyle shaded his eyes and squinted toward the bay and then looked back at Alex. "Well, sir, I know that your father was the same as mine. And so that makes us brothers. Halfway, that is. 'Cause our mothers were different."

Alex studied him, disbelieving that the boy could have known this and not have said something. "When, lad? Did you know of our connection when you joined my service?"

"Aye." The boy rubbed the back of his head, wincing some. "I don't recall ever not knowing."

"Christ, Kyle. You knew all this time, and you said nothing to me?"

He drew back, startled, worry creasing his forehead. "It wasn't my place to bring up such a thing, my lord. It was yours."

"Why the devil would you think that?"

The boy drew back further, shoulders hunched as though Alex had just struck him, and frowning down at his feet. "Well, because you are my liege lord, sir. I was plenty glad enough just to be near you."

Bloody hell. Just to be near? What a sorry ass he'd been to the boy.

"And you were willing to settle for that little? For my unconscionable anger toward you, my coldness, when you knew all along that we were brothers." Alex watched helplessly as huge tears gathered in his brother's eyes.

Kyle sniffed them back and stiffened his chin. "Oh, but I wasn't settling, my lord, I was proud of you."

Damnation. "You'll call me Alex, like a proper brother. Do you hear me?"

The boy's eyes grew wide, terrified. "Yes, but I—" He swallowed loudly. "In public, sir? I couldn't!"

"You will." Which only made the boy recoil. Small steps would have to do. But there was plenty of time for that. He had begun to believe he had plenty of time for a lot of things. "All right, then. But you'll work on it, Kyle."

He nodded. "Aye, I will."

"So how's your head?"

A smile quivered at the corners of his mouth. "Hard. Like yours, I suspect."

Alex roared with laughter. He took in great, delicious, salt-sprayed gulps of it, wondering why he'd waited so long. How he could have been so very stupid, so blind, in so very many ways.

And if Talia could possibly forgive him for it.

Talia didn't know whether to be blisteringly angry at Alex, or sad or grateful or pleased, for leaving her with Conrad all night.

The man had been everything that Alex had promised. Kind and generous, honorable and intelligent, blessed with good looks and a sense of humor.

Making all the right overtures about marriage and children and Carrisford—

And it didn't matter at all.

The king and his entourage were gone now, and the castle was beginning to show its fatal flaws. A day or two longer and it would be nothing but a fiery rubble.

Like the coward she was, she had evaded Alex all day, absenting herself from the king's hurried leave-taking, avoiding the great hall, taking meals while hiding here in a corner of the cellar like the rat she was.

"Ah, there you are, my lady."

"Jasper!"

"Hiding, I see, and well you should be."

"I'll thank you to keep your opinions to yourself." She popped the corner of bread into her mouth and stood up, brushing the crumbs off her hands. "What can I do for you?"

"I think you ought to come take a look at the east-facing loop passage. Doesn't look good to me."

"Show me." Feeling as though she were skulking, she followed Jasper through the cellars and up a set of stairs into the east tower, and finally out into the dimly lighted corridor of arrow loops that ran between the towers.

"See right here. I think this doorway's just about ready to go, my lady."

Talia came around the corner of the corridor and stopped in her tracks. Jasper was pointing up at the empty keystone in the sagging arch not two feet above his head.

"Holy Mother of Jesus, Jasper, get back over here, right now!"

"It's ready to go, ain't it?" A thin stream of stone dust poured down onto his forehead and he frowned at her.

"Come here, Jasper!" Talia darted toward him, grabbed his hand and yanked him to safety.

An instant later the arch fell in, as though Jasper had been holding it up by sheer ignorance of the danger.

They both stared at the small pile of stones at their feet.

"You saved my life, my lady!"

"What's happened here, Jasper?"

"Dunno, my lady. Leod's been working here . . ."

Talia heard a shift of stones above them and pulled Jasper out of the way again, just as the rest of the ceiling began to fall in, the corbels giving way first, and then the flat cross-slabs, pitching into the corridor, one after the other, each landing just behind them, as Talia pulled Jasper with her, until they reached the safety of the tower.

"Dear God! Go, Jasper! Check from the opposite tower, but take care." Her heart in her throat, Talia sent Jasper outside and waited in the archway while the dust cleared, terrified that one of the watchmen above might have fallen through.

"Hello?" she shouted into the lifting dust, finally clambering over the fall. Wondering if her undermining had done this and what other dangerous traps she might have set around the castle without realizing it.

"Is anyone hurt?" she called again into the distance. "Helllloooo!"

"Hello?" Giddrey was right above her on the sill of the wall, peering into the breach. "Anyone hurt? Oh, my lady! Good God! Stay right there!"

Talia heard his footfalls on the tower stairs and met him on wobbling legs as he came flying into the room.

"Thank God, you're all right."

"Was anyone on the walk?"

"One very quick-footed watchman who ran like a hare. And, meaning no disrespect to you, my lady, but I'm getting you out of here before His Lordship has my hide."

Giddrey shoved her the few steps down through the filtering dust and into the courtyard.

Into a very crowded courtyard, with Alex storming toward her at full tilt at the head of the mob, his face a fierce but unreadable mask.

One that would quickly turn to anger, when he discovered the cause.

And he would discover it, because he was a thorough man who would inspect every inch of the foundation.

Because he had a castle to sell.

And the evidence of all her digging—her treachery—was just waiting for him to discover it.

She'd be convicted and locked in his dungeon within the hour, and her neck in the noose by nightfall.

Running away seemed pointless.

Besides, Alex would be on her in the next breath, and her heart was already skipping and stuttering. Because she was madly in love with a dear man who needed so much more than she could give him.

The very man who was lifting her into his arms, enfolding her, holding her tightly against him. "Christ God, Talia! You could have been killed."

Then his mouth was everywhere across her face—her eyelids and her temple and finally her mouth.

A long, deeply plundering, soul-melting kiss that struck the breath from her and left her weak-kneed and her head spinning when he held her at arm's length from him as the others reached them.

"What the hell happened, Talia?" His eyes were hot and intense and traveling all over her as he turned her, went around her, feeling of her arms, her legs, her ribs, finally taking her head in both his hands and tilting her chin to him.

"Alex, I'm sorry, I—"

He grabbed her against him and held her as though he would never let go. And he whispered the most marvelous thing she'd ever heard, "Lord, if I'd lost you, Talia . . ."

And then he kissed her again, right there in

front of everyone. Hardly chaste, not for public display, but he didn't seem to be considering anything but the two of them, though lots of people had gathered around them.

And then he pulled away again sharply, huge and powerful in all his fury, a new dusting of mortar on his cheek and across his broad chest. "Stay right here, madam; I don't want you in there again, do you hear?"

"Yes, Alex." She felt meek and obedient, stunned at the change in the man. His smile looked a bit crazed, wild and reckless.

"Giddrey, come with me," he said, speeding off toward the tower.

There came a warrior's shout and a half dozen others followed Alex, as though they were off to do battle against some terrible foe.

"What happened, my lady?" Leod whispered, as Quigley handed her a damp rag.

"Overeagerness, Leod," she said, weeping as she wiped her face of the dust, watching the tower door for Alex to come roaring out with his accusations. "We're on the brink."

Jasper appeared at her side. "The other tower looks sturdy enough, my lady. No other cave-ins."

"Not till it's time."

"When, then?" Quigley asked, picking a chunk of plaster out of her hair.

"In the next few days. Unless Alex realizes before then what we've been doing and tosses me into the dungeon." Which seemed a perfect place at the moment, dark and isolated. "I just need to keep him from seeing the extent of the excavation for himself."

Jasper brushed at his hair, raising a cloud of dust. "I'll go see if I can explain away the cave-in to His Lordship, my lady. And anything else he might find."

Like his entire castle ready to fall.

"And while you do, Jasper, I'll try to think of a reasonable excuse that will get everyone safely out of the castle before we set her afire." What a ghastly calamity it had all become. "Please tell Alex that I've gone to clean up. That I'll see him at supper."

If I'd lost you, Talia . . .

Oh, Alex, but you have lost me. I'm afraid we lost each other long ago.

But the man wasn't at supper, or in his chamber afterward, or in the guardhouse. Not anywhere.

And that could only mean that he'd found out and now was so angry with her that he couldn't even look at her. She'd waited all day for his ser-geants to come arrest her, but nothing seemed amiss—they were ever the gentlemen.

And as she finally climbed the stairs to her own chamber, a guilty coldness clung to her shoulders, stained the air and made her ache all over.

It wasn't that she was secretly tearing down her

castle, piece by piece; indeed, that was a covenant between her and the people she loved.

The coldness came from the undeniable fact that Alex was the most honorable man she'd ever met. Stone-headed and stubborn, and no sense of just how good a man he was.

Which left Talia feeling empty and grieving for the fullness of the life they could have had together had things been different.

She slipped into her nearly dark chamber and stumbled her way toward the table, wondering how Alex's scent had gotten in here, the sharp bay and cinnamon of him. Sifting through the drapes and the tapestries, caught up in the counterpane like a dear memory.

She sighed and sniffed back her misery then picked up a fat candle and started toward the red glow of the brazier.

A voice rumbled toward her from the shadows, reached out and stopped her. "So, my dear lady, what did you think of FitzWarren?"

"Alex!" Her heart went skidding wildly off its course with a crazy kind of relief, of a great tragedy postponed for a brief moment.

"Well, madam?" He was lounging long-legged in a chair in the near darkness beyond the brazier, an engulfing power that enfolded her, that shimmered against her skin and slipped through her veins. "What did you think?"

"Of Conrad?" she asked as she lit the candle,

trying to steady her hand and read his mood, the curious ease of it, wondering why he hadn't confronted her immediately with the cave-in, with her betrayal.

The whole foundation of the castle—his fortune and his future—was on the brink of sliding into the bay. He must have noticed.

"Was he everything you expected in a potential husband, Talia?" The chair creaked as he rose, his darkness filling the rafters as he stepped just into the candlelight.

This wasn't the fiercely impassioned man she'd last seen in the courtyard. Or the one who ought to be ranting. Something was wrong.

And right and simple. His eyes clear and piercing, haunting. Devastatingly handsome in his hip-short tunic and a pair of long braes. His work clothes, clean and smelling of cedar shavings.

"Alex, where have you been?"

He paused and considered her before he said, "Seeing to things."

"What things, Alex?" Trying to sound unconcerned, Talia wedged the candle into its stick on the table, then stood back from him to more carefully examine this uncommon mood of his. He looked . . . artful, as though he was holding back a secret from her.

Doubtless a dark secret.

"Why?" One of his brows made a wry arch. "Were you worried about me, Talia?"

"Just . . ." She swallowed, bewitched by the low roughness of his voice, the intimacy it conjured. "Just that you disappeared completely after"—she felt guilty even saying it— "after the cave-in."

He smiled sideways at her, charming, sly, smelling of soap and leather as he stepped toward her, caught her fingers in his and whispered, "I like that."

"What?" Though she liked this breathtaking connection between them, fingers laced, his rough thumb rubbing lightly against her palm.

"I like that you worried about me, Talia. I could get used to that."

Nothing he was saying made any sense. Nothing in the way he tilted his head and gazed at her through wickedly smiling eyes that said everything but *you betrayed me, Talia*.

Those same dark eyes became quite serious suddenly, and then a little cocky. "I told him, Talia."

More puzzles. "Told who what, Alex?"

He dropped onto the bench in front of her and looked her squarely in the eye, a challenge, a promise. "I told Kyle that we . . . that he and I are brothers."

Happy beyond measure, Talia knelt between his spread thighs. She took his hands between hers, her throat closing over. "You really did? I'm so glad."

He gave a short laugh. "Hell, the lad could have told me himself."

"What do you mean?"

"He already knew."

"What? Oh, Alex, no. Poor Kyle must have been devastated to know—"

"He wasn't, Talia." He brought their clasped hands to his lips and set a kiss between her fingers as he thought, one finger then the next, his gaze fastened fiercely to hers. "He's a wiser lad than I was at his age."

"And far luckier. To have you."

He sliced her a self-directed indictment, then stood up and paced toward the casement window.

"You haven't answered my question, Talia." His voice had roughened, filled with a longing.

"About . . . what?" She'd forgotten everything but the thrilling sound of him, his scent. Nothing else seemed to matter.

He wasn't acting anything like she'd expected. Wasn't shouting or threatening or demanding. He was simply gazing at her mouth as though he'd been without food and water for a lifetime.

But her question seemed to bemuse him, to pull him back to her. He caught both her hands and drew her to her feet. And then he was lifting her against the length of him, embracing her against all that hardness, his chest, his thighs, and that wonderfully thick rigidness that fit so perfectly against her belly.

"Ask me again, Alex."

He was making soft, nuzzling noises, had cocooned her nearly completely against the table, resting his hands against her hips at the edge of the table. He bent his head and whispered against her ear, "FitzWarren."

"What about him again?"

He made a dizzying, deeply satisfied sound in his throat, as breathtaking as the brush of his tongue along the ridge of her ear. "How did I do?"

"Do? Oh, Alex—" He was doing so marvelously well that she couldn't catch her breath. She grabbed a fistful of the front of his tunic, offering more of her ear to him, her mouth, and her sigh, taking in his breath with her own, as he brushed at the edge of her lips.

"Tell me, beautiful Talia . . ." He tilted her chin with his thumb, a beguiling smile lifting the corners of his eyes. He spoke against her temple, the heat of his words sending shivers dancing across her shoulders. Said something about last night. Their guest.

"About Conrad." She remembered now, but only barely. "He was . . ."

He loosened his embrace enough to study her, his eyes intent upon hers when he asked, "He was what?"

She caught her lower lip, because she couldn't quite remember this Conrad fellow, not with Alex framing and filling her world.

I love you, Alex.

Oh, no! Not that!

Her eyes stung, welled inexplicably with hot tears. "He was . . . well—"

He would do.

"He was what, Talia?"

"Blond . . ." Then her blasted tears spilled over and ran down her cheeks, and a hiccoughing sound came coursing out of her. Because it didn't matter if Conrad's hair was brown or green or if he was bald.

Alex stepped away, still holding her hand, as though he wanted to see her more fully, his face a range of keen edges and devilishly dark orange. "And?"

Her heart stalled at the sudden change in him. He was Alex again, and the blackguard had been plying her, deliberately setting her off-balance with his seduction.

Well, let him believe that he'd succeeded. Because he had so thoroughly.

"Well, he was nearly as tall as you." She put the brazier between them, adding wood to the embers. "But you already knew that."

He was looking at her from beneath an ever-darkening brow. "And what else?"

"He has sisters."

"Did you talk of marriage?"

"Well . . . we . . . he . . ." How could she possibly answer clearly when he had started toward her again, relentlessly, rounding the brazier, his eyes fixed on hers, making her pulse thunder against her throat?

"Did you?"

"Some, yes."

A frown flickered across his brow, tightened his mouth briefly. "What does that mean?"

"Uhm, well . . ." She backed away from him, stubbing the heel of her slipper against the table leg. "We talked about my wardship, certainly."

He kept coming, and she kept backing away, thoroughly confused by his interrogation, the seduction of it. "What about your wardship, Talia?"

"Well, about the castle—" Oh, Lord, here it comes: his pronouncement against her. That she would dare to scuttle the sale of Carrisford by destroying it.

"What about the castle, Talia?"

What the devil did the man want from her? "Its history, of course. Did you know that the Conqueror slept here on his way to Bristol? Though it was merely a mote and bailey at the time . . . but you don't want to know that."

"No."

"Well, then what, Alex? You've confused me completely." She was beginning to think that he hadn't come here to accuse her of treason against him. Maybe he didn't know.

"Aye, Talia, I was confused, too. Before."

Before. And then what? Enlightenment? She

was suddenly exhausted. "Alex, maybe this should wait until the morning. It's been a long day and we're both . . ."

He shook his head sternly. "This isn't something that can wait a day between us, Talia. Or even an hour. I doubt even another minute should pass."

"Well then, just tell me, Alex. Stop this dallying, because I can't bear any more of it."

He grinned, made a delicious yummm sort of sound way deep in his throat. "That's part of my plan, Talia. Dallying with you of an evening."

God, he looked wonderful, solid and pliable. His smile so crookedly grand she could stand here and look at him forever. "Dally with me? On purpose?"

"Oh, yes, madam."

"Isn't that cruel?"

He actually stopped in his slow, sinuous pursuit of her and thought about it. "Mmmm, not entirely cruel, I think. But a kind of torment."

"You'd actually do that to me, Alex? Torment me?"

Again with that distracting smile, alive with his secrets. "In my way."

His way? She swallowed hard, wondering what that would be, putting herself safely behind the chair, though she could imagine all sorts of ways he might torment her. "After all we've meant to each other?"

"What have we meant, Talia?"

That stopped her short, because he'd meant so many remarkable things to her—rainbows and the tide and the apple harvest. But she could hardly confess that, so she shrugged. "Well . . . you know."

"I do, Talia, at long last. A recently discovered truth. But do *you* know, I wonder? As I continue to wonder what happened last night between you and FitzWarren."

She laughed because this whole horrid mess had become so absurd, and all about Conrad, it seemed. "Nothing happened between us, Alex."

He scrunched up a thoroughly disgusted frown. "He didn't kiss you?"

"Never once. Didn't even try."

"Ha! The fool." It was a prideful, possessive laugh that made her feel beautiful, cherished. And then he leveled an eye at her. "So you didn't take a fancy to him?"

"A fancy to Conrad? Good Lord, no."

"Not your ideal bridegroom?"

Foolish man. She was looking at her ideal. The sort of perfection that wasn't allowed in this world. "Not even close, Alex."

"That's good. Because I wasn't going to let you marry him anyway."

What an awful, pride-leveling game he was playing. "But he'll do after all, Alex."

His brow furrowed. "Do?"

He's not you, Alex. "After all, he seems thoughtful and intelligent, and I can't truthfully think of a
single reason why I should refuse him and risk another monster like Rufus. A perfectly reasonable
choice." Wasn't that what he wanted from her?
"So, I accept him, Alex. I approve of Conrad."

He just stood there for a moment, a mystery
caught up in the rise and fall of his chest.

"Do you approve of . . . me, Talia?"

"As . . . ?" A tiny part of her heart went sailing
out over the moon.

"As a husband, Talia."

"Oh!" *Oh, no. Not that!* "Why?"

"Why?" He looked suddenly lost, helpless and
dear. And then he grew big and blustery. "Damnation, Talia, I thought you'd be pleased."

"Well, I—" *should be. Want to be.* "You want to
marry me, Alex?"

"You're damn right I do. Right here, right now."

"But, Alex, I . . ."

"Will you have me, Talia?"

Have him. Hold him, for all the rest of her days.

Her eyes began to puddle again. "What about
your lovely heiress, Alex? And your gigantic castle and your vast holdings and all those influential
titles?"

He smiled ruefully, wolfish. "Remind me often
of what a fool I was, my love."

His love.

"Thinking that I could blithely give you away to someone else when you are my heart."

His heart, too.

"Oh, Alex." It was too late.

"Marry me . . . please."

Please?

"Oh, Alex. No one's ever said *please* before."

She'd stopped running from him sometime back, and now he merely slipped his fingers through her hair, tilted her face to him, and said so simply.

"I love you, Talia. And I'm asking. I'll beg, if you wish it. From right here on my knee." He kissed her lightly on her mouth and then knelt on one knee, enveloping both her hands in one of his. "Will you have me, sweet? Marry me and make me whole."

"Oh, dear. My love." *I can't.*

Though she wanted him completely, and forever, wanted him to stay and stay, wanted children with him and orchards and a full tithe barn for her people.

But not even Alex could stop the killing tide of the war. Could he?

"There, Talia, you love me."

"Alex, I—"

"You do, sweet. Though I don't quite understand your resistance." His grin grew wolfish as he scooped her up into his arms. "But I think you may be right to make absolutely sure. You'd best try me out first, before you go marrying me."

"Try you out?" He'd gone completely mad.

"Just like you would good horseflesh, Talia."

"Whatever do you mean, Alex?" And why were they on the way to the bed?

"Ride me hard, madam."

"What? To where?"

He laughed broadly, the sound of him rumbling through her. "Right here in this bridal bed of ours."

Our bed.

"Test my gait, sweet," he said, shifting her weight in his arms then letting her slide slowly, wondrously down the length of him until she was standing on the bedside step, at eye level with him.

"Alex, I—"

"Do check my teeth on your ride, my lady"— he caught her earlobe and nibbled, tugged— "my tongue"—he trailed his lightly along her shoulder—"oh, and my . . . spur"—his grin grew wickedly wise as he held her hips against his, against the perfect outline of him.

"Your . . . oh, Alex!"

"My prick, then, love." It was lovely and hot and full of life. "Rock-hard and ready for your pleasure, as you can feel for yourself."

She'd never seen him like this, never felt such breathless ecstasy. "Alex, I shouldn't!"

Oh, but how she wanted to, wanted him with all her heart. Couldn't help arching her back toward him, or her sigh, long and deep as he trailed his bewitching mouth along her jaw and down her neck, nibbling and laving and kissing.

"I want you all for myself, Talia. To taste you here—" He lingered as he untied the lacing at her breasts that had so confounded them both the night before, leaving his steamy kiss in the hollow there.

"And touch you, Talia." She watched in shameless fascination as he then untied the drawstring at the neck of her chemise.

"To fill you with myself." He looked directly into her eyes. "Marry me, my love."

"Oh, Alex, if only—"

"Aye, if only I hadn't been so stubborn and arrogant." He took his sweet time working his fingers down the front of her kirtle, tugging out the laces, tantalizing her with unspoken promises, lighting her imagination.

And her belief in miracles, because that's all they had left.

"You've been perfect, Alex."

He hummed his approval against her throat, slipping his hand between her chemise and her kirtle to cup her breast. "And you are beautiful, my love."

She might as well have been as naked as a dewy spring morning for the shimmering bliss he was causing with his audacious kiss, for the exquisite aching between her legs, as though his hand was playing there.

Or his mouth.

"Alex!" She stopped herself from asking him if such kisses were possible, or proper, or if he'd consider it, because he was bending her backward over his arm, his spicy breath steaming hot against her nipple, fire flickering from the end of his tongue, right through two layers of cloth, and all she could do was to cling to his neck and press herself against his mouth, her hips against his hardness, his lovely spur.

She wanted more of his delicious torment—to feel his skin against hers, but couldn't think beyond grabbing fistfuls of his tunic and urging his hips and his feral hardness against her, which seemed to make him growl.

And then she finally realized his meaning, his threat to dally with her, to torment her.

"Is this what you meant by dallying, Alex?"

He lifted her upright, and smiled, skiffing his fingers through her hair. "First, the wedding night, my love, and then the wedding. Is that all right with you?"

She nodded, banishing the chiding voices that warned her to run from her lies, from him, the man she loved, who made her laugh and who rescued rabbits.

Who might have been able to talk the king into

turning the war, turning their lives around to the sunlight. She hadn't asked and couldn't now, for the lump in her throat.

And the bed had never seemed so vast and inviting. Four-posted, and lushly draped, heaped with pillows and her counterpane.

A perfect dallying place, where she could welcome his impossible madness, where she could cling to him and pretend it would all last forever.

"I love you, Alex."

"I know." He grinned, then pressed his mouth against hers, again and again, slippery hot and slanting, breathing like a hunted stag.

And she was quite sure that he did love her as dearly as she loved him.

"Then dally with me tonight, my love."

Because it was the only night they'd ever have.

Chapter 20

❦

"**O**h, my dear love," Alex said, feeling greedy and unworthy of the remarkable woman, dizzy and aching with the need for her, "I'm going to do far more than just dally with you."

Her eyes grew wide and welcoming, her fingertips toying at his nape, raking through his hair. "You plan to torment me then?"

"Till you're crying out for me to stop."

He heard the hot little sigh that caught in her throat and sent a surge of fire zinging through his groin. A sure warning to him that if he didn't take his time, if he didn't focus clearly on the journey instead of on the prize, he might just lose it all.

"You're amazing to me, Alex. So different than I'd first imagined."

He couldn't help preening under all that heat,

or thinking himself the luckiest man on the great, green earth.

"God, Talia, you're beautiful."

She was so much more than just that; but she shied some as she stood in front of him on the bed-step, then smiled and threaded her fingers through his hair, drawing him closer, her eyes brook-clear as she whispered,

"So far I like this dallying, Alex. I'm looking forward to being tormented by you." And then she kissed him, fully and fiercely, dancing her tongue against his, leading him and then following.

"And riding you here, Alex." She moved her hips against him. "Riding this."

"Talia!" He groaned and pulled well out of her reach, his restraint at the edge of its limits.

She stood there looking innocent and well kissed. He'd managed to loosen the lacing of her kirtle all the way down to her waist, her soft linen chemise beneath that, hanging deliciously off one shoulder, bunching where he'd been exploring her breast.

An unwrapped package, waiting just for him.

"You've too many clothes on, my love," he said, not knowing until too late that his brain would seize up completely as he watched her shrug out of her kirtle in a single motion, the bulk of it landing in a heap around the bedstep.

"Better?" she asked, tossing him a flirting smile.

"Oh, much." He slipped his hands around her

waist, then lifted her off the step and set her on her feet. He'd been aroused by the woman since the moment she first smacked him in the helm, roused and ready to fill her with himself, to lose himself inside her.

She took an unsteady breath as he brushed her chemise off her shoulders and let it slip down her arms. The sleeves caught up at her elbows, her breasts bobbing, beckoning.

"Oh, God, Talia." He stopped just to stare at them, to marvel at the ivory softness, a perfect fit for his palms, at the dark rosy tips, crested and so sweetly ready for him.

He caught her waist between his hands and tasted her throat, kneeling slowly as he followed a steaming trail over her collarbone and then down the vanilla fragrant vale between her softly rising breasts.

She hummed as he traveled, trailing her fingers through his hair, swaying against him in a rhythm that matched his own heartbeat.

"Are you dallying with me now, Alex, or tormenting?" Another singing sigh. "Because what you're doing feels a whole lot like torment to me."

"Dallying only, my love." Her nipples were but a breath away from his mouth, teasing and taunting him. He cupped the buoyant shapes, then caught a bud between his lips and drew her inside his mouth.

"Oh, Alex, that's—" She gasped and blew out a

long sigh. "Oh! Ohhhhh!" She grabbed the back of his head, pulled him closer.

She tasted of her bath, honey sweet and heated, grew impatient with her arms trapped by her sleeves.

She shrugged them off, letting the linen bunch at her hips, then fall to her ankles, all the while keeping hold of whole hanks of his hair, pleading with him to continue, when he couldn't stop if he tried.

"I want to feel you, Alex!" She was thoroughly naked and moving against him like a warm, springtime breeze.

"Oh, my dear Talia, I don't know if I can take much more of this." He was rock-hard and throbbing, on the verge of taking her here on the floor, sitting or standing—needing to thrust himself into her.

"I do recall that you're the one who's being given a trial run, Alex." She grinned as she shoved at his shoulder and stood free of him, leaving him breathless and grunting like a bull. "And I think you've got too many clothes on."

Alex staggered to his feet, stunned by her boldness, pleased to his bones to have a wife who would seduce him. He reached for his tunic, but she stayed his hand.

"Let me, my lord." She was sloe-eyed and impatient as she unbuckled his belt and helped him out of his tunic, then his linen shirt, leaving his erection straining against his leggings and braes.

"Oh, my!" she said when she saw it. She looked up at him and smiled, her eyes bright with pure, lustful admiration.

"Take care, Talia," he said, knowing that he ought just to shuck the lot without her help. But she was purring, slipping her arms around his waist.

"You're so warm," she said, sliding her palms down his hips and over his backside, pressing her cheek against his chest. "And hard, Alex, everywhere."

"And you're softer than down, Talia." Drawing a breath was difficult; his hands played at her hips, freely fondling her, meeting her rhythm.

"These go too, Alex. Your braes." She planted a long, succulent kiss in the center of his chest, then stepped back and studied him. The tops of his braes, the drawstring that held them up.

And his erection.

"Your spur, Alex?" She looked up at him from beneath her dark lashes, spots of color high on her cheeks. "Larger than I'd imagined."

"You've imagined me? My . . . spur?"

A shy smile flitted across her cheeks. "Aye, Alex. And it looks to have a mind of its own."

"God, yes it does, love. Though we are in perfect agreement at the moment." He drew a deep breath through his nostrils and gathered her against him, the closeness keeping her in check.

He slanted a kiss across her mouth and then another, just that, kisses only while he shuddered and slowly regained control of his senses.

"Your braes, Alex," she whispered amongst all that deep kissing, nibbling at his lips, nuzzling his chin. "You're still wearing them."

He gazed down at her, at all that eagerness. "So I am, my love."

"I want to see what you're offering."

"Oh, Talia, as you wish." Great God, he'd almost given her away to some ungrateful baron.

Her quick fingers went searching, found the drawstring and tugged. That would have been bearable, just, had she stopped then and there. But the knot held stubbornly, and she was far too curious.

"Oh, Alex." She covered him with her hand through the bulging linen.

Alex took a breath the moment he could, then clamped his hand over hers to stop her exploring. But that seemed only to encourage her.

"Oh, I like you here, Alex." She made an admiring little sigh and squeezed him lightly, shaped her fingers around him.

"Talia, stop!" He grabbed her hands safely away, kissed her fingers.

"But, Alex, I've seen nothing of you yet. Your teeth, of course— they're straight and white and strong and, well, you nibble with skill. And your tongue is excellent. But your spur, Alex, remains a mystery. And hardly something that you can hide from me."

He couldn't find breath or brains enough to reply. But when she reached for him again, he held out his hand and stopped her in her tracks.

"You'll wait there, Talia." He bent and shucked his hosen and braes, braced himself for any reaction.

But when he looked up at her, she was boldly appraising him, from head to toe to erection.

"Well, you can do a whole lot of dallying with all that, Alex." The woman was mischief to her soul, grinning at him in triumph.

"Talia!" He lifted her into his arms, and she climbed eagerly into his embrace, wrapping her bare legs around his waist as though it were the most natural thing in the world, sultry where her desire met the hot length of him, staggering him with the need to plunge, to stroke and taste her where his hands were laced together, where she was soft and slick.

"We've been in this position once before, Alex." But that particular time she wasn't naked or rocking against him, or making love to his mouth, or murmuring something about her dreams and their children.

"You won't clout me in the head this time?" he asked as he collected her kisses.

"As long as you behave."

"I don't plan to do anything of the sort."

She grinned. "I was hoping so."

Talia had been taught not to stare at extraordinary sights, oh, but this male part of Alex had been too spectacular to look away.

His spur, indeed! Provocatively rigid, dramatically displayed below his slender waist, thick-veined and pulsing.

And now he'd fit the length of it along her cleaving, and she could hardly breathe for the hot bliss of it.

The man himself was bronze-muscled, his eyes as hungry as his mouth as she clung to him, and he carried her to the edge of the bed.

"I love you, Alex."

His smile went crooked as he lay her back against the mattress and braced his hands on either side of her head. "That's some kind of miracle, sweet."

"Oh, yes, Alex!"

He hovered for a long time, kissing her, dallying with his mouth while the humid heat of him brushed against the inside of her thighs.

"Tell me, love, why you and Jasper were in the collapsed passage?" The man asked that kind of a question, then planted a distracting kiss on her nipple, nuzzled there until she could barely breathe.

The passage.

Please God, don't let him be merely taunting me here.

"Jasper had come to show me the trouble there. Heavens, Alex." His touch fuddled her completely, struck the breath from her. He teased at her breasts, made her squirm and rise up to meet him while he pulled and licked, sending bits of starlight from her fingers.

"You terrified me today, my love."

"I'm sorry." She slipped her fingers through his hair and pulled him closer.

"When I heard that you were somewhere inside the collapse, I came running." He was so large as he leaned down to kiss her mouth, his arm muscles bunching and quaking, his breath coming in ragged bursts.

"I didn't mean to worry you." She hadn't meant to love him either, but some things were just so easy to do.

"Let me take care of it next time, Talia." He began trailing his kiss downward, from one rib to the next.

"Aye, Alex. I promise."

"But as punishment, my love, I'm going to have to torment you." She felt the smile he was trying to hide against the underslope of her breast.

"I was hoping so." Though she couldn't imagine what he could possibly mean.

She had spread her legs indelicately around his, and now he was doing something that had altered her pulse. She felt soft and pliable and wondered what he was thinking, where he was going when he knelt between her thighs.

She sat up on her elbows, her imagination running quickly alongside his large hands as he brushed them across her belly. "Alex?"

He was smiling at her, a cagey look in his eyes. Another of his secrets that left her light-headed and aching.

"Your promise, Talia, before I continue."

"Promise? What do you mean?"

But he was already landing a kiss on her knee—on the *inside* of her knee. And then the inside of her thigh.

"That, you'll come find me when you see problems at Carrisford." He'd spoken this across her belly, sent his words steaming through her most private curls, dancing them there.

Tormenting her. "Oh, yesssss, Alex!"

"Your promise, love."

"Carrisford." She'd heard that. And something about her problems belonging to him now. "I'll come find you, Alex. Alex! Oh! Was that your tongue?"

It was. The tip of it. And then his kiss and his nuzzling. Right down there at the very joining of her thighs.

"You taste of sunlight, Talia." His words broke against her curls. And another kiss. A searing, slick bolt of fire.

"I think I'm going to faint, Alex."

"You won't if you just breathe, my love. Now your promise, Talia, or I'll stop."

"You wouldn't." But he did, and she raised up on her elbows, to stare right into his eyes.

"Trust me, Talia. Let me take care of you and these people you love like I should have done. Let me love them, too."

What an impossible man. "I promise to try my best, Alex. By my heart, I will do my best."

He spent a very long time looking into her eyes, surely finding love enough there to blind him to her horrible deceit. He smiled, the devil in him returned.

"Well, then, my love, just to show you how deeply I accept your best promise . . ." He seemed to take great pleasure in parting her slowly with his fingers, in seeking something else from her.

"Oh, Alex, please!"

"I warned you that I'd be tormenting you." Another of his kisses, deeper yet, probing, his fingers inside her, sliding and slipping, nuzzling her as though he were kissing her mouth until she was ready to explode.

"Enough, Alex!"

He raised his head from his tormenting her, smiling, leaving her limp and unfulfilled, craving him as he caught her hips and carried them up against the pillows.

"Not nearly enough, Talia. Though I'm nearly

out of self-restraint." He was kneeling on the mattress, in the space between her thighs, braced on his hands, his great staff, his spur, dazzlingly large.

She reached out to touch him there, but Alex grabbed her hand and pinned it to the pillow. "God bless you for the thought, my love, but I would not last a second longer if you did what I think you were going to do."

"I was just going to wrap my fingers around you, Alex." She raised her hips to try to meet the heat of him.

"As I thought." He rested his forehead against hers.

"And kiss you as you just did me."

He drew in a deep breath, then opened his eyes to hers. "I love you, Talia."

Alex couldn't have dared hope for all this ungoverned curiosity in a wife. Just now his joints ached, and his muscles had long ago cramped into thick knots. He wanted her like he wanted sunlight, wanted to be inside her.

To be the man who claimed her and her love and all of her cares.

She sighed against his mouth and called out his name when he found her with his fingers, opened herself to him, her eyes half-lidded and following his.

"Be with me, Alex." She wrapped her legs around his waist and tucked him closer, the tip of him meeting her, unerringly, the way she'd found his heart.

"Oh, my love." He shuddered with the need to plunge forward and plunder her, but he held back, slowing against the irresistible tide.

But Talia seemed as eager as he, tilting her hips and holding his, taking the tip of him as far as she could, until he met her maiden's barrier.

She laughed with her eyes, tears glinting at their corners. "Make me yours, Alex, make me believe, for all the rest of my days." And all the while she was rocking in her steady rhythm, her heartbeat and his.

"And be my wife, Talia." Then, like a man with a single feral thought, he thrust in and upward, breaching her swiftly, the pleasure fragile and fierce as she took him tightly inside her, more deeply, more fully with each cry of his name, and he was buried to the shank.

He kissed her eyelids, then stilled completely, terrified that he'd hurt her. But she wore her fox's sly smile, was stretching languidly beneath him, a riverweed, a willow, breathing deeply, her eyes alight with pleasure.

"You're very large, Alex."

"I can leave you, love."

She tightened her heels against his buttocks. "No, you can't."

His heart gave a thudding leap. "Vixen."

"My wild stallion." She ran her fingers through

his hair, kept hold at his nape, then began that earthy rhythm again.

He met her long, measuring strokes, keeping her close to him, his weight sheltered on his elbows.

And they rocked. Lingered.

"Are we dallying, Alex?"

"As we will every night of our lives." There was nothing left of his restraint, all of it spent on Talia, because he loved her more than his life.

He slipped his hand along her hip to her belly, found where she was wet and ready for him, where they were one.

A simple touch where she was the warmest, then her sigh caught against his chin and became a lingering, throaty, "Ohhhhh, mmmmy! My Alex!"

Her Alex. Could a man be happier?

Alex rode the full, fathoms deep force of her pleasure, holding back his own until it finally came roaring out of nowhere.

"God, I love you, Talia."

Talia felt every inch of him, soared alongside him into the clearest, starriest part of the sky, unable to get enough of him, riding his glorious rhythms, until her marvelous Alex reared up, his nostrils flaring and full, the magnificent thickness of him arching within her.

He kissed her madly, the deep pulsing of him lifting her again toward another release, until he bellowed her name and spilled his seed into her, flooding her with his life.

Her great, handsome, wild-haired beast. Her magnificent warlord, falling back to earth, his heart thudding against her chest as she soothed him, as she wept.

"I love you, Alex." She kissed his cheek, where he tasted of salt and their lovemaking, lifted his damp hair off his forehead.

He looked sated, sloe-eyed. Cocky as he brushed a kiss across her mouth. "And I you, my love."

She'd remembered something that she'd meant to ask him so long ago, a plaguing question she'd have asked him at supper if he'd been there. But then she'd found him lounging in her chamber.

And her life had changed. At least she hoped it had. One last chance to save them all. "About your counsel with the king."

"God save me from kings and their ministers." His eyes darkened as he shifted onto his elbow.

"What did you learn of Stephen's spring campaign?"

He shifted his eyes from hers. "Ah, love. That."

She wiggled out from under him, sat up on her knees, searching Alex's face for any sign of hope that things might turn out well. "What happened in there, Alex?"

"Carrisford is in a strategic position."

She shook her head, wanting to disbelieve the inescapable truth. "Strategic, in what way?"

"I'm sorry, my love, but it's a factor of armies and alliances."

"And not a single thought toward the people who live in the village. I should have taken the king there to show him."

"Sweet, I think he knows." He caught her hand in his, but she yanked it away.

"As you do as well, Alex, and yet you both can continue this—"

"We have little choice, Talia. Stephen especially. The moment he lets down his guard, Maud and her rebels are on his flanks."

"So what you're saying, Alex, is that the war is coming to my valley and there's nothing you can do to protect my people, my family." She shivered, held back a crippling sob.

"And *mine*, now, Talia. From this day onward." He lifted the edge of the counterpane and draped it over her shoulders. "The castle garrison will—"

"Will be busy, won't they? Protecting the castle, the king's interests. Yours."

"*Our* interests, Talia." He lifted her chin with his bent knuckle and made her look into his eyes. So honest and determined that she wanted to weep. "Yours and mine. Stephen is sending troops and arms and cavalry."

"Dear God!" She swallowed hard and drew the

counterpane around her. "So there's no hope for any kind of peace."

"There's plenty of it between you and me, my love." He slipped his hand beneath the blanket and around her waist. "Oceans of it. I've a strong, loyal garrison, who've pledged themselves to me—and thereby to you."

How could a powerful warrior be such an innocent? "Oh, Alex, I wish—"

"Believe in me, love." She wanted to believe in him. That would be plenty enough. He stopped her wish with another ravishing kiss, softly, slowly. Then, rising up on his knees, he lifted her fingers to his lips and gazed at her through his sooty lashes.

"Marry me, Talia." He was waiting for her answer, this very impatient man whose heart she would eventually break. Whether now or in a few days didn't matter.

She offered a smile to him and a prayer to the mother of all women that she would understand why she had to deceive the man she adored.

"On one condition."

He sat up, grinning like a madman, one eyebrow cocked. "Does that mean yes?"

"It means on one condition, Alex."

He caught her chin, planted a smiling kiss on her nose. "Your wish is my greatest pleasure, my love."

And her greatest regret.

"Well, my mother and father were married at the market cross in the village . . ."

An awful lie; they were married in the chapel. But this wedding-that-would-never-be was the perfect excuse for emptying the castle, from battlement to cellar, so that no one would be hurt when she set her home and all of his dreams ablaze.

"And?" he asked, so sweetly impatient that tears sprang to her eyes.

"I'd like us to be married there, too."

He smiled. "Consider it done. Is tomorrow morning too soon?"

"Two days." That would be enough time to prepare the castle for its end.

"I'll be aching for you by then, my love. As I am now."

He carried her up onto his lap, the counterpane making a tent around them. She gladly took him inside her again, rocked with him, rode her magnificent steed until he was roaring out her name and holding her as though he'd never let go.

"I love you, Alex."

Now, and for all the nights that are never to be.

Chapter 21

"**A** mighty fine day for a wedding, my lord."

"Aye, it is, Father John," Alex said, glancing up at the castle for the hundredth time, surprised at the churning in his guts, that he'd be subject to the simple vagaries of his wedding day. The pleasure of it, the anticipation. The beginning of his life with his love.

The sky glowed azure, and the sun was remarkably warm for nearly November. The village was thronged with people, everyone but the few guards he'd left in the main gatehouse. All waiting for the wedding to begin.

Waiting for Talia. A lady worth waiting a lifetime for.

"You're looking like a merry bridegroom, my

lord," Leod said. "Not a bit nervous, I'm sure?"

"Only that Talia might change her mind." Alex had only been jesting, but couldn't help noticing Quigley's quick frown—the look he shot to Leod and Leod's belly laugh.

"Ah, now, the lady Talia wouldn't go changing her mind about you, my lord. Not on your life. Never met a man so worthy, nor seen our girl so in love."

Quigley looked overwhelmed, pleading. "You'll remember that always, won't you, my lord? No matter what. That she loves you more than you'll ever know."

No matter what.

Quigley's encouragement should have comforted him, instead it made him look again toward the battlements, his banner flying there.

Something had been missing all through the day, like birdsong, or the breeze off the bay.

The girls.

"Where are Brenna and the girls?"

Quigley and Leod shook their heads at each other, then Quigley brightened, and said broadly, "With Her Ladyship. Helping her with her primping, I expect. You know how it is with the ladies."

"Especially on a young woman's wedding day."

Aye, he knew well how it was with his lady. Organized down to the tiniest detail, even this hurried wedding of theirs.

With cider and ale enough for the celebration, the cross decorated with greenery and ribbons.

And her bride bed as well.

Their marriage bed.

He'd come upon her draping fresh garlands this morning, and weeping as she did. She'd bawled like a babe when she saw him, filling his arms with her fragrant embrace and covering his mouth with her kisses.

"Go now, Alex," she'd said, shoving him out of her chamber and into the tower stairwell. " 'Tis unlucky for us to see each other before the wedding."

"Ah, love, I've never felt more lucky in all my life." He'd kissed her once again, and then he'd idled away the rest of the morning.

And now he was idling away his wedding day under the watchful eyes of Quigley and Leod.

Like a pair of dogged nursemaids.

Or guards.

His hackles rose, a sharp prickling, a soldier's warning that he had never in his life dismissed.

"Ah, good! There's Dougal," he said, pointing into the most dense part of the crowd. "I've a favor to ask of him. Watch for my lady, will you?"

When neither of the old men followed, Alex wondered if he'd been overreacting.

Then he decided to go hurry the woman on his own, bad luck or no.

* * *

"Will you be all right, my lady?"

Jasper must have seen Talia's hands shaking even in the dimness of the cellar, and she loved him for asking, for caring. "As right as I need to be."

"Well, the girls are safe out at the limeworks."

"And Alex is waiting down there in the village for me to come marry him."

Jasper rubbed his knuckles across her cheek, the way he'd done for all her life. "I'm sorry to my soul that it had to be this way, my dear girl. He did turn out to be the best of them, didn't he?"

"Lord, yes, Jasper." She caught a sob in her chest and blinked back her tears. "But it's time. Wait here for my signal. And then we'll clear the guardhouse of the watchmen and be done with it."

She kissed him on his cheek and left the cellar so he wouldn't see her weeping.

She dodged through the silent, utterly empty courtyard, reached the family quarters, and stumbled down the stairs into the cellar, scrubbing tears from her eyes.

The round room smelled of wool and linseed and the bristling pile of kindling leaning against the timber post in the center. And the rushlight she'd left waiting for her.

Oh, what a terrible price she was exacting from the man she loved.

Who loved her, and her family, and who would have been a fine steward for Carrisford if it hadn't been for Stephen's war with his cousin.

Mother Mary, protect us all.

Talia picked up the rushlight, steadied her hand to keep the flame upright and was just bending down to the sacks of wool and linseed oil when she felt a warm, familiar shadow cross her shoulders.

She knew whose it was by his scent and his size and the heartbreaking sound of him.

"What are you doing, Talia?"

She set the pale rushlight down on a chest, scrambling for some suitable lie as she turned toward him.

Toward his stark silhouette on the bottom step, limned by the spill of afternoon light that should have bathed their wedding celebration.

"Well, Alex, I'm . . . looking for"—something for the wedding— "an oyster-shell clip for my hair. Somewhere here in one of my mother's coffers."

"Ah." The air stilled, cooled like a tomb, before he stepped into the circle of rushlight, huge in his quiet fury, flinty as the winter.

"I wanted to wear it . . . the clip—"

"At our wedding, I vow?" His voice came from somewhere she'd heard before, bitter and cold.

"Well, yes, I was hoping to wear something of my mother's. A sudden need to feel her close to me."

He stepped into the center of the room, almost too tall for its ceiling, his gaze sliding efficiently over everything, missing nothing. He looked so very fine in his wedding clothes, all leather and velvet and shiny gold buckles.

"Taking your time preparing for our nuptials, I see."

She swallow hard, breathless. "Yes."

"I thought you might want to know that the market square is full to bursting with our well-wishers." He paused overlong. "Friends and family, Talia."

There was nothing but lies and emptiness left between them, because no matter what happened now, she couldn't stay, could hardly breathe for fear of sobbing.

But she let out a frivolous sigh, and he turned his broad back to her. She reached out to touch him, felt the heat and brought her hand back.

"I'm sorry I kept you waiting, my love," she said, as blithely as she could manage. "Wedding day nerves, I guess. I . . . well, I just lost track of time, that's all. But if you'll hurry back to the village and let Father John know that I'll be right there—"

"Christ, stop it, Talia." He whirled on her, his eyes piercing, as brittle as glass. "Please. Before you dig yourself an even deeper hole."

She'd never seen him so angry, could only stammer and try to stall his inevitable hatred of her. "Well, I . . . I don't know what you mean."

A hard-edged muscle moved in his jaw, his bronze skin clean-shaven for his wedding day. So soft it would be to touch. "Tell me what you're doing down here."

It wasn't his anger that she regretted, but the cold, unrelenting disappointment in his eyes. He was waiting for her to answer him, his chest rising and falling in his tightly tethered wrath.

"Alex, I—" Her stomach churned; her heart tattered and aching. "This is a storage cellar. My mother's things are here. . . ."

"I know the signs of sabotage, madam." He grabbed up a bundle of sticks. "You've made this place a tinderbox. Linseed and wool sacks and wood."

"I told you wh—"

"I'm not a fool," he hissed, tossing the bundle aside.

"I'm painfully aware of that, Alex." And so painfully in love with him.

And yet she couldn't think of any elaboration at all, not with the naked truth laid out before them, not with him bearing down on her, brimstone seeping from his every seam.

"You were just about to set fire to this cellar, weren't you, Talia?" He caught her back against the center pole, trapped her firmly there with his bent thigh against hers. "It's been your plan all along."

"Alex, I didn't—"

"Christ, Talia, don't bother trying any of your pretty falsehoods on me, I know them all, and I'm sick to death of them."

Resentment and outrage went off like rockets inside her, sizzled down her spine. She grabbed hold of the front of his tunic and pulled him close.

"And I am sick to death of your wars and the devastation you bring. Tired of hiding my family and sending innocent villagers to the woods to save their lives. Tired of running just ahead of the next horror."

"And so your answer is deception? To leave me waiting to marry you in the village like a fool, while you set my castle ablaze?"

"It's *mine*, Alex!"

"Damnation, woman!" He reached behind her, cradled her head against the post for all his anger, and leaned as close as the kiss he'd given her that morning. "And I'm supposed to do what, Talia? To just stand back and allow it? Allow you to raze a castle I hold in wardship to the king?"

"I don't care about the king."

"Or about me?"

"Oh, I . . . Alex, you couldn't possibly understand."

"I understand that you made a promise to me the night we made love." He touched his mouth against her temple, breathing deeply—a dear intimacy that she moaned against, a richly scented memory of him that swept her along with the slamming of his heart. "The night you told me that you would be my wife. That you loved me. Do you even remember it?"

"Indelibly, Alex." Burned into her heart. "I promised you that I would come to you whenever I saw problems with Carrisford."

"And you promised this because . . . ?"

"Because I love you."

"A hell of a sobering thought, Talia. That you can love me and still burn down my castle. God knows what you'd have done if you'd taken a dislike to me."

"This has nothing at all to do with you and me, Alex. I should have done this years ago long before Aymon or Rufus."

"Or me?" His eyes glittered with molten fury, were red-rimmed and wounded. "Do I so remind you of them? Do I disgust you so much that you'd burn me out, Talia, just to spite me?"

"I would never do that, Alex. Please believe me, I had no choice. I haven't for a long time."

"You're right there, madam." He snatched the rushlight by its flame, unflinching as he crushed its brightness inside his palm. "You've made your last choice."

He grabbed her wrist and started up the stairs.

"Where are you taking me? To your dungeon?"

She hunkered down and dragged her heels, but he merely scooped her up like a sack of grain.

"You can't stop me, Alex. Not unless you lock me up or hang me."

"The court of law is the king's business, madam. This is mine."

Alex could barely manage his temper at the moment, could barely see for the blackness of his anger.

He felt like a damned fool, had gone in search of his beloved, expecting to find her still at her toilette, surrounded by the girls.

Her chamber alive with flowers and giggling and those damn rabbits.

He'd expected to wed her at the foot of their castle and bed her and make children with her and love her until the end of time.

Yet, all the while she'd been plotting her intricate betrayal of him. She was very good at it. Masquerading all this with her beguiling smile.

Destroying the very things she loved.

Carrisford.

Me.

Holy hell. He shoved open the door to his chamber, and stood her on her feet, then slammed the door behind them.

He wanted most of all to let go of her and walk away, but her eyes were wide and weepy, and his heart was slamming against his ribs.

And she smelled of the day that should have

been theirs, of leafy garlands and weddings, the spicy scent of apples caught up in the curls at her temple.

He wanted her as he wanted air. "Dammit, Talia, do you know what I gave up for you?"

She gave an angry little stamp and swabbed her sleeve across her eyes. "You gave up nothing more than you wanted to give up, Alex."

"What the hell is that supposed to mean?"

"That you are the same man, in the same place, that you were when you came storming through my gates and into my heart. And now you're free again to do anything you'd like."

He opened his mouth to deny her, grasping at any hint of logic, feeling selfish and shallow even before the words left his mouth.

Because none of it seemed like Talia.

"You knew what I wanted for my life, madam. Knew exactly why I didn't want to stay here with you."

"Well, good. Now you don't have to stay; you have your excuse. I'm sure there's an heiress out there somewhere for you. One far better for your purposes than I am. A far less troublesome castle to seize. I'll be hanged and you can have your perfect future."

A coldness settled over his shoulders, the prospect of life without Talia. "Christ, Talia, how long have you been conspiring to bring it down?"

"I wasn't conspiring, Alex. Carrisford is my birthright, I can do whatever I think best with it."

"And so you'd burn it down? When I'd promise on my life that I would protect you."

"But you can't possibly, Alex. Not even you." She was sobbing softly, scrubbing the streaming of tears from her cheeks. "I'm sorry. I didn't want to hurt you. You can't know how much I love you."

So that's what Jasper had meant: a subtle warning from one of her confederates. To beware, to believe, to trust where he shouldn't.

Where he could not.

He whirled away from her so that he couldn't see her tears, because they looked so real, dredged up from her deepest sorrows. He braced his hands against the cool sandstone near the window, wondering how he could have been so blinded.

"I suppose Jasper is out there somewhere, ready to fulfill his part in your little plan. Shall I send someone to stop him before he starts a conflagration?"

"No. There's no one but me."

Finally, the answer he'd been expecting—and yet something deep inside of him knew that there was something dreadfully wrong. This was Talia, taking all the blame, protecting the people she loved no matter the cost.

"You're such a beautiful liar, Talia. There isn't a man, woman, or child within leagues of Carrisford who wouldn't offer up their lives for you. Including me, God help me. Because I love you."

A horrible, howling sob tore out of her. "Oh, Alex, please don't—"

"Damn it, Talia, why couldn't you have just believed in me. You couldn't just trust me to protect you?"

"Alex, there's nothing you can do. It doesn't matter who holds Carrisford, or how good his intentions or how much I love you; it's the way of war. And it's killing us, little by little, year after year. And for what? For this tired old castle, who's done her finest and deserves her rest. Oh, God, Alex, it hurts me so much to think about what I have to do." He'd never seen her so defeated, grieving as though she'd lost someone dear to her, her whole body wracked with howling sobs. "But I can't stand to see any more suffering."

"Talia, what the devil are you saying?"

She turned away from him to stare out the window. "Carrisford stopped being a place of strength and security sometime ago, and I was just too blind to notice."

"To notice what, Talia?"

"That if it weren't for the castle itself, the village would be safe, and my family, too." She leaned against the wall, sobbing, hugging herself, looking so alone. "No one would pay a moment's attention to the little valley that rolled peacefully down into the ocean."

"And?"

"And so I realized that if the castle weren't sitting here on the rise above the bay, like some pitiful prize, then the war and all the trouble would just pass us by unnoticed. And so"—she lifted her teary eyes to him—"I set about tearing the walls down from the inside."

"You did what?" The woman was mad.

"Excavating our way from the tower cellars and strategically along some of the walls. I thought you must have realized that already."

"My God, Talia, you weren't just going to burn me out—"

"If you're going to try to live here after I'm gone, Alex, then you'll have to do quite a bit of shoring up. And remove the fuel from the cellars—I'm afraid they're quite a danger at the moment, but I thought we'd be done by now."

"What do you mean 'gone'?"

"The keystones are missing in most of the arches—"

"Dammit to hell, Talia, that was your doing? The wall walk falling in."

"That was us. Me. I thought I had taken care of the possibility. I was terrified that someone had gotten hurt from my carelessness." The sun stole in through the casement window, lighting the streams of tears that just kept streaming down her cheeks. "I've muddled everything."

"You damn well have." She'd turned his world

on its heel, this clear-hearted woman who loved so completely.

Who had defied a king and held off seven invasions.

Who had waited for him as long as she could.

She stood and crossed her arms over her breasts. "So, what are you going to do now, Alex?"

Damned if he knew *what* to do with a woman like this. Prepared to sacrifice her own life to protect her family. Confessing that she loved him just as deeply.

But she stood her ground in her plain brown kirtle, jutting her chin out at him, her face streaked with tears. "Whatever you choose to do, Alex, I doubt it will include me."

"What the hell do you mean by that?"

"You obviously don't understand yet. And I doubt you will. You have three choices. And I have but one; and that means leaving here."

"You're not going anywhere."

"Yes, that's one of your choices, Alex; making me stay here in a dangerous castle and forcing me to marry some fool husband of your choosing."

Bloody hell!

"But I promise you, Alex, that I will escape him at the first opportunity and take the villagers and my family with me, because that would leave the castle standing and we wouldn't be safe here."

"You'll marry no one but me, Talia, and we will

stay right here." He didn't know when he'd decided that course, but it made perfect sense. Though he'd have to keep a guard on her.

"That's your second of three choices, Alex: force me to marry you and live in the castle."

"That's not a choice, madam, that is fact."

"Well, then I'll escape you at the first opportunity and take the villagers and my family with me."

Her hair had come free of its circlet. She was beautiful in her cobwebs and bits of straw, in her pacing and methodical finger waggling.

"Your third choice, Alex—"

"—I don't need a third choice—"

"—is to marry me and help me tear down this dear old place. So the village will be safe. And the orchards will thrive, and our children will run free in woods and we can live in one of Father's old manor houses—"

"Enough, Talia!"

"We've two manors to choose from, and stolen goods stashed all over the estate."

"Stolen from whom?" She studied her fingertips, a confession if he'd ever seen one. "From *me*?"

She nodded. "And strangers, and the king. And lots of things from that Gloucester fellow."

"The earl?"

Another nod.

"Christ, in heaven, Talia."

"Those are all your choices, Alex. Oh, but . . .

you have more, don't you?" She frowned, and held out her wrists. "Arrest me and charge me with treason and let Stephen take care of the rest."

"You plan to live in an old manor house."

"Just beyond the orchards. It isn't much, but it's never been touched." Her eyes filled with tears again. "And I love you, Alex."

"I know."

"I didn't want to, but I couldn't help myself."

"God help me, my love, I know what you mean."

Her eyes brightened with the teetering kind of hope he'd seen dozens of times but had never recognized.

Trust and love and all of her dreams.

What the beautiful woman didn't realize was that choosing between her love for him and the grandest title, the largest castle in the world was the simplest thing he'd ever done.

Talia watched Alex with every part of her, hoping that he didn't hate her, not knowing quite what to make of the smile that came over him.

Or the way he was stalking toward her, looking perfectly pleased with himself, reckless.

"Well, Alex, what did you decide?"

Instead of answering, he lifted her high into his arms, then kissed her madly and everywhere. Doubtless to disorient her and try to influence her determination.

"You're a very stubborn woman, Talia." He

started toward the door with her, his fingers spread indelicately across her bottom.

"What have you decided, Alex?" She pushed back off his shoulders. *Stubborn.*

"Duck down, my love." He covered the top of her head as they passed through the doorway, and started up the stairs.

His love!

"Where are you taking me?" And where the devil was he going with his other hand riding up her leg? "Alex . . . oh!"

He was going *there.*

And so she let him, sighing all the way up the stairs, and into her chamber, all the way to the bed and its sprinkling of flower petals, carrying her all the way back against the pillows, certain, without even asking what her magnificent husband-to-be had decided.

"Do you suppose, my love," he asked, smiling his kisses against her mouth as he gathered her into his arms, "that we have time enough before we light that blaze to save our marriage bed?"

She would have answered sooner, but she was humming to his delicious music and crooning against his ear.

"Oh, Alex, and time enough to be married, too."

Four stars of romance soar this November!

WHEN IT'S PERFECT by Adele Ashworth
An Avon Romantic Treasure

Miss Mary Marsh's quiet world is sent spinning the moment dashing Marcus Longfellow comes striding into her life. The Earl of Renn believes the young miss is hiding something, and a sensuous seduction will surely reveal her secrets. But is his growing passion for her interfering with his perfect plan?

I'VE GOT YOU, BABE by Karen Kendall
An Avon Contemporary Romance

Vanessa Tower has never met anyone like Christopher "Crash" Dunmoor, the sexy adventurer who can ignite sparks in her with just a smile. Will the gorgeous bookworm convince the confirmed loner that love is the most tantalizing adventure of all?

HIGHLAND ROGUES: THE WARRIOR BRIDE
by Lois Greiman
An Avon Romance

Lachlan MacGowan is suspicious of the mysterious "Hunter"—and shocked to discover this warrior is really a woman! Beneath the soldier's garb, Rhona is a proud beauty . . . and she is determined to resist the striking rogue who has laid siege to her heart.

HIS BRIDE by Gayle Callen
An Avon Romance

Gwyneth Hall has heard the dark rumors about Sir Edmund Blackwell, the man she is betrothed to but has never seen. Yet burning kisses from the gorgeous "devil" may be more than she bargained for . . .

REL 1002

*Avon Romances—
the best in exceptional authors
and unforgettable novels!*

Have you ever dreamed of writing a romance?

*And have you ever wanted
to get a romance published?*

Perhaps you have always wondered how to
become an Avon romance writer?
We are now seeking the best and brightest undiscovered
voices. We invite you to send us your query letter to
avonromance@harpercollins.com

What do you need to do?

Please send no more than two pages telling us
about your book. We'd like to know its setting—is it
contemporary or historical—and a bit about the hero,
heroine, and what happens to them.

Then, if it is right for Avon we'll ask to see part of the
manuscript. Remember, it's important that you have
material to send, in case we want to see your story quickly.

Of course, there are no guarantees of publication,
but you never know unless you try!

*We know there is new talent just waiting
to be found! Don't hesitate . . . send us
your query letter today.*

*The Editors
Avon Romance*